Cherrington Academy

Rebecca Caffery

SRL Publishing

www.srlpublishing.co.uk

SRL Publishing Ltd
42 Braziers Quay
Bishop's Stortford
Herts, CM23 3YW

First published worldwide by SRL Publishing in 2020

ISBN: 978-191633734-3

SRL Publishing's policy is not to use papers that are sourced from the Amazon Basin or from rainforests of exceptional value. Printed on paper which has achieved Chain of Custody certification.

This book is for everyone who is different in the world or who have struggled to find their place and their people. There is help out there, there is support and there is light in this life, sometimes finding it just takes a 2000-mile journey.

~ Chapter One ~

One red brick dormitory had the power to change everything.

I'd ran two thousand miles across the country for this singular building. Not literally, there had been two planes and a bus involved, but it had felt like a cross country sprint to get here.

I had arrived though. My fresh start, everything I deserved after the awful couple of years I'd had before this. The scars of tenth grade still engraved across my lip and around the back of my head, thank god for a full head of thick curls that covered the five-inch indent.

The dormitory looked like something from a Disney movie rather than a school building. It looked more like a castle with its huge bay windows, tall tower expanding from the roof of the building and how every room at the front seemed to have gold window frames. At least I could finally see where all the money my parents had spent to send me here had gone.

I dragged my suitcase behind me on the cobbled driveway as a gleaming gold sign caught my eye. *'Viribus'*. I made a mental note to Google that later. A wide tugging smile pulled at my lips as I passed the *'Welcome to Cherrington Academy'* sign and crossed over the threshold, this was it. I promised myself a big change, to reinvent myself, build myself back up and be the best version of myself. No longer afraid, no longer flinching at every loud sound. This was my chance and I was going to take it.

The school brochure said it was a safe haven and for the price of the tuition I expected it to be a freaking

1

resort, but I'd take some serenity and a place to heal right now.

I wanted to be shocked when I presented said brochure to my parents, and their reactions were just *'how much'*, not *'why'* or *'no we aren't sending our son two thousand miles across the country'*. But, as they paid for my bus and plane tickets to get here, without even offering to help me move, no shock ran through my veins. More like pure relief that I was escaping, and I hadn't had to pay a single dime to do so.

Although, as I looked down at the map and envelope of keys I held in my hands, I wondered if my parents had overpaid for me to be here. E28A. My new home according to the circle on the map and the note on the envelope. The whole walk from the accommodation office, I'd been repeating what the receptionist had told me - Edwards dormitory, floor two, room eight, bed A. Bed A was what made me question the price of this place and had the potential to be terrifying. It meant that I had a roommate, something I had yet to experience in my sixteen years of life.

The dorm was dramatically big, it had a staircase that spiralled up its six levels, and each floor spanned out into several wings with huge oak doors that led to each bedroom that housed the three hundred boys who resided here. I should have expected this from the brochure, but the vastness of the building had still caught me by surprise, so much so my suitcases toppled to the floor.

Artwork lined the staircase walls as I hauled my cases up the stairs to the second floor. They were all beautifully framed by thick pieces of gold, we had fancy things in my family home, but nothing this extravagant. Although my parents could definitely afford stuff like this, they just chose not to. Hardly worth it when they were rarely home.

Room eight was directly in front of the top of the staircase. Whatever and whoever was behind that door wasn't going to spoil my fresh start.

I pushed down the handle to see if the door was locked and when it opened a crack, I peered in and to my delight it looked empty, this was a result. I could settle in in peace and work up a little more nerve to meet the guy I'd be sharing with for this academic year.

I pushed the curls that had tousled over my face, settled down my cases and surveyed my room. I could work with it. There was a huge open space between my double bed and the big wooden desk, enough space for a rug and once I'd removed the blue and white pinstripe canape from over my bed, I could definitely see myself snuggled up in it after a long day of classes.

The images I'd started to conjure up of the perfect decor and a homely environment were disturbed by the opening of the bathroom door and a half-naked guy, who, I presumed to be my roommate, stepping out with just a towel hung low around his hips. A further towel was being used to dry a mound of hair that flowed from his head. I knew not to stare, but this boy's body was one I'd only ever dreamed of. What looked like hand-carved abs, a splattering of blonde hair up his snail trail and a jaw that could cut ice. A body pure of imperfections.

I mentally shook myself; this was not the time for ogling. I had to will myself to stop, to look away and focus on something else, but as he spoke, he pulled me back in with his emerald eyes and sharp nose.

"Ah, the roomie has arrived. You know you're two months late, right? I was quite enjoying having this place to myself." There was a hint of sarcasm to his words, but the icy air that cut a path around us told me he meant it more than I wanted him to.

I could push past that though, we had to be civil if we were to live together for at least the next seven months. "I'm Logan, Logan Shields. You must be Noah, right?" I stuck my hand out to be courteous, but as he turned his back on me to wander to his chest of drawers, I knew not to expect much from this guy.

"Noah Castle," he confirmed as he slipped on a pair of boxers under his towel. "I apologise, I can't promise you this level of entertainment every day," he added, his hands gesturing up and down his body, his lips tugged into a smirk as the towel dropped to the floor.

I turned away quickly; my whole body scorched by his words. My cheeks burned rouge as I realised he'd caught me checking him out, not the start I wanted to make with my roommate. I surveyed the mess I'd made with my open cases on the floor to distract myself from him as he changed behind me. There wasn't a huge amount of furniture here - a bed, a dresser with matching wardrobe and a desk that sat on the opposite wall to my bed, but the brochure did say as most boys lived in the same room for eleventh and twelfth grade, you could bring more furniture and decor.

Not that the emptiness mattered, it was mine and I could work my magic with it. I'd rather live in a bare room than be back in the coldness of my old house in Calgary.

I tugged down the draping canape over my bed, only to be grossly disturbed by how similar the pattern was to the tie I would now be forced to wear every day. Apart from the roommate, that was my only other complaint so far about the school. I'd spent the last couple of years building a wardrobe of designer brands and stunning patterns that I'd thrifted from every goodwill, boot sale

and vintage store I could find in
Alberta. That would all have to be locked away for the
weekends now and to say I was gutted would be an
understatement.

As I finished jailing my clothes, in the small space the
three carbon copies of uniform weren't taking up inside
my wardrobe, Noah spoke again. "Look, Logan, this has
been my room for the last two years. It's going to take a
bit of getting used to for both of us, but rest assured I
won't be here half as much as you think."

I wanted to question that, but I'd take him not being
here if it meant we didn't have to have any more of these
exchanges. "You don't have to worry either. I'm so quiet
you'll probably not even know I'm here," I replied.

"That, I doubt. Your dreadful cologne has already
wafted over here and infected my side of the room," he
laughed, and not in the 'haha I'm joking' kind of way, it
was a thick, spiteful laugh. One that splintered my spine
and stung the back of my eyes, but I cleared my throat
and pushed past the urge to let any tears fall. His words
may have been uncalled for, but I wouldn't show him that
they got to me.

Instead, I set to work with my bed as I covered the
soft mattress with navy blue, Egyptian cotton sheets that
I'd splurged on with my savings from my summer job
before I left. However, he didn't quite take the hint. As I
pushed the comforter into its cover, he disturbed me
once more.

"God, do you plan to be this unresponsive all the
time?" he asked. "If so, I'm not sure I'll be able to stand
you."

Even though my chest began to tighten, I looked up
at his face, Cheshire grin spread across it. I pinched the
flesh between my index finger and thumb and willed the
pounding in my heart to stop, I stood up to him. "Look, I

just travelled two thousand miles to get here. I just want to get unpacked, climb into bed and pass out." I was a new version of Logan Shields and I wasn't going to allow myself to be spoken to like that anymore.

"Two thousand miles?" he questioned. "What the fuck? I was wondering where the rest of your boxes were, but I guess you can't get them on a plane. Where are your parents?"

That stung deep in my chest. Where were my parents? If I went by their calendar that they shared with me on Gmail, they were in the States arguing some big case. What he meant was why aren't they here. "They couldn't get the time off work, they are lawyers. But yes, two thousand miles. I'm from a place called Grande Prairie in Calgary."

"Alberta?"

I nodded and tidied up the sheets so they were ready for me to get into and grabbed some sweats from my dresser so I could get some well-earned shuteye.

"Jeez," Noah whistled. "No wonder you're tired. Well, before you pass out you need to get and check in with the prefect, he lives on the top floor. You won't be able to miss his room."

Noah hadn't been wrong. The prefect plaque on the door in front of me stuck out like a sore thumb amidst the other doors I'd passed on the way up to the sixth floor. This floor was completely different to all others, all the rest had thirty or forty rooms to them, but this one had just three. The prefect's room and two others down the corridor.

I hovered my fist in the knocking position for what felt like an eternity before I worked up the courage to wrap it against the door. I could hear movement on the other side and my thoughts whirled in my head, making me question why I was even here? What if he didn't like me? What if he was another homophobe? Or one of those guys who didn't like the thought of having a gay guy in an all-male dormitory?

With a shaky breath, I connected my fist with the door and knocked lightly, the sound of my racing heart louder than the knock.

"You must be Logan?" the prefect said as he opened the door and took me completely by surprise. He was shorter than me by at least an inch, had warm chocolate brown eyes framed by thick black frames and a head of messy, mousy brown hair that hadn't been styled today. Nothing like the scary figure I'd imagined to be the leader of this dormitory. "You're already being described as a rarity you know? A boy hasn't moved into this house as an eleventh grader in the last twenty-five years, according to Julian."

I had no idea who Julian was, and I didn't want to, not when he was bigging me up like this. I wanted to remain under the radar here, grow, but still be unknown to prevent any further bullying or garner any attention from the wrong people.

"Now that's a title to live up to," I half-joked, hoping he didn't notice how I wrung my sweaty hands out behind my back. "But yes, I'm Logan Shields. It's nice to meet you."

"Where are my manners? I'm Charlie Montgomery, Edwards prefect, just in case you hadn't gathered that from the ridiculous sign glued to the door. I don't know what they stuck that one with, but it doesn't budge. Trust me, we've tried."

A laugh escaped my lips and a chunk of tension resided in my neck; he hadn't been what I'd expected at all. There was already an easiness between us and I relished in it.

7

"Nothing a few power tools couldn't fix," I said feeling slightly more confident in my words. The new version of myself could do this.

"Don't mention that to my friends, you really wouldn't want power tools falling into their hands," he grinned back at me, his friends sounded kind of wild.

"I won't don't you worry. Wouldn't want to cause chaos on my first day," I joked in reply. Internally, however, I was freaking out, this was going so much better than I thought it would. Charlie had the sweetest of smiles and with his tousled hair, it was hard to be scared of him.

"Actually, come to think of it, I haven't seen those lazy gits today. You'll understand the definition of wrong hands when I drag them two out of bed. Wait here a sec."

Wait here for what? I wanted to ask as he headed down the corridor towards the other two doors. I stepped into his room to search for a mirror, after twelve hours I must have looked such a state and whilst I was okay just signing in with the prefect like this, I didn't want it to be my first impression to his friends. As my eyes travelled to his mirror, I was caught off guard by a flurry of coloured paperbacks splayed across a shelf. I looked closer and noticed they were arranged beautifully in alphabetical order. There was an open copy of the wonderful Rainbow Rowell's 'Fangirl' on his bed, and I couldn't help but nod in approval at his choice.

It was in that moment someone cleared their throat from behind me and pulled me from where I was surveying his book selection. I turned round to be met with not only Charlie but two other boys one either side of him.

Gunmetal eyes. That was the first thing that caught my attention about him. The taller of the boys, dressed in just a crumpled vest and gym shorts. Not that anything else mattered about him when had had the most beautiful steely orbs. I'd have taken him in a waste bin bag if I got to look into those eyes every day.

"This is Isaac Wells," Charlie stated as he clapped his hands on Isaac's bare shoulders. "And this is Joshua Havana," he said pointing his thumb at the other boy. Joshua just yawned, his fingers trying to fix the frizzy mess of an afro on his head.

"You sound as tired as I feel," I replied trying to stifle back my own yawn, it really was contagious.

"Sorry, late night, we didn't get back from Toronto till like three am last night, October and the girls dragged us to some ridiculous make-up convention," Isaac replied as he rubbed the sleep from his eyes.

"His girlfriend has him whipped," Joshua added with a cheeky smile.

"Yeah, you idiots both broke curfew again. Thanks for not even letting me know, I had to bullshit with Julian to keep you out of trouble," Charlie said as he clipped the back of both boys' heads.

All three of them laughed and a wave of jealousy hit me as I had no idea who these girls were or what was really funny. I had to reassure myself it would just take time, that I wouldn't just slot in automatically to their inside jokes or their friendship group.

I suddenly realised, with expectant eyes upon me, that this was probably the moment I should have been introducing myself. Not just standing there looking like a deer caught in headlights. I was supposed to be making a good first impression to give myself a shot at friends here.

"I'm Logan Shields," I began. "I'm uh new here."
Good job Logan, like they don't already know that.

"He's a year below us, just moved in on the second floor with Noah," Charlie added to my stupid

9

introduction.

Isaac let out an overdramatic gasp that filled me with a cold sensation of dread. If my anxiety hadn't already been through the roof after my first encounter with Noah, it was sky high now.

Before I even had a chance to question his reaction, Charlie had continued his spiel. "He just moved here from Calgary, so try and be helpful, you know like seniors who have been here for the last three years."

Isaac smacked his shoulder and his face mocked disbelief. "As if we would be anything other than helpful," he scoffed.

"No stunts. No breaking curfew. No alcohol," Charlie said with a glare Isaacs way, his eyes scorned the tan-skinned boy before he turned back to smile at me. "Look, if you need anything just let us know. We are the only people up here so you'll always find one of us around."

His smile and words reassured me and put my mind at rest. Hopefully, their help would make my transition here somewhat smoother.

"Thank you," I replied as Isaac's phone beeped in his shorts pocket.

His eyes lit up like lightning on a stormy night as he read the text. I guessed it must be his girlfriend.

"October and the girls are in the dining hall. Let's go," he commanded, not looking up from his phone. He didn't wait for a reply as he turned towards the stairs the other two following after him as I stared down at the floor, forgotten.

I wasn't expecting them to befriend me straight away, but I didn't expect them to just walk away. I'd wait till they were out of the building and then I'd scuttle down to the second floor again. I went to pull the door behind me when I felt an arm wrap around my neck.

"Hey new kid, you're coming too, we all gotta eat," Joshua replied, as he guided me out of the room and down to the dining hall.

~ Chapter Two ~

Two hundred sets of eyes hit me like a tonne of bricks as I stepped into the dining room. Charlie was right, people had already started talking about me. Being new was never fun, but being new halfway through the first semester of eleventh grade was never going to be a barrel of laughs.

I braced myself for the disgusted stares and the hushed whispers of insults, but they never came. A couple of the older looking guys and girls smiled at me cheerfully, others nodded welcoming me and one boy even shook my hand and introduced himself to me. It was a shame that I was in so much shock I couldn't even conjure up my own name as me, Charlie, Isaac, and Joshua joined the dining room queue.

The dread I felt about being surrounded by so many people seeped out of me and resentment rushed through me towards all the bullies at my previous school who'd made me think that I was only ever going to receive a negative reaction from other students. Any normal person would bask in being the new kid, everyone excited about you being there, not me, I couldn't even enjoy this moment.

When I finally had a chance to catch my breath, I took in the dining room and was completely stunned. It was like the grand hall from Hogwarts. Dark oak tables were scattered around the floor, wooden benches sat either side of them to match. Framed artwork hung on

12

every wall and the ceilings were so high you could fit a skyscraper underneath them. It made my High School look like a plastic playhouse in comparison.

Groups of friends were dotted around the room, sharing food at the table, conversations bounding off every wall. The atmosphere was electric, the kind of atmosphere I'd never been a part of.

It wasn't that I hadn't had friends at my old school. That hadn't been the case at all. Karina Jenkinson had been my best friend from grade five through to the middle of grade nine and then she'd blossomed as a girl, became popular and was pretty enough in the cheerleader's eyes to join their squad. She'd left me behind. I had to come out on my own and face all the backlash without her support. No one came near me after that, it was like there was a warning sign above my head that said, '*he has gay cooties, don't come near*'. So I learned to hide, I ate lunch in the corners of the library, I made zero eye contact in the corridors at school and I made sure, or well everyone around me made sure, I sat alone in class. That's why the next words that spilled out of Charlie's mouth as we waited in line shocked me to my core.

"I feel like I should prepare you for having lunch with us." My mouth actually gaped open like I was about to catch some flies for my dinner, and I shook myself internally a little to make sure this was real life. "The gang are great, but they can be a little much especially because you're new. Just to warn you, Libby is going to drool over you because she has a thing for gingers, October will be all over Isaac but if you close your eyes you can't hear them making out and Ameliah, whilst she's quiet and sometimes a bit icy, she knows what's what and will always tell you straight."

I nodded at his words and tried to memorise their names, repeated them over and over in my head before I

13

was completely distracted by the extensive menu they had on offer. There was every kind of dish you could dream of. Pizzas, stir fry's, burgers, burritos, grilled meats and veggies, curries, noodles and so much more. According to the welcome pack I'd read through on the final coach from Toronto Airport, I could order whatever and however much of what I wanted and just tap my card to pay for it.

"This is incredible," I commented to Charlie and his grin said everything, he must have seen how overwhelmed I'd felt and maybe as prefect he'd been told a little about why I'd moved here.

"I recommend any of the Mexican dishes they have to offer. The nachos are amazing, but the burritos are better than anything I've ever had from Taco Bell or Burrito Boyz. You're going to love every mouthful," he commented and clapped a reassuring hand on my shoulder and squeezed in a loving manner

My spine bristled at the contact, my eyes scouted the rest of the dining hall for everyone's reaction, for the fake gags and revolt in people's eyes. No one even blinked, there wasn't a single person looking at us as Charlie rested his free hand on the back of my elbow and guided me towards their table after we'd both ordered a burrito each. It was a small taste of freedom, but I clung to it and desperately hoped to find more of it here.

We arrived at a table already inhabited by both the other boys and the three girls I was yet to meet. A girl with long, curly blonde locks had her legs draped over Isaac's lap as she dug her fork into her salad, I assumed she was October, his girlfriend. To her left was a rounder girl with a short brown bob, who flashed the most beautiful, pearly white smile at me as she unnervingly looked me up and down. Definitely Libby. Whilst

14

opposite Libby and beside Joshua was a petite girl with a pixie cut, her nose buried in a worn copy of *Harry Potter and the Chamber of Secrets*. She must be Ameliah.

As I sat down opposite Isaac, between Joshua and Charlie I surveyed the group. They were such a misfit bunch that sat amongst them I could see how I would belong here. The gay ginger amongst the nerd, the flirt, and the boys who I couldn't decide if they were athletic or geeky or somewhere in-between.

"Introduce us to the newbie then, Mr Prefect," Isaacs girlfriend said with a sarcastic tone as she finally peeled herself out of his lap.

"Give me a chance," Charlie replied as he started to un-peel the foil around his burrito. After a single bite, he finally gave the girl what she wanted. "This is Logan Shields just transferred from Grand Prairie High in Calgary, so he's a long way from home. Try and be nice to him girls as he's in eleventh grade like yourself. You ladies can introduce yourselves, right? You don't need me to do that for you too."

October, I assumed, rolled her eyes at him and laughed. "I'm October or Toby for short." She wrapped her arm around Isaac's waist and added, "This one's girlfriend as I'm sure you've already figured out. Don't let him get you into any trouble, okay?" She smiled at me, but the warning had an underlying message of sternness, and I couldn't help but wonder what that was about. It wasn't the first time today I'd heard a similar warning.

"Libby," the girl with the blunt bob said as she presented a hand across the table to me. "Cheerleading captain and your English Lit partner. The second Mrs Salam mentioned a newbie joining us in mid- November I volunteered myself." She smiled even wider at me than I thought possible, as her hand still hung in mid-air across the table as Charlie's words replayed in my head about her. The poor girl. If only she knew I wasn't on the market for

her. I quickly took her hand after far too long and she squeezed it with purpose before she pulled away, cheeks flushed and her eyes anywhere but on me.

That only left one. "Saving the best till last," Ameliah commented as she looked up from her book and gave me a chance to notice her vintage nude glasses that accentuated her caramel eyes beautifully. "I'm Ameliah Jones, Junior class president and debate team co-captain with your wonderful prefect," she added as she side-eyed Charlie.

Now that really had me intrigued. I wondered if there was tension there between the two of them. My mind wandered to the endless possibilities of why that tension could be there. Had they previously dated? Was this just co-captain rivalry? I watched Charlie do nothing but smile back at the girl. Very interesting. This was one of the bonuses of always being on the outsides of groups, I'd gotten really good at watching and reading people.

"So, why the move mid-semester?" Libby asked like it was completely okay to get started with the toughest of questions.

"Hey," Charlie warned. "Let him settle in before you ask for his life story." Thank god for him, because I had no desire in that moment to get into the darkness that led me here.

"This school has an amazing reputation for its education standard," I replied, the line sounded perfectly polished and practised. I'd prepared it for moments like this.

"Even so, Alberta must have schools like this?" Libby pushed and I let out the shakiest of breaths as I wished she'd just drop it.

16

"I fancied a change," I shrugged. "Honestly, I'm here to get through my classes and graduate."

"He's serious as well, this guy is about to be in my twelfth grade Physics class. It's practically unheard of," Joshua chimed in and thankfully took all the heat away from me.

"He's in my Bio class as well," Charlie said and even though I hated the spotlight, I couldn't help the small smile that tugged at my lips. I'd worked damn hard at the entrance exams for this place to be allowed to take two higher credits to have the chance to graduate in the winter semester of twelfth grade.

"God, I haven't even started to think about graduation or leaving here." Libby chuckled.

"It's nothing against this place, I'm just done with high school. It hasn't exactly been the greatest experience for me." I added before my brain had chance to catch up with my tongue. Before they had the chance to comment I spoke again. "So, is this the only place to eat on campus?"

"There's also a Denny's at the bottom of the drive," Charlie replied. "We go there regularly for Saturday brunch; you'll see this weekend that these idiots…" he thumbed to the two other guys… "can demolish almost half the menu. Stick with us and we'll show you all the secret things you can get there."

A wave of nausea hit me. He wanted me to stick around. To be part of his friendship group, to go for brunch on a Saturday. The words were like a wrench at my gut. If I wasn't so worried about being completely alone here, I might have cried a little.

"Hey, new kid. Don't look so worried," Isaac said as his smile transformed into the coyest of smirks. "Like Char said, stick with us and you'll be absolutely fine, you may even enjoy yourself." I caught the warning glare that

17

Charlie shot Isaac.

"Don't even think about recruiting him, Isaac. I'm serious, I'd like to get through the next six months without having to pull you out of the Deans office every other weekend." His tone was far too serious for an eighteen-year-old and I really felt for him, for whatever Isaac had clearly put him through.

"No promises Char, he may seem quiet now, but I'm sure he has a wild side under all that. I sense it." Isaac mocked as he sniffed the air and winked at me.

Not once in my life had I ever been considered 'wild'. Even as a child I made safe and calculated decisions. Never swinging too high on the swings or daring to join in with the pre-schoolers who chewed worms like candy.

"Leave it out, Issy," his girlfriend said, pushing his shoulder. "Ignore him okay, Logan? He just gets excitable."

"Hey, I'm not a dog," Isaac protested, wrapping his arms around his girlfriend's waist, pulling her closer to his side.

"I'm going to end up vomiting up my lunch if you don't put her down Isaac. Whilst this PDA is completely delightful, please tone it down for all the singletons around this table." Libby fake gagged. "You single?" Libby asked, eyes fixed on me, almost uncomfortably

"Intrusive much?" Ameliah replied, before I could get a word in.

"Like it wasn't what we were all thinking," Libby retorted, snorting a little.

"Well, I definitely wasn't," Charlie added.

"I'm surprised," Ameliah muttered, but I'd heard the words and so did Charlie if the brief panic that danced across his eyes was anything to go by.

"Well, are you?" Libby asked again.

"I am very much single," I admitted.

"Now that's something we can definitely help you with." The Cheshire grin that spread across Libby's face disturbed me. "Every girl loves a ginger nowadays; we'll have you coupled up in no time."

She hadn't even sensed that I was gay, that was somewhat a good thing, but I had no desire to mess around any girl like that. I'd done a good job at blending in though, I almost wanted to pat myself on the back.

"God, please don't set him up with anyone Libs. We don't need a repeat of what happened when you tried to couple up Joshua and that nutter Betsy, she damn near erected a statue of him in her room," Charlie said as all of the group took a sharp breath in. There was a story there that I hoped to hear one day.

"She wasn't even the worst of the bunch," Joshua said pointedly addressing me more than anyone else. "Libby made me go out with Quinnie, you'll see her around in classes. she's the same grade as you. She's head of the track team and there's a good reason for it, she drills those girls like they are marines. She had me up at four am every morning before school making me do some killer boot camp. I'm a lacrosse player and she nearly killed me with some of it."

I chuckled at that vision. Joshua was the tallest of the guys with at least two inches on Isaac who must be at least six foot two, he was also the bulkiest. Isaac had nice lean muscles, but Joshua was ripped, veins highlighted across his muscles as he flexed. It was hard to imagine a girl pushing him to exhaustion. "She's not the kind of girl I'd like to meet. I don't think I'm even capable of doing a single push up."

Everyone laughed around me and for the first time I allowed myself to bask in it. To soak it up and reveal in the fact that I might have finally started to make friends.

They probably thought I was joking, but I'd have done anything to get out of the two physical education classes I was being forced to take at Cherrington Academy.

Through the laughter I looked down at my watch, it was past seven and shit I'd missed my boxes of things being delivered. "It was really nice to meet you guys," I said abruptly as I crumpled the foil over the end of my half-eaten burrito. "But I'm nowhere near unpacked and I'm still so tired from travelling so I should probably head back to my room." I hated that I had to leave so quickly, but I didn't want to keep Noah up all night with my unpacking. I just hoped they didn't think this was rude of me.

"You need any help?" Isaac asked. It hadn't gone unnoticed that he'd been watching me with his steely eyes since he'd joked about recruiting me. I'd chosen not to over analyse it, he was probably just sussing me out.

Charlie started to choke on a chunk of burrito, Joshua rushed to pat his back and when he finally swallowed he said, "am I dreaming or did Isaac just offer to do something nice for someone else?"

"Are you feeling okay, sweetie?" October asked as she mockingly placed her hand across his forehead to feel for his temperature.

"I can't do anything right," Isaac replied with a roll of his eyes. "Take it or leave it new kid, either way, these guys will rib me for it."

"I'd love your help," I replied quickly, I sensed this wasn't something he did often so I'd jumped at the offer. "I'll have you know I'm quite meticulous with my organisation though." My boxes were all labelled with detailed names of where I wanted to put everything.

"Been there, done that. Charlie made me alphabetise his books in eighth grade all like one hundred of them. If

I can do that, I'm sure I can help you unpack whatever bits you've managed to bring from Alberta." He grabbed his tray from the table and gestured for the door. "Shall we?"

I nodded and waved to the group as I followed after his long-legged strides. "Bye guys, I'll see you tomorrow if unpacking hasn't killed the both of us." I aimed my wrapper for the bin and chased him out the door.

"Sorry," he apologised, voice strained like it was hard for him to say, or that he didn't say the word very much. "So, second floor with Noah, right?" He asked almost rhetorically as we slipped through the Edward dormitory doors.

"Room eight," I added as he took the stairs two at a time. "I have to warn you although I could only bring two suitcases on the plane with me, I shipped like four boxes of books, DVDs and other bits of decor to unpack."

He looked at me like I'd just shot him, but it didn't break his pace as he bounded up the of stairs in front of us to my door. He went to push it open, but it was locked. Noah was gone.

I heaved out a sigh of relief, we could unpack in peace. I slipped my key into the lock and felt even more relief that all my boxes have now been brought up and sat waiting for me on my bedroom floor.

"Okay, so maybe it was a few more than four." I chuckled as the boxes took up most of my side of the carpet.

"We are gonna be here all night," he confirmed and subconsciously I cheered, I had no quarrels towards him being in my bedroom all night. None at all.

~ Chapter Three ~

The first three days passed in a mixture of classes and settling in and already I was feeling more at home than I had ever done at my old school.

My social status, even before I came out, hadn't been great but it tanked the second people had confirmation that I was gay. I already stuck out like a sore thumb in my vintage designer clothes and the high-pitched voice that didn't drop until I was fifteen. I was all about the choir, when the rest of the boys were trying out for the sports teams. It isolated me completely from fifty percent of the school straight away.

Things had felt easier here from the second I'd met Charlie, kids were welcoming in the hallways and I fell into a routine of getting up, going to classes, talking to people at my table and not feeling like they were going to beat me up when the bell rang.

I'd spent every mealtime so far with Charlie and the rest of the gang, settling in was coming easier to me than I expected. I just prayed they felt as happy to have me around as I felt to be there.

On the morning of my fourth day of classes, I got to witness exactly what October and Charlie had tried to warn me against getting roped into. Six am, and the loudest of foghorns blasted throughout every floor of the dorm. Me, being the lightest of sleepers, woke up violently and shot out of bed like the house was burning down. Only to be rained on by hundreds of packs of condoms being tipped from Isaac on the top floor balcony, the button to the horns gripped in his hand.

Most of the ever-hopeful boys grabbed at handfuls of the condoms that fell above us, but I just looked up, bleary-eyed, at Isaac and shook my head when he winked at me.

Just before I headed back to bed for the extra hours sleep I desperately craved, I caught sight of a very red-faced Charlie as he snatched the bucket from Isaac's hand and reprimanded him loudly in front of all the weary boys. Isaac just smirked his natural smirk in reply and I had to bite my lip to keep myself from laughing. I'd never experienced this level of crazy and it felt somewhat thrilling to be this close to the action.

I finally dragged myself down to breakfast way too late, to find only Ameliah at our table, everyone else having already headed to their eight am classes or cheer practice in October and Libby's case.

It didn't unnerve me like I thought it would eating alone with one of the others, I had this silent appreciation towards Ameliah as the quieter one of the group, more indie than popular in comparison to the other two girls. We followed similar mantras in life, speak only when we had something to offer, not just for the sake of it.

"Penny for your thoughts?" she asked as I slid onto the bench across from her, cream cheese bagel in hand.

"Oh, don't mind me. Just thinking about my timetable for the day, I have double French this afternoon? What the hell? I've never experienced a double period of a language in my life."

"Welcome to Cherrington Academy," she chuckled as she closed the book she'd been reading.

"It's intense, the last three days have been a huge change for me. I have to take Sociology here, that's a new one."

"Try not to stress, you'll get used to it. You're clearly

23

smart enough to be here if they've let you into two twelfth grade classes."

In the weeks leading up to the entrance exams for Cherrington Academy, I'd probably had ten hours sleep max. I'd spent every waking minute cramming in all the studying I possibly could as I downed coffee like it was going out of fashion to get me through all five exams to get in. When I received the acceptance letter it'd all felt worth it, plus the Dean had personally written back to me to tell me how impressed he'd been with my scores and that he would honour my request to fill my two twelfth grade science credits this year.

"I hope so, I feel like I already have a lot to live up to moving here halfway through the year and my parents forking out to send me." No matter how I felt about them I still didn't want to have wasted their money.

"Did you go to private school before?" she asked straight up.

I shook my head. "No, a state school. Classes were easier there and there were fewer requirements."

She sighed almost wistfully. "Sounds like bliss."

If only she knew the truth. "Trust me. It really wasn't," I replied. Although, with the good mood I'd been in since I moved in, it didn't pay for me to think about the past right now.

"Why the move?"

I hadn't told any of the group about why I'd actually moved here yet, except Isaac and even then, it was an edited version of the truth. I could easily just tell Ameliah what I'd said to him.

Me and Isaac had been four boxes deep into the night of unpacking when he'd asked the same question. I hadn't been sure what to say to him at first, but he'd made me so comfortable that eventually the conversation had flowed

24

smoothly between us. So, I told him why I moved.

"I was bullied through the last half of ninth grade and all of tenth, and this semester it eventually got too much." My tongue darted out over the deep scar on my lip, I could still feel the pain from where it had been busted open. "Things weren't great at home either, my parents travel a lot for their job, so getting away from them was a bonus too."

I hadn't been sure how to get out, I'd been looking up boarding schools when I stumbled upon an ad for the prestigious Cherrington Academy.

"The bullies give you those scars?" he asked as he gestured to my face. He hadn't been prying, there was genuine concern laced around his tone as he reached out, almost close enough to touch my face.

I nodded. "They did. They fucking sucked," I replied with a soft sigh, as I leant against the side of my bed, his hand retracted quickly back into his side.

"That won't happen here you know?" he said firmly. "There's a strict no bullying policy, plus me and the other guys would kick their asses. Trust me." The no bullying policy had enticed me in the first place, but he'd offered me the protection I hadn't found at my old school and just like that, on day one, I'd felt somewhat safe in my new home.

His reaction spurred me to tell Ameliah, so I retold her in the exact words I said to Isaac. His eyes had danced with concern, whereas hers had been more empathetic as she sat quietly through my story. She asked no questions like Isaac did, but as I finished speaking she voiced her opinion.

"I actually hate people," she took a stab at her eggs. "Like who gives them the right to treat others like that? It's just bull shit."

"Tell me about it, but I just don't wanna have to keep

reliving it. Nothing against you, I just want to move on here."

She smiled at me in agreement. "I get that, don't worry, tell people whatever you want it's not my place to spill the beans. We are friends, I was just curious about your transfer, that's all."

She wanted to be my friend. That's what I'd taken from her reply and it was all I wanted from this place, except a good education of course. "Thank you, Ameliah, honestly you have no idea how much I needed to hear that right now."

My phone vibrated on the table and Libby's name lit up the screen. It was my third text from her in the space of an hour and I hadn't even replied to the first two yet. Last night her texts had gotten flirty so I'd turned my phone to *do not disturb* and closed my eyes, then used the excuse this morning that I'd fallen asleep.

"She has a crush on you," Ameliah commented as the screen lit up once more with her name. "You look like she's about to kill you."

"It's just, I know she's your friend, but I'm just not…" I searched for the word that would be the least offensive in this situation.

"Interested?" Ameliah offered up and I nodded, relieved. "Don't look so worried, Lo. Libby does this all the time; she's had more crushes than I've had hot meals. Just be honest with her and let her down gently." With her tray in hand, she pushed off the bench and stood up. "Don't overthink about it okay? I'll see you at lunch." She headed towards the bin and I was alone at the breakfast table with my half-eaten bagel and a whirlwind of thoughts.

English Lit with Libby next, gonna tell her I'm not interested, if you don't see me at lunch please search for my body

I fired the text off to Isaac and his reply was almost instant.

You're screwed man. Hope you have a good excuse; maybe tell her you're still getting over someone from home and aren't looking for anything else right now

You may be lazy, but you're an absolute lifesaver. Thank you

Enjoy English Lit.

I took his advice hard. I walked straight into English, dropped down into the seat next to her and sighed heavily.

Immediately I earned the reaction I desired as she draped her arm around my tight shoulders and asked me what was wrong.

"Just, you know, missing home," I lied with an even deeper sigh.

"Home home or someone at home?" Her eyes glazed over me curiously and although something bit at my gut out of guilt, the fact she didn't look too upset justified the lie for me slightly.

"Somebody," I confirmed. "It's long over, but I miss them and it's strange not seeing them here. I think I just need like a tonne of time to fully get over them."

She nodded understandably and squeezed the hand I had laid on the desk we shared. The world didn't end, she didn't cry like I'd seen a couple of girls do when they'd been rejected at my old school, she just smiled in sympathy, before her pearly white smile took over her face again and she squeezed my cheeks in a lovingly way.

"Don't worry, Lo. Plenty more fish in the sea for both of us." She replied and I exhaled like I was never

27

going to breathe out again and laughed with her.

The rest of the day had been just as good, I'd eaten lunch with the gang and actually enjoyed my drama class, it was on another level in comparison to what it had been like at my public school. The budget here for the arts astounded me, normal drama classes had proper costumes, props, and stage sets. This school had all the fancy lighting and tech equipment, the class had the potential to become my favourite. By the end of the day though I was exhausted, my bag weighed down with all the catch-up work I had for being a transfer student.

My plan was to go back to my room, change into comfy sweats and sit at my desk till bedtime and tackle as much of it as possible. On the way back to my room I'd grabbed a burrito to go and text the group chat that I'd see them at breakfast if I hadn't drowned in all the homework I had.

That plan went completely down the drain when I entered the room to find Noah packing his suitcase. My hands felt clammy as I shut the door behind myself. I knew things were a bit awkward in here and I wasn't his favourite person in the world, but I didn't want him to have to move out because of it. Surely *I* should leave if that was the case.

"Hey, going somewhere?" I tried to keep my tone light and comical, but the panic was there. It was still early days; I didn't think he'd concede this easy.

"Home?" he asked it like it was a question, like why the hell would I have not realised he was going home.

"It's only Thursday though?" I dropped my messenger bag onto the desk, it clunked from the weight of the textbooks I should have been studying right now, not worrying about Noah and him going home.

"For the long weekend? Don't ask me why we have

one, because I don't know. Guess you're stuck here if you have no plans." His tone was malicious, it made me want to throw a textbook at his head. But, how the heck was I supposed to have known about some random long weekend.

Well at least if the dorm were empty I'd have four days to do my catch-up work and get ahead for the last bit of the semester. I had to find some kind of positive from spending my first period of time alone here.

~ Chapter Four ~

Noah was gone in almost a blink of an eye. His case had hit the floor and he'd taken off. I hadn't even had the chance to ask him if I could stay here on my own or even what his plans were for the long weekend. I knew so little about the person I now lived with, I didn't even know where home was for him.

I had to go in search of Charlie, find out what I needed to do whilst everyone was gone for four days.

I found him in prefect mode at the main entrance to Edwards dormitory, an A4 pad of paper in one hand, his school tablet in the other. A pen dangled between his fingers as he kept a steady, well-practised grip on everything. It was beyond impressive.

"What time you leaving?" he asked, his gaze only on me for a second as a student tried to breeze past him without signing out properly.

His arm had shot out to block the boy's path before he'd even taken two steps across the driveway, he was way too good at his job. Within seconds he had the ninth grader all signed out properly and off down the drive with his weekend bag to his parent's car.

"So?" Charlie asked as if the question he posed had been forgotten and not just ignored by myself.

"I'm not," I half mumbled as I tried to get around him, only to have my path blocked in exactly the same way as the previous guy. Except I was smarter than the ninth grader and ducked under his arm but Charlie, being

30

the expert prefect he was, was one step ahead and lightly grabbed the back of my blazer to stop me.

"Hold up, what do you mean?" he asked me with pitiful eyes that I so hated to see. Like I must be some kind of sad sap that had nowhere to go for a long weekend that I had no idea existed before an hour ago.

"I'm not going home. I just got here and I doubt my parents are up for paying for another return flight to Calgary. So I'm staying here, I just need to know if that's okay and that the canteen will be open like normal?" I hadn't even asked them if it was a possibility, I knew the answer and if I was honest with myself, I had no desire to go back to the place I just escaped from.

"You're coming home with me then," he replied his face a blaze of determination as his grip on my blazer tightened like I was going to wriggle away.

"Char," I tried to protest, but he just cut me off with a wave of his hand.

"I'm going to call my mom and let her know, she'll be totally okay with it though. She loves when I bring Isaac or Jay home with me. Oh my god, my sisters will love you as well they are twelve and crazy about clothes right now, they will adore your fashionista ways."

The pure glee in his eyes told me I had to just resign to going home with him. "Fine, I'll go pack a bag."

He clapped like an idiot, before he signalled to the queue of students lined up behind me. "I'll meet you back down here in a half-hour."

I sprinted back up the stairs and packed the quickest bag of my life. Normally it would have taken me at least a couple of hours to pack for a weekend with a friend I hardly knew and a family I'd never met.

"You ready?" he asked as he slipped his duffel bag over his shoulder and gestured to his car now parked at

31

the curb.

I nodded and he took my bag, dropped it in the trunk and we were off to his hometown of Mississauga. I marvelled as we passed the airport I'd landed in just a week ago and how I felt so much less anxious then when I'd arrived. As we drove he told me everything I'd need to know for a weekend with his family. How it was just his mom and his twin sisters at home as his dad had been killed in a drink driving accident when he was ten. How his mom worked her ass off working two jobs and a weekend job to send him to Cherrington and how the twins were the cutest girls alive.

The moment we pulled up outside his house a wave of relief pushed the flood of nerves out of me. His house was the sweetest family home I'd ever seen; net curtains in the window, old Halloween decorations still laced around the fence that lined the front lawn, and a homemade fall wreath hung from the knocker of the rusting front door.

It was nothing like the ceiling to floor windowed apartment we lived in, in Calgary inside a small gated community. We never decorated for any seasons except Christmas when mom hired a decorator to hang pristine silver decorations on an expensive tree to keep up appearances with her colleagues.

Charlie killed the engine and turned to me across the console. "Okay, so it isn't much, not like if you went to Isaacs or Jay's, but there is a spare room because my sisters still insist on sharing." He scratched the back of his neck and laughed nervously as he looked up at the house once more.

"You don't have to explain anything to me. I'm just so grateful you invited me and your mom was okay with having a house guest." On my way over I'd text my parents to let them know the plan, they hadn't replied.

His smile was grateful as he nodded at me and climbed out of the car before retrieving our bags from the trunk. "Jeez, what is actually in this bag? I didn't realise how heavy it was when I chucked it in there."

My bag hit the floor with a thump and I winced at the thought of my Tom Ford aftershave smashing all over my clothes. "Sorry," I replied quickly as I retrieved it from the floor. "You didn't give me enough time to form a packing list to make this ten times lighter."

"You look like you need some help their young man," Charlie's mom called from the front step, arms outstretched ready for her son's arrival. "Hey baby," she cooed as she pulled her son, that towered over her, into a bear hug.

"All good, Mrs Montgomery," I replied as I stopped behind Charlie. "I'm Logan, thank you so much for having me for the weekend.

She let go of Charlie and pulled me into the tightest of hugs. "It's so lovely to meet you, Charlie hasn't stopped talking about you since you transferred to Cherrington. Please, call me Anne, me and the girls are so excited to have you here," she said with a grin as she led us into the house and told us about the plans she had for the weekend.

**

Turns out those plans definitely included all of us. On Friday we'd gone with her to the office she now managed and put us through our paces with some filing and admin. Then on Saturday, she dragged Charlie around the Mall, as I'd come willingly when she'd mentioned both of the girls had grown so much since their last shopping trip and needed some new pieces. Sunday afternoon we'd gone

out for dinner with all of Charlie's extended family. I had
never seen a restaurant make room for thirty people
before, it had been completely overwhelming at first but
when I'd got to grips with the names of all thirteen of his
cousins it was less scary. On the final day of the holiday,
there'd been no plans so I'd given myself a lie in, only to
be disrupted at ten AM by my phone vibrating with a
string of texts.

> *Been dragged to the mall with mom and my auntie, so I'm
> taking advantage ;P* -Isaac.

I opened the multiple attachments to find photos of just
his bottom half in some straight leg black jeans, shots
taken from every angle. The jeans were ugly but poking
out the top of the jeans and up his toned stomach was a
thick snail trail of dark hair that really caught my
attention. Damn this boy, he made me drool over even
the grossest items of clothing.

He had such incredibly toned legs that would look
perfect in something more fitting.

> *If I'm honest, I'd recommend you get slim fit or skinny, they'll
> look ten times better.* -Logan.

I stared at my phone for a solid ten minutes waiting for a
reply, swiping in and out of every other app before
hopping back to our conversation only to see my message
had been read as soon as I'd sent it. I hated myself, it was
a push too far, he hadn't been asking for my opinion, he
was probably just bored of being dragged around the
shops by his family.

I scrolled aimlessly through my Instagram, anything
to get the picture out of my head, only to stumble onto

his page. There wasn't much on there; a couple photos of
him and the boys from 9th and 10th grade, some more
recent ones of him and October in couple-like poses, but
no selfies, nothing of him on his own. Not that I needed
them, because his name popped up on my screen, a
message with another photo attachment.

Better? ;P - Isaac.

Not much of a conversation, but then I saw the photo
and hot damn he was in skinny black jeans that perfectly
outlined every muscle of his quads and calves. My skin
prickled rouge as I zoomed in on his legs, not at all close
to his crotch, but enough to see how snug the jeans were,
maybe I should become a stylist.

Much :) - Logan.

"Don't let him suck you in," Charlie commented from
behind me and I practically jumped ten feet in the air
from where I'd been laid on the bed,
   "Uh, uh, what do you mean?" I quickly locked my
phone and dashed it down onto the other side of the
guest bed.
   "He's a great friend, but don't get caught up in his
plans, trust me Isaac will have you in Julian's office before
you can say the words detention or suspension."
   It was then I started to picture Isaac 'having' me in
Julian's office. That had to stop.
   "You don't have to worry about that. All those
pranks? Not my thing." My phone vibrated on the sheets,
the nerve endings in my fingers itching to open the
message and see what he'd replied, but I'd already drawn
enough attention to it. Instead, I ignored him and kept
my focus on Charlie.

35

"Good, because you don't want to be on Julian's radar." There it was again, that wistful look in his eyes like he'd recalled a memory but kept it to himself. "So, do you fancy a trip into the six?" He asked before he pulled out a pair of tickets I hadn't even noticed he was hiding behind his back, the gold of them gleamed in the cool November sun.

"No way!" I reached to snatch the ticket from him. "Hamilton?" The tickets were for the lower balcony, they were perfect. So perfect I wanted to cradle them in my arms like a child.

"You know it. Evening showing, we'll get food at this cute pub and then stroll up to the theatre. I can't wait to get another poster for my wall."

This would be my first, although I couldn't quite see Noah letting me put up a huge poster in our room and ruining the hardly lived in vibe he had going.

I threw my arms around his shoulders and then my whole body froze. My mind was abuzz with the fact I had my arms wrapped around another male. Thankfully less than a second later he pulled me in tighter. "You're welcome," he offered up and I spluttered into his shoulder as I start to laugh.

I pulled away. "I'm sorry, I've just never been to a big show like this, not many theatres in Grand Prairie." He only grinned harder, as he clapped my shoulder and rubbed softly.

"Well, I'm glad I'm getting to enjoy this experience with you." He crossed his legs at the end of my bed to get comfy. "Look, I'm off duty as prefect but I do wanna check in. Julian told me that before you transferred here that you dealt with a lot of shit at your old school. He didn't give specifics, but I know how hard it can be."

He was the first person who didn't look at me

36

expectantly, like he was waiting for me to spill my guts, but I could still see the concern in his eyes as they lingered on me for an intimate second.

"I'm okay, I'm settling in, I think. You guys befriending me has helped, I don't feel so alone at this school." That was as far as I wanted to reveal, anymore and I would be in the territory of giving the reasons why I had left and well, I wasn't quite there yet. I couldn't face another coming out that only left me in the mud, literally. Karina had been my best friend in 9th and 10th grade, we spent every second at school together that we could and even more so out of school. However, when the cheer team had come knocking for her dance moves, despite her being an outsider at school, she tossed our friendship away to save her popularity status.

"I'm glad, and what I said about Isaac? He really isn't that bad, it's just what he does. You get used to him."

"You guys are quite different huh? How did you become friends?" I asked, because when I looked at the three of them, I saw how Joshua fit into both of their lives, but Isaac and Charlie were on different paths.

"Roommates in the ninth grade. He was my first friend at Cherrington. He, just, I don't know." He lent back on to the bedpost, arms tucked behind his neck. "He got me I guess? I was comfortable around him. Middle school was not a fun time for me, I came out in 7th grade as bi and it all went downhill from there. Isaac never once judged, I guess that's why..." he paused and I could see the wall go up as his fists clenched the comforter, his eyes wet. He snuffled it all back quickly and continued. "I guess that's why we became friends, then we met Joshua because he lived next door and we became three. Inseparable since. I know we are different, but those two would do anything for me and me for them, we've never been a four though, so I'm excited for this year."

I had never been a part of anything like this, in my elementary school there were 15 of us in my class, we all ran around together like a pack. There were no differences that could separate us all then. We all went to the same middle school and that pack was broken, more so as they found new friends and I didn't. "I get that, more than you could understand." He leant over and hugged me again and the pounding in my chest began to calm.

"Okay, you need to get ready so we can go get the subway into Toronto." He pushed up off the bed and I was alone again.

I contemplated the outfits I could wear in my head. I'd bought some perfect black cigarette pants with me that would work for a night at the theatre and so many shirt combinations that could go with it. As I started to think of accessories my phone vibrated again and I was hit with the reminder that Isaac had text me earlier.

I'll wear them out next week. See if they really are perfect for dancing in ;) - Isaac

...

What about this shirt? - Isaac.

He'd attached a picture of him in a burgundy, short sleeve shirt. He'd left a couple of buttons undone and I could see patches of dark chest hair that covered the top of his chest. Heat shot up my neck and I was glad that I hadn't opened the messages in front of Charlie, because I would have been facing a problem that only a cold shower could sort out. He looked incredible, his arms were made to wear short-sleeved shirts and the tone complimented his skin perfectly, maybe he had been

38

listening to my lesson in fashion for him.

Buy it :P - Logan.

My body temperature tripled with his reply.

Just for you - Isaac.

~ Chapter Five ~

The long weekend hadn't been long enough. The relaxed feeling I'd returned to Cherrington Academy with had only lasted till period one, where I was handed even more catch up work. Every class throughout the week had been the same, and it had me curled up in bed on Saturday evening procrastinating the six projects due in the next couple of weeks with an episode of *Keeping up with the Kardashians*.

It may be trashy reality, but I was totally engrossed in all the drama until a green sticky note being slid under my door drew my attention from the screen. I huffed at the thought of getting up to retrieve it but paused the show and trudged over to the note. I had come to learn to expect anything from this school.

The note read *we'll pick you up at 10* with a ridiculous winky face after it. I peeled back the note only to see my own reflection on a pink driving license. My baby blue eyes stared up at me, my pale lips tugged into a tight smile and my burnt ginger curls swept across my forehead. It was a perfect mirror image, but it wasn't my license, I couldn't drive yet.

I let out a snort as I studied the license further and realised that this evening Joshua and Isaac expected me to be Aubrey Fiscal, a twenty-two-year-old from Albany. I'd overheard their plans to sneak out to a club tonight when they were being far from discrete at dinner, I just had no idea that their plans included me.

I couldn't imagine myself in a club. I hardly drank, I

didn't do drugs and did I want to dance in front of Joshua and Isaac after only knowing them for a couple of weeks? Not really. I had literally no idea how to behave in a club. The last time I'd consumed alcohol was at my cousin's birthday and I'd thought I was invincible. Which had led me to believe I could somersault off a trampoline and not end up in the hospital with a broken ankle.

It was a lot to think about; what it would be like to be drunk with Joshua and Isaac, they had definitely been drunk before.

What would I do in a club if someone tried to talk to me? Or if someone tried to come on to me? I mean that was laughable, but I was a virgin to all this both the club and people coming on to me. I hadn't even had my first kiss yet.

I sat back down on my bed, my head in my hands as I tugged them through my lamely gelled curls, my brain in complete overdrive at a simple teenage decision.

I desperately wanted to be normal like Isaac and Joshua and take off to a club without a care. Not be sat here trying to find a reason not to go.

I could go to a club. Right? Easy. Dancing, a few drinks, not too many. Have fun. Easy peasy.

A glance at the clock told me it was just after half-past eight. I had two options either formulate a plan to get out of this or try and get 'club' ready in the next hour and a half. I looked down at my state of undress, Noah had been true to his word and had hardly been around since the long weekend, so I'd felt comfortable lounging around in just a vest and gym shorts I never used.

He'd told me for certain he wouldn't be home this evening. I hadn't asked why, just nodded and silently cheered that I wouldn't have to hang around under his judgmental stare and pretend to study when all I really wanted to be doing was putting on a face mask and watching a rom-com.

It didn't stop me thinking about where he'd spent almost every night this week. However, I never questioned his whereabouts even when he'd woke me up returning home one morning at six am, deep black hollows surrounding his eyes. If I was honest with myself, I was concerned, maybe even a little worried, but too afraid of rocking the boat with my roomie to ask.

Despite my reservations about the evening ahead I hopped in the shower, washed and conditioned my hair and proceeded with all seven steps of my skincare routine before towel drying my tight curls into a more laid-back state. All of this left me with only ten minutes to pick the perfect outfit and as I stood, panicked, in front of my closet, nothing jumping out at me, I wondered if it was even worth going.

Then my rational side kicked in and I reminded myself it was supposed to be a new start here, so I shuffled myself into my tightest black jeans, buttoned up a teal shirt and slipped my feet into patent Chelsea boots.

A final spritz of hair spray and a glance in the mirror told me I was ready, well at least physically, mentally I was still completely freaking out about entering a club that evening. Thankfully, a knock on the door pulled me from my spiralling thoughts. They were bang on time.

My door creaked open to present a pretty well-dressed Joshua in his navy bomber jacket and dark chinos and damn, wow, shit, Isaac in the combination of clothes he'd asked for my opinion on. I couldn't deny they looked even better on him in person. I quickly locked away the thought of fawning over his arms in the burgundy button down before I consumed any alcohol this evening and plastered on a smile.

"Time to go, we need to be quick before Julian locks the gate for curfew," Isaac said as I patted down my pockets feeling for the outlines of my phone, wallet and keys. "Please turn off that whole deer in the headlight look you have going on, I'd really like to be able to get into the club tonight," he teased with a stunning grin.

Joshua elbowed him in the stomach and Isaac yelped before he covered his mouth in remembrance that this was supposed to be a covert operation. "Is Noah not here?" Joshua asked as I locked the door behind me.

"No," I stammered out keeping my eyes focused on the keys. "Said something about studying I'm sure he'll be back soon." I really needed to get better at lying if Noah planned to be MIA as much as this in the future, Julian would not be as easy as Joshua to fool.

They crept down the driveway towards the Uber that waited for us and I followed suit as we snuck out the front gate. "So, what's the plan?" I asked as we slid into the back of the taxi, our shoulders bumping together messily.

"Just you wait and see kid," Isaac replied, a glint in his eye that sent a rush of panic down my spine.

"Isaac," Joshua warned. "He already looks freaked out, we don't need a meltdown here. I really wanna get into L3 tonight."

L3? I thought aloud. I'd seen the club when I'd been Downtown at the Crafts Market. It looked sketchy in the daylight when it was closed, I hated to imagine what it was like at night packed with rowdy drunks.

"Maybe we should have given him the option not to come," Joshua suggested as his teeth withered at his bottom lip.

"I'm not a child you know? If I didn't want to come, I wouldn't have," I replied in protest, arms crossed over my chest. I was too desperate to be part of this friendship group that I couldn't help how childish it looked.

"Joshy is just being a mother hen, don't worry. Let's just enjoy the night, hey?" Isaac cocked his head at Joshua and the boy sighed and nodded. "Good, now let's get the party started," he grinned and produced a small bottle of vodka from his jacket pocket and took a long swig before he handed it over to me.

I twisted the bottle around in my sweaty palms and for a second stared at it like it might magically disappear or turn to water. I'd had vodka before, a shot of it moments prior to the trampoline experience, probably why it scared me so much.

I willed my hands to bring the bottle to my lips, my brain chanted over and over that I could do it, just take the sip. Swiftly I gulped down a couple of mouthfuls before the burn forced me to splutter some of it over the back of the seat in front of me.

Isaac's eyes glowed at me in amazement and when I looked down, I realised I'd drank almost half of the small bottle. He clapped his large hands on my shoulders and smirked. "That's my boy."

I wished.

Joshua just shook his head at the both of us before he stole the bottle from me and took his own shot. I watched as his throat took the liquid effortlessly, they clearly did this a lot. "I hope you know, Isaac, that when Charlie kills us for this, I'm offering you up for bait first."

"Stop worrying. I'll just remind Charlie of the time he drank all that gin in ninth grade when he was trying to befriend Benjie our old prefect," he turned to me to tell the story, a catty grin spread across his face. "It was hilarious, he dropped down a whole flight of stairs on his ass and who was waiting at the bottom? Only bloody Julian. We thought he was a goner."

I struggled to imagine Charlie like that. Even when we'd been at home with his family, he still looked stressed out, like something could go wrong at any minute. I guess that's what you got when you lived with this pair and they pulled stunts like this. He'd loosened up when we'd gone to Toronto, but I could still sense something was heavily weighing on his mind. He'd refreshed his emails constantly on the train to the city like a problem was going to pop up. "You two were a bad influence on him from the very start, huh?"

"Hey, I was pretty much an angel back then." Me and Joshua both looked at him with our best 'are you kidding' faces. "Well, if you compare me to how I am now."

The two of them burst into laughter, I'd only known Isaac for a few weeks but every man and his dog knew he didn't have an angelic bone in his body.

"Also, don't be so rude. I got you the best gift ever tonight."

I raised my eyebrow at him. "Which was?"

"That brand-new shiny ID sitting in your pocket, Aubrey," he patted the pocket of my trousers and my skin sizzled. "That was a quick turnaround even for me. We are almost there, drink up," he handed the almost empty bottle to me and I guzzled it down hoping to burn away the feel of his fingertips on me.

Out the window I could see the blur of Downtown, the vodka vibrated inside me and I was almost buzzing as we clambered out of the taxi and joined the back of the queue for the club.

The buzz turned to a cold drip of dread as I locked eyes with the big, broad shouldered bouncer monitoring the door. This was a mistake. I clung to Joshua's arm for dear life as we moved slowly up the queue.

Isaac swatted at my arm and pulled me into an upright position. "Stop it. If you cower like that, we definitely ain't getting in."

I wrung my hands out in front of me as we reached the front of the queue, however, I had no reason to worry, as with a flash of my ID I was in. The guy merely waved at me to move to the next window to pay. You had to pay?

I must have spoken that part out loud, because the woman behind the desk said, "ten-dollar entry fee before midnight." Jeez, how much was it after? I dug in my pocket for my wallet, but Isaac held out three ten-dollar bills in the woman's direction before I had the chance to retrieve it.

"My treat," was all he said as the lady stamped our hands and motioned us into the club.

The dance floor was already packed with a variety of people, I spotted people that looked almost as young as us, to some older people who were dancing drunkenly in the middle of the floor. Neon lights flashed around us and the vodka in my system had already begun to swirl into a bit of a haze. The pounding music practically shook the ground I was frozen to, my mouth hanging open like a goldfish as I gawped at my surroundings. Even when Isaac stepped in front of me I still didn't blink.

"Jaeger-bombs?" he shouted in my face over the music. I had zero idea what they were, but I gulped down any panic I had about the club and let him lead us to the bar to order.

"Take it slow, okay?" Joshua suggested as he handed me a glass inside a glass, which wasn't strange at all, but again I just nodded and took it.

I'd watched the bartender pour it though, just to check that it wasn't going to kill me. It was just energy drink and a small amount of dark liquor, how much damage could it really do?

"Cheers," Isaac yelled as we clinked our glasses together. "To the new kid's first adventure, may there be many more."

I mumbled my own cheers before I followed suit and hastily tossed back the liquid. It slid down my throat much easier than the vodka. The sweet liquid was warm but didn't burn my throat, it tasted like boozy almonds.

"Whatever that was?" I pointed to the glass that now rested on the sticky surface of the bar. "I'll take another."

Both boys doubled over in front of me, cackling in delight before Isaac wrapped his arm around my shoulders. "So much for slow, ay Jay. I think we just found the kids poison."

Joshua shook his head disapprovingly at the pair of us but ordered another round nonetheless. "Drink this and then we'll head to the dance floor to sweat out some of this alcohol. Don't want you getting wasted before the night has even begun."

Too late. My body swayed a little as I clutched on to the bar, not that it stopped me eagerly chugging down the second drink. I felt weightless, like my limbs had disappeared from beneath me.

Isaac signalled towards the dance floor and I followed as Rihanna's *Please Don't Stop the Music* bellowed from the speakers. All the worry about dancing in front of the pair drained out of me as the alcohol forced my hips to sway in a way I normally saved for when I was locked away in my room. My hands waved in the air in time to the beat of the music as I thrusted my hips with great rhythm. It felt like complete freedom till I whirled round to catch both Joshua and Isaac gawking at me.

"So he can actually dance, who knew?" Isaac commented loudly over the music.

"Who knew indeed."

47

"I can still hear you, you know," I replied

"Those are some moves, Lo. You'd put Shakira to shame with those hips," Isaac grinned as his eyes glanced up and down my body.

The words just fuelled me to pick up pace as the chorus kicks in, sashaying my hips with every beat of the song. I could have done that all night, it was like being on cloud nine and I didn't want to come down.

"Damn boy, you're making us look like amateurs." Joshua wasn't wrong, they were both too stiff, no fluidity to their moves.

I tossed him a wink before I bent my knees slightly to perform a perfect body roll.

"So mysterious," Isaac replied, but my focus was on Joshua as he headed towards a woman who looked at least five years older than us. I gripped Isaac's shoulders and turned him in that direction.

"Don't stress, this always happens, let him do his thing, he'll be back." He reassured me as he tried to copy the body roll I had just perfectly carried out.

"Well, at least you still have me for company." I demonstrated the body roll again, but he just looked as though he was trying to do the worm standing up.

"For now."

I came to a complete stop at his words. "What do you mean?" He said nothing, just glared at someone at the bar and as I followed his line of sight my eyes landed on a burly older man. He was practically ravishing me with his eyes as he scaled the length of my body approvingly. I couldn't say I wanted to return the gesture as he sat there with a greying beard and fine lines under his eyes.

"Not my type," I commented as I turned back to Isaac.

"Not the right gender or just not your kind of man?"

Isaac asked as he clutched my elbow to keep me upright, the alcohol taking over my balance.

I tried to swallow, but my throat was as rough as a cheese grater. Had I heard him right? How did he know?

"Not my kind of man," I croaked out, spluttering up a cough. My brain didn't even have time to catch up with my words, but when it did, I stood waiting for the ground to open up below me, for the world to end. I wanted to have faith in Isaac, in the group, but even as the physical scars healed here, the mental ones were engraved into my brain.

"Good to know will help with the wingman process." Wow. Wow. I let out a shaky breath. I'd just came out to a man, a male who I was becoming good friends with. Came out to a good reaction, no beatings or put-downs. This was a moment I'd savour forever.

A familiar song came on and I let out a high pitch scream. "This is my jam." A remix of Halsey's *Without Me* blared across the dance floor. I grabbed Isaac by the hand before I dropped my hips to the floor, a move if I saw someone else doing I'd definitely describe it as 'stripper-esque'.

Amid my turns I caught Isaac nodding in approval, I allowed myself just for a brief second to consider him to be checking me out. Appreciating every time I curved my ass out or rolled my chest.

I shimmied my hips millimetres from his crotch. His face twitched, eyebrows shooting up and for a second his eyes questioned the roll of my hips, before a smirk broke out across his face. For tonight, I was going to let myself believe that this was real. That someone like Isaac would admire a boy like me.

He desperately tried to keep up with me for the next few songs but sweat trickled down his forehead matting his hair into a fringe. "I think I need another drink," he mumbled into my ear before he pulled away from where our bodies had been slotted up against each other.

I was so stupid, I'd gotten caught up in the music and his approving eyes and had forgotten who he was. My straight friend whom I'd been grinding against like there was no tomorrow. I couldn't watch him walk away, it was too embarrassing. The back of my neck cringed into my head and I let my eyes fall shut for a moment to think about what had just happened. The second my eyes shut I felt Isaacs hand back on mine as he pulled me towards the bar.

"Where the hell did those moves come from?" he asked, a smug grin pulling at the corner of his lips, that sent shivers down my spine.

"No idea," I shrugged, as we lent against the bar.

"Stay here, okay?" Isaac commanded before he walked further down the bar to fetch us a drink.

"What's your poison?" a deep voice murmured from behind me, so close I felt his hot breath ghost my ear.

I whipped around, a little frantically, only to end up face to face with the bearded man. He was so close to me our noses almost touched. I took a step back, my shoulders bristling into a rigid position. "It's okay, he's buying my drinks tonight," I gestured my thumbs behind me to Isaac who was hopefully ordering me a strong drink.

"On a promise is he?" the older man purred.

"God no. Nothing like that, I'm just new in town."

"Oh, sorry, I assumed with all that was going on there he was your boyfriend."

"Yet you were still trying to hit on me?" I rolled my eyes, what a jerk.

"Well, you never know if you don't try. Am I right?"

50

He shrugged his broad shoulders, he probably did this every night.

"If that's what floats your boat I guess."

"I could definitely float your boat if your boyfriend's happy to let you out of his sight for an hour." He attempted to slide his hand up my right thigh, but Isaac was already stepping in, our drinks now on the bar as he swatted the older man's hand away.

"I don't think that will be happening," he replied as he curled his arm tightly around my waist. "I got you a drink, babe," he kissed the side of my cheek, as he slid his free hand into mine. "Let's take these to a booth."

"Lead the way." I let him pull me behind him until we arrived at a plush purple booth as far away from the creepy guy as possible. I gulped half my drink before I dug my fingers through my curls. "I think that guy just propositioned me?"

"Oh, I know he did," Isaac drawled from behind his glass. "If I'd waited just one more second I think he'd have been dragging you into a bathroom stall."

I scrunched up my face and punched the boy in the shoulder. "Gross. Why did you let him go on for so long, idiot?"

"Gross indeed, I've seen those stalls, definitely not a place you want to find yourself on your knees. Your face was just too priceless, Lo, you would have thought he was offering to saw off all your limbs in a slow and unbearable process."

My cheeks were as hot as sunburn at that thought. Me. Down on my knees. In a bathroom stall. Not something I wanted to envision. Not right now anyway, not when all I could see in the flickering lights of the club were a pair of smoky eyes that had me ensnared.

"Yeah, definitely not, no thank you." I raised the glass of dark liquid with a funky neon straw in it, up to him.

51

"What is this?"

"That's a double Disaronno and Coke. I thought if you appreciated a Jager bomb, you'd appreciate this sweet almond liquor."

I took a small sip to test the waters. Pleasantly surprised as it tasted more like juice than alcohol. A dangerous concept with how tipsy I already was.

"Slowly, slowly," Isaac smirked, as he placed his hand over the glass and lowered it to our table.

"It was you who ordered me a double," I shot back.

"Clearly I forgot I was ordering for a lightweight," he chuckled.

"Or you were just distracted by the guy flirting with me at the bar."

"What the hell do you mean by that?" Isaac slid back further into the booth, away from me.

Shit. Too far. "Well, you said you were listening." I tried to tease, to cut the thick heavy air that had started to form between us in less than half a second.

"Oh. Oh yeah," Isaac replied before he downed almost all of his drink.

There was no way he could actually be jealous, right? I was crazy to think that, that was what was happening. He was straight and taken and I was delusional. "I think I'm drunk," I sighed

"You're definitely drunk. Charlie is going to kill me for bringing you here."

"Charlie, Schmarlie. He isn't the boss of us. Plus, he loves us, he'll forgive us for one night of fun." I grinned, lopsidedly as I leant back in the booth.

"I'll remember to use that line when he's screaming at us later. I knew there was a mischievous side lurking in you somewhere." He lent back on his elbows in the booth and if I'd been braver I would have admired him for longer than I should in that position.

If only he knew of all the mischievous thoughts I had been having all night, they were enough to make a sinner blush. The position he was in really hadn't helped.

"Another one of these please?" I smirked as I downed the rest of the drink.

It was too late though, the lights were flickering on and Isaac was grabbing me by the hand, pulling me up out of the booth. "That's the end of the night I'm afraid."

I didn't want to leave. In there, with a tonne of alcohol inside of me, I was freer than I'd ever been. I was defying all the laws I had ever set myself. I'd been hit on. Flirted with a boy. Drank alcohol and not actually embarrassed myself too much.

I stumbled a little as we moved away from the booth, but in my almost fall I spotted Joshua, lips swollen and the flies of his pants undone as he strode toward us. Me and Isaac shared a knowing look before we burst into hysterics. Joshua shoved both of us before leading us out of the club and into a taxi.

It was three am when the cab finally approached the gates. The locked gates. "Fuck, how the hell do the two of you plan on getting us through them?" I screamed in my drunken state.

"Calm yourself, we are experts at this." Isaac paid the driver, before guiding us to the edge of the gate. I glanced behind myself at Joshua and he didn't look worried, so I settled on the fact that it would be fine.

"Shit," Isaac grunted "They've already repaired the hinges I unscrewed last week. I can't open this."

I gulped, hard, I could have cried "What's your big plan now then?" I asked, a little choked.

"I don't have one. We're screwed."

"Just call Charlie, we've already triggered the motion censored lights, if he hasn't already been alerted, Julian defo will have." Great optimism there, Joshua, just what I needed

"I don't think there will be a need for that boys." Just like that, all three of us were met with our red-faced head of house and our prefect, staring us down from where they stood on the other side of the gates. "Which one of you wants to start explaining then?" Julian glowered in on Isaac, fingers tapping his elbow. "Not that I'm surprised to be meeting you, Mr Wells and you, Mr Havana. But I had been hoping not to have to meet you like this, Mr Shields."

My eyes scanned the ground, not even risking a glance up at the older man. I couldn't justify anything; my brain was too foggy for such an activity. So the silence just hung between us like a bad smell.

"Look." Isaac finally jumped in. "Don't blame Logan for this, it was my idea and I just roped him in."

"Are you saying Mr Shields isn't capable of thinking for himself?" Julian shot back,

"What Isaac is trying to say." Joshua stepped up. "Is that we didn't explicitly tell Logan that we were going to be out this late."

"I do not wish to hear your nonsense lies, Mr Yates. I'm sure your prefect here is tired of hearing them too."

I took this opportunity to look up at Charlie, his hair splaying in different directions, his eyes surrounded by sunken pits of black. Charlie had been telling me just a few days ago all the shit he'd had to deal with already this week. "Sorry sir, sorry Charlie. We are all really sorry," I grovelled, Isaac and Joshua both nodded in agreement next to me.

"Very sorry," Isaac added, and I had to hold back the urge to thump him.

"Whilst I appreciate your apologies, as sincere as they

seem." Julian shot a dark look at Isaac. "You've broken a multitude of school rules *and* the law. That must be punished. Nothing but classes, sports and extra-curriculars. No leaving campus."

Isaac moved to protest, but Joshua just pushed his shoulders down. "We understand, sorry sir."

Julian didn't care, he had already walked away. "Mr Montgomery, I assume you can make sure the three of them make it to bed without causing any more trouble," he called over his shoulder.

If looks could kill, Charlie's glare alone would have found the three of us six feet under. "I have nothing to say to all of you right now, you're lucky Julian isn't calling the Dean or even the police. You reek of alcohol, you should be getting suspended right now. And you." He prodded Joshua's shoulder until he stumbled backwards. "I expected better, especially dragging Logan into this. He doesn't need this on his record already." I blanched at that, would that really happen?

He walked us back into the house, but he stopped at the foot of the stairs. "If any of you do this again, I'll shop you to the Dean myself. You hear me?" Acid burnt the back of my throat and before he could step away my sick began to spray everywhere, all over him. "I'm so fucking done," he all but growled as he took off up the stairs, leaving the three of us just stood there, my sick and our guilt surrounding us.

"At least it was a good night, right?" Isaac offered up. Joshua just shook his head and followed the path up the stairs Charlie had just taken.

Isaac looked at me, a little pitifully before he walked towards the cupboard on the ground floor and opened it up, pulling out a mop. "I'm going to do this one decent thing for you, it's the only thing you're ever going to get from me, okay?"

I just bobbed my head in reply, clouds fogged my vision, my throat felt completely red raw.

"You're going to go to bed before you pass out. I'll clean up here and you are to never mention that I did this to anyone."

~Chapter Six ~

House arrest was unamusing. Although, House head Julian had been less amused at all of us for sneaking out.

The first few days had been somewhat easy. I'd had a hangover the size of Jupiter and had spent most of the day after with my head in the toilet. Noah really hadn't appreciated that.

Trying to complete homework when I wanted to be out with the girls and Charlie at dinner was definitely the worst part of house arrest. I slammed the textbook shut for the hundredth time that evening. I needed a break, but Joshua was at Lacrosse training and Isaac hadn't replied to my text to hang out.

As if he was a mind reader my phone pinged with his reply.

Just got out of detention, could use a chance to vent if you're up for it? I'll bring the coffee. - Isaac

Perfect, black coffee, two sugars. - Logan

I shot back but tutted at his text. Isaac had this reputation for being a troublemaker. I'd heard about it in almost every class, even amongst some of the eleventh graders who didn't really know him. Yet he still got almost perfect grades, despite giving the teachers constant stick. I couldn't figure out how he did it.

I caught a glimpse of myself as I stood up from my

desk. I looked horrendous, I'd been slobbing around in my boxers and an over-sized t-shirt whilst Noah hadn't been around. He hadn't been joking when he said he'd never be here. None the less, I couldn't really let Isaac see me like this, we'd still only been friends for a few weeks. I pulled on a pair of jeans and a hooded sweatshirt just in time for Isaacs entrance to my room, he'd foregone knocking before the first week of our friendship was over.

"I'm so done with Garrison's English class, he can shove his nouns and his similes up his ass, I refuse to go any more," Isaac erupted, throwing himself down onto the bed next to where I was sat the second he'd handed me my coffee.

I snorted around the lid of my coffee as the steam hit my face. "You're under a two-week house arrest and that was your second detention of the week. I really don't think you need to add truancy to your current resume."

The side-eye I received from him tickled me, but all the stress I felt towards homework eased from my shoulders. The anxiety that had forced the sweatshirt over my head melted away with him in close proximity. It was a feeling I constantly wanted to cling to when it wasn't just me and him in a room.

"I'm just saying," he drawled out with a coy smile. "He's lucky to have me in that class."

I rolled my eyes hard which only caused the smirk to tug harder at Isaac's lips. In reality, he was a straight A English student and it was what he would most likely be majoring in at University.

"I don't dispute that. The poetry you let me read that you'd written was crazy good. You're clearly a talented writer, I was actually a little gobsmacked." His ears turned the lightest shade of pink and a real smile appeared, which he soon laughed off.

"Don't go exposing me to anybody else, not even Jay or Charlie have read any of that." I was pretty proud of that, to be honest. Considering I'd only been here for a few weeks it was nice to know I was getting to see a part of Isaac that his friends of three years didn't even know.

"Don't worry, your secret is safe with me," I said with my hand across my heart before I reached for my sociology textbook on the side table. "Why did you take this class as your social sciences option for twelfth grade, I literally can't even get through the basic material."

He pried the book from my hands and slid it onto the floor. "What you need is a break," he said simply like I hadn't procrastinated the whole afternoon away.

But maybe if I took a break I'd feel more refreshed and after coffee and chats I'd be able to go back to it energised and with a clear mind. "I think my schedule is just still so unorganised. It's strange living at school so I have no clue anymore when I should be studying and whatnot. Plus the extra language and social science classes are killing me."

Isaac just laughed as his eyes scanned my walls before he peeled a timetable off it. "Get organised?" he asked as he dangled it in front of me. "Says here you've scheduled time to piss."

I snatched the timetable out of his hand and re-pinned it to the corkboard before I thumped his shoulder. "You deserved that," I added as he winced.

"Oh yeah?" he replied, swiping a pillow swiftly from behind my back. "Just like you deserve this," he said thwacking the pillow across my face.

"Two can play at that game." I grabbed the other pillow and took a shot at him in the stomach which sent him tumbling back down the bed. I took the power of being in the upper hand position and swiped at him another couple of times catching him on the side of the leg as he shuffled right to the end of the bed.

I went to smack him one more time in the shoulder to get him to admit defeat, but instead of hitting him straight on, his hand gripped the pillow to stop my follow-through.

"You really want to carry on now?" he grinned as he clutched at the pillow before he tore it from my fingers.

I shook my head almost frantically and scuttled back up the bed as far away as possible from him, but he only shot me a daring grin and crawled towards me before pounding me with the pillow once more.

"Stopppp!" I yelled, squirming underneath where he was hitting me.

"You started this Lo, what did you expect?" He widened his grin as he hovered over me, pillow raised threatening to smack me again. "You know what would make me stop? If you ordered us The Works from Skip the Dishes and didn't tell Charlie about it. You know how he gets mad about take out." I rolled my eyes because Charlie really hated all the grease from take away food, his OCD was ten times worse than mine.

"You'll be thankful for him when you still have the same great body after your metabolism has slowed down."

"You think I have a great body?" Isaac mocked.

"Oh be quiet," I said as I swatted him away from me. I never said no to a burger from The Works, the restaurant practically lived in my dreams. "I'll probably either get the Nacho Libre with extra avocado or the Hipster with added cream cheese. You wanna split a tower of onion rings?"

"I'll get a ring of fire, because I'm super-hot, but make sure you get me parmesan fries instead of regular and I definitely need some of the bacon aioli you got last time it was so damn good. Yes to the onions rings as well, because why the hell not, and then you can answer my question," he added relentlessly.

"Your persistence is admirable," I responded. "You play soccer and work out, I'm sure you have a good body. It wasn't an observation, it was a presumption." I shrugged.

"A correct presumption."

"You're so bloody vain Isaac. Now hand me your phone so I can order this food, mines on charge at my desk."

"You're so lazy, if you want a burger stand up and get it yourself."

"Do you want a burger or not?"

He waved his phone above his head, sardonic eyes teasing me. "If you want it, you'll have to come and get it."

I shuffled quickly to my knees and dived for the phone, missing only narrowly. "Ordering food was your fricking idea, why are you making this so difficult for me. Make your damn mind up," I panted, before jumping to reach the phone again. Not only missing again, but this time I smacked his chin with my elbow.

Isaac yelled out in pain, reaching, instantly, to clutch at his jaw.

"Jesus, Isaac. Now look what you've made me do. I swear you have some kind of death wish." I pried his hands from his chin to survey the damage.

His chin trembled and I couldn't tell if he was about to laugh or cry, so I gently pressed at the bruise to test the pain only for him to yelp. His jaw had already started to bruise and the swelling around it did not look good.

A smile ghosted over Isaac's lips and a chuckle slipped from his mouth and I finally let out the deep shaky breath I'd been holding in since the collision.

"You're so much stronger than you actually look, Lo. I feel like my jaws freaking broken."

This time, I reached out more tentatively, tilting his jaw cautiously so I could inspect it. "I genuinely think we may have to take you to the nurse though. I don't think it's broken, but I'd rather be safe than sorry.

"Does it really look that bad?" Isaac asked, his brows knitted together.

"Of course all you care about is how your face looks," I said with a roll of my eyes, typical Isaac.

"I can't wait to explain this to our friends, how you punched me because I wouldn't let you use my phone to order a burger."

"Oh, because that's definitely how it happened," I countered, sarcasm dripping from my voice.

"Logan was soooooooooo desperate for The Works, that he punched me when I wouldn't let him order it."

"Oh be quiet. No-one would believe that. You'd just be exposing yourself to everyone, especially Charlie, that you were sneaking down here to order yet another take-away this week."

"I have that prefect of ours wrapped around my little finger, I'll have you know. He'd defend me over anything."

"Bullshit. He's not an idiot."

"The bruise speaks for itself, Lo," he said gesturing dramatically to the shadow forming across his jawline.

"You're really going to milk this aren't you?" I leaned in to flick the bruise, but Isaac quickly caught my hand to keep me from getting any closer to his face. I squirmed in protest, trying to wriggle free, but his hold on my hand was solid. "You can't pin me down forever you know. Look what just happened the last time you tried to stop

me. I'll probably end up kicking you in the balls," I
chuckled.

"If only I had video evidence of how violent you
actually are, not this sweet quiet guy everyone else knows
you to be."

"What can I say? You bring out the worst in me," I
replied childishly as I stuck my tongue out at him.

"Is that right?" He looked down at me with a
dangerously coy smile. I cocked my head, he was taunting
me, trying to get me to play this game with him.

I went to reply. Even opened my mouth to try and
force out a reply, but I was just met with tongue
vigorously swiping against mine. Our lips were touching,
fuck our lips were touching.

I kissed him back. Kissed him back with the same
amount of force he had me pinned down with. I let our
lips slot perfectly together, not even flinching when Isaac
threaded his fingers through the curls at the nape of my
neck. Heat crept up my whole body as I slid my hands up
to cup his face, pulling him closer if that was even
possible.

It was all wet and sloppy and I felt completely out of
control, but I loved every single second of it. My first kiss.
My first hot, messy kiss with one of the most stunning
boys I'd ever met.

He tugged at my curls, desperate to keep us moulded
together, although I couldn't talk, my fingers were caught
up in the boy's shirt to stop him going anywhere. Every
now and then I'd go to reach under, but the anxious soul
in me hesitated before my fingers could even come into
contact with his olive skin. I wanted so badly not to be
scared, to rip his shirt off like a normal sixteen-year-old,
but that was too out of control for me.

Isaac took control of the kiss again as he pushed my
sweatshirt up over my arms and head and tossed it to

the floor. It felt like years as he peppered kisses down my chest before he finally pulled away, eyes wide and startled as they darted in every direction but my face. I looked down at him, his shirt a crumpled mess, his lips a brighter red than I'd ever seen before, his phone now discarded on the floor.

I was frozen, not even sure that in that moment I was breathing, only reassured by the pounding of my heart in my chest. I desperately needed Isaac to say something, anything, but he couldn't even look at me.

"What the fuck?" I squeaked out, still struggling to comprehend what had just happened.

Not that I had time to comprehend it as Isaac re-attached his lips to mine. We rolled over and he pulled me down on top of him, our bodies even closer than the first time. This time the kiss was soft, measured, like Isaac knew what he was doing, but I couldn't concentrate on that my subconscious a mess with the fact that I was kissing Isaac. Straight Isaac. Isaac who had a girlfriend.

My mind begged me to stop, but as he dominated me with a kiss I was a goner. I shuffled slightly underneath the boy to allow our knees to slot together in a more comfortable way. I never even thought about protesting when he began to kiss down my neck, chest and down towards my waistband. Heat tingled across my chest, each kiss burnt an imprint into the skin, but my brain was only burnt by the potential consequences if these kisses left marks.

That thought clearly hadn't crossed Isaac's mind as he began to suck on a sensitive spot just under my ear. It was a different kind of pleasure to anything I'd ever felt. It hurt slightly as my nerve endings tinged with fire, but the burning sensation only made me feel more alive.

I was sure when this finally ended I'd feel several

layers of regret. But in that moment, I felt ecstatic.

Isaac kissed my lips again, as if this were a thought we'd just shared.

This time it felt like he was searching, every now and then pressing his lips a little harder, or swiping his tongue across my bottom lip, asking for entrance. I'd kiss him every which way if it meant that I could keep doing this.

The warmth of his fingertips glided against my stomach, goose bumps pimpled my skin and that was what pulled me from the trance of the kiss. I pushed him away sharply, roughly, pulling at the sheet to cover my bare skin.

His gunmetal eyes, that had first caught my attention, filled with realisation and hurt, that I wish I hadn't seen.

"I can't," I mumbled and wrapped my arms around my stomach. "Not like this, Isaac. I'm sorry."

"Can't what?" he asked, his eyes still scanning me like he was trying to bore into my soul to find the answer.

"You know, do that."

"Do what?"

I couldn't say it, didn't want to have to embarrass myself with the revelation that I was an almost seventeen-year-old virgin in front of the boy that just five seconds ago I'd been kissing so hungrily.

"Look Isaac, it must be obvious that I'm a virgin. It's not that I'm someone who's waiting for marriage or any of that bullshit. I just don't want to lose it to a quickie or whatever."

"Right. Message read loud and clear." I couldn't bear to look at him. Couldn't bear to see the disappointment or amusement, or whatever way Isaac would probably be looking at me right now after hearing that embarrassing statement. "I can stick to kissing," Isaac then added and I turned my head so quickly I almost gave myself whiplash.

"What?" I stared at him, not even blinking.

"Kissing is okay, right?" Isaac confirmed, his voice a level of soft I'd never heard him speak in. Dare I say I'd never even heard him speak to October like that.

"October," Was all I could manage to say. It was like a light bulb had just lit up in my head. By the looks of it Isaacs light bulb had just gone off too, his eyes wide with panic. That one word stopping him stone cold. The bubble bursting around us.

"Shit," Isaac swore. "Fuck. I'm sorry. Jesus. Please, don't say anything about this to anyone, okay?"

Isaac had already climbed off of the bed and grabbed his bag and shoes, not even putting them on his feet, as he left the room.

The moment was over. All that remained was me lying there wondering how it had even started.

~ Chapter Seven ~

"What the hell happened to you, man?" Charlie asked as we walked to breakfast the next morning. Thankfully, things were feeling a little less tense between all of us. The look of worried on Charlie's face definitely said he was more concerned about the black bruise that spread across Isaacs jaw, than the fact that we'd snuck out last week.

"I don't want to talk about it," Isaac said with a warning glare my way like I planned on exposing us. I wasn't that stupid.

Charlie had then proceeded to pester Isaac all the way to the dining hall. With every question Isaac getting more and more agitated. By the time we actually sat down for breakfast I thought Isaac might be about explode and actually punch Charlie. His nostrils flared and his fists were balled and I almost felt the need to go over there and try and calm him down. Almost.

"Look, Charlie. I told you to fucking leave it. I'm already going to have to hear this about ten thousand times from October, I don't need it from you. So calm your mother hen ass down and let me just eat my breakfast." Isaac slammed his fist down on the table, before un-balling his fists to flex his fingers. "I'm sorry," he quickly apologised.

I couldn't help but think his dramatics were only bringing more attention to the bruise the size of China across his jaw. If he had just made up some excuse as to how he'd gotten it, none of this would be necessary.

I glanced at him, I couldn't help but notice the dark circles that had formed under his eyes. That I could relate to. I hadn't slept a wink last night. I'd laid there in the darkness for hours, just starring at the ceiling, the images of us kissing replaying in my mind over and over again. The heat of his lips on my neck, the taste of his coffee-stained breath, his gorgeous Tom Ford cologne all over my body. It'd taken all my might to stifle the wood in my pants that had threatened to rise multiple times last night. Was that what kept him awake too? I had so many questions for him. So many things I needed to know. Why had he kissed me? Was it his intention to kiss me or was it just the heat of the moment? Why? Why? Why? I knew I hadn't been imagining things that night at the club. He had been semi flirting with me then and I'd just blamed it on the alcohol?

Not that I could ask those questions right here though, especially with how October was flying towards our table. She slammed herself down on the bench next to her boyfriend and pulled him into the tightest of hugs.

"Baby, what the hell happened to you?" she cooed. Now I liked October and I could see myself being good friends with her, but damn that voice. It needed to be taken down a few octave levels. Especially at this time of the morning.

"He won't tell any of us. Said we need to leave it. He's a right moody pants this morning. I'd just leave it alone if I were you," Charlie commented to her. He sounded pained. Like he was gutted that Isaac wasn't going to tell him something. If only he knew. He definitely didn't want to know. I wish *I* didn't know.

"Don't fret about me, babe. It'll heal, you know how sensitive my skin is. I always bruise like this. Remember how bad my stomach was when I got tackled last year

68

during that soccer match."

"Still, this is bad. Have you been to the nurse? It might be seriously damaged."

"I've been. She said I just need to ice it and take painkillers regularly."

"That's it?"

"That's it."

Ameliah cleared her throat, her eyes darting between me and Isaac and then to October. Fuck, I'd been staring.

My phone vibrated and before I could even look at it, I knew it was her. Ameliah the observant. I looked down at the message, my palms sweaty as I gripped the phone, fingers hovering over the screen as I tried to think of a reply.

What do you know, Lo? - Ameliah.

She was way too good at this. She always seemed to know what was going on. I thought I could work things like that out about people, although I was still yet to work out why there was sometimes this foggy air that lurked between her and Charlie.

What do you mean? - Logan.

About Isaac. You know something. Make an excuse, we're going for a walk. - Ameliah.

I looked up at her across the table, her stonewall stare telling me she was serious about this. How exactly did she want me to get out of breakfast? If anything I was an awful liar. Maybe I could tell them I was feeling sick and then Ameliah could offer to come look after me. Would that be weird? That would definitely be weird. What else could I say? Then it came to me. "Ameliah, you said you'd help me out with that application form. Can we go do it now?"

"What application form?" Libby quizzed from beside me.

Now *that* I definitely hadn't thought through. What the hell could I possibly be applying for right now? God was this the really the time for me to even try and talk about what I'd been thinking about for the last few nights. "Choir. I'm going to petition to start up the choir."

"That's such a good idea, Lo. Let me know if you need to get my Prefect signature on that petition," Charlie replied, beaming a proud smile at me.

"We will do, but as Ameliah is class President I thought she'd be able to help me out. Especially as she sits on the board that ratifies these clubs."

"Let's go then." Ameliah stood up, grabbing her tray off the table, before heading to the bin with me trailing behind her.

"Bye guys, see you all later."

After we quickly emptied our trays into the bin, we headed out into the gardens of the grounds surrounding the dormitory. "Spill then," she said as soon as we were out of the dining hall.

"I'm not sure what you think I know?" My voice was harsh, almost defensive and I knew I was going to have to reign that in if she was going to believe me.

"Don't bullshit me, Lo. I saw how you were looking at him. You definitely know more than you're letting on to." She stopped in front of me, arms folded across her chest.

Why had I agreed to this walk? There was no way I could lie my way out of this one. Her death glare was making me want to shrivel into a ball on the floor. There

70

was just no way I could tell her the truth. I'd have to tell her some version of the truth that didn't incorporate all the kissing that happened after I basically punched Isaac in the face. "I was teaching him how to dance."

"You were doing what?" she asked, her tone high pitched as her eyes narrowed in on what I was telling her.

"I was teaching him how to dance," I repeated, this time more firmly.

"Yes, I heard you, I'm just trying to imagine your awkward ass teaching Isaac how to dance," she said as she imitated my walk, hips swaying and feet stumbling all over the place, never sticking to a straight line.

"Well, I'll have you know that I'm actually a great dancer, Isaac and Joshua were very impressed with my dancing when they took me to the club."

"Damn, I wish I'd seen that. I just can't imagine you dancing, Lo. You walk so awkwardly." She was almost balled over laughing as she walked like someone with a huge wedgie.

"I do not walk like that," I replied, as I showed her exactly how I walked. Okay, maybe I did, but now was not the time.

"That still doesn't explain how he got that massive bruise on his face?" Her head was tilted to the side, her eyebrow raised. She clearly wasn't planning on dropping this anytime soon.

"Well, I started telling him how I didn't just know like club style dance and that I actually went to ballroom classes once upon a time. So, I tried to demonstrate to him how to ballroom dance so he could use it on October one day, he thought he was capable of leading way too quickly and I ended up elbowing him in the chin." None of that was really a lie. I did know how to ballroom dance and I could probably show Isaac how to do it and I had elbowed him in the face.

"Probably for homecoming I'm guessing. It's coming up and he's always taken Toby to those kinds of things, but they've never ended up dancing at them," she replied and I almost let out a deep sigh of relief. "But, why was he being so defensive about it?"

"Embarrassed, I guess." I shrugged my shoulders with more force than was probably necessary. My mind was racing with how much I needed to fill Isaac in on this plan as soon as possible, we definitely did not need him coming up with his own version of the story of how he got that bruise.

"That's really strange. I don't get him at all. October has never really moaned about the lack of dancing."

"It's the last homecoming dance he'll take her to. He's graduating, maybe he just wants this to be a dance to remember." She was making me sweat. I could feel droplets of it running down my neck and it had nothing to do with this ridiculous heat we were currently experiencing in the middle of Fall. I stood still for a moment, pulling the hoodie I was wearing over my head, leaving me in just the v neck t-shirt I had on underneath.

"Who the hell has been sucking your neck?" She reached out to touch the bruises Isaac had maimed on to my neck. In all of the chaos about Isaac's bruises, I'd forgotten about the ones he'd left for me all over my chest and neck. This was not going to end well at all.

I swatted away her prying hands, scrambling to cover the dark bruises that were littering my neck. Before I'd had Isaac sucking all over my neck, I thought hickies were possibly the grossest and least classy things you could sport. But, when his lips were all over my neck, shots of desire shooting up and down my body, how could I say no?

"You can't tell anyone okay?" Because that didn't

sound suspicious at all. I really hadn't prepared for this at all. How had one kiss already caused so many lies to spiral? "Not that it's a secret or anything," I wrestled out, trying to redeem myself as much as possible. "It's just someone from the school in Thorold. It's really, really early days and we aren't telling anyone yet, we've only been out once and it's just so new. So can you, uh, keep this to yourself?"

Her eyes were still inquisitive, like she wasn't quite sure that I was telling the truth. But, eventually, a small, tight smile tugged at her lips and she pulled me into a one-armed hug. "I'm happy for you, Lo. I won't tell anyone, take all the time you need, okay?"

I nodded and pulled her into my side, letting her rest her head on my shoulder. As she pulled away from me I averted my gaze, my eyesight following the trickle of students that were leaving the dining hall on the way to first period if they were seniors, or back to the dorm to finish getting ready. I was in desperate need of a 'Tums' to settle the burning in my stomach, it was almost enough to make me throw up. I couldn't believe I'd just had to lie to someone I was trying to maintain a friendship with.

"I need to go get into my uniform, but I'll see you at lunch, okay Lo?"

I just nodded in reply. Thankful that, for now, she'd bought my dumb excuse of a lie. I wasn't quite sure how, when I'd been spending every waking minute with the gang, she thought I'd had time to sneak out to meet another boy. What I did know, was that I really needed to speak to Isaac. We had to get our stories straight.

73

~ Chapter Eight ~

I'd made a decision; today would be the day I'd come out to the group. It was time, I couldn't keep it from them anymore, I didn't want to feel like I was lying to them all of the time. It felt wrong.

I wanted to be excited about it, but Isaac had put a huge dampener on my moment last night after I made him privy to the dancing excuse I'd fed to Ameliah. I'd told him straight up that I was going to come out today, he hadn't been happy.

"Is this because we kissed?" he'd asked as he paced around his room. I'd only gone up there to give him the courtesy of knowing it was coming, so it wasn't such a shock when everyone knew tomorrow. "Because I already told you it was a mistake and that I was sorry, does it really need to be such a big deal?"

I wanted to scream at him, that it wasn't about him or our stupid kiss or whatever else had happened between us. That it was about me and only me and me being able to own who I was. To take my chance to do what Simon from my favourite film hadn't got to do and come out on my own terms. I wanted to hit him again for being an ass about it, but I could see all kinds of worry and trepidation in his eyes and I knew that he didn't mean to be such a dick.

I didn't though. I calmly told him that it was my choice and I'd made it and I gave no shits what he thought about it. Of course I reassured him that I wasn't about to expose him or our kiss, I didn't out people.

I'd slept on the decision and even though he hadn't text to let me know he was okay, today was still the day.

"It's time to leave it all behind," I sang softly to myself, the Lea Michelle lyrics feeling perfect for this exact moment.

I picked up my phone and shot off a text to our group chat on WhatsApp. I was tired of coming out being such a big deal. This would be it. A text. Plain and simple.

Not that it needs to be said. But, I'm gay. Just want y'all to know so that I'm not keeping it from you guys, as you're my best friends. Honesty is the best policy and all that.

I pressed send and flung the phone on to the bed. I paced up and down the small amount of floor space between mine and Noah's bed as I waited for a reply. It felt good, yet nerve-wracking, to be owning this in my own way. I didn't need to throw myself a coming out party. I just wanted to let my closest friends know that this was who I was.

I could hear the phone vibrating on my bed. The replies rolling in thick and fast. With the third vibration I darted to my phone, scrambling to pick it up and open the group chat.

Good to know. Although, I was already sure of this when I heard you whistling seasons of love at the urinals last weekend ;) - Joshua.

Not even going to ask why that was necessary to say, Joshua. Now I'm guessing that's why you were asking me if I was gay when we first met in Freshman year. You stereotypical twat. Happy for you though, Lo, welcome to the club. Unless anyone else is about to throw themselves out of the closet right now? - Charlie

All of us girls are proud of you. We love you Loggie. - Libby.

I'm hungry. Anyone wanna go get Denny's? - Isaac.

I chuckled and rolled my eyes at Isaacs message. That boy was always hungry. The bruises I'd covered on my neck with concealer this morning were definitely were evidence for that.

That had been a fun experience. Having to ask to borrow Ameliah's concealer. She'd just nodded whilst she eyed the bruises, clearly loving how she was the only one I'd chosen to share my secret with. Well, part of it.

I laced up my converse and threw on a jacket. I couldn't think of anything better than Denny's right now. I was ready to destroy a stack of strawberry cheesecake pancakes.

I'll meet you there, I quickly sent back, before I stuffed my wallet into my back pocket and locked my bedroom door behind me.

I heard them before I could even see them. I turned to see the three lads, whooping, and hollering at me as they pounded down the stairs. Charlie running straight up to me, crushing me into a hug.

"How does it feel to be an out man?" Charlie asked, grinning boyishly at me with Joshua and Isaac laughing behind us.

I pushed him away, my face beet red. "Oh shut up," I said as I punched him in the shoulder lightly. "We aren't going to make a big deal of this, right?" I asked. I knew in the back of my mind the teasing was completely light-hearted. but the memories of coming out last time still haunted me.

"Of course we aren't," Isaac clapped his hand on my shoulder. "You know us, we don't care whether you're gay, straight or a bloody purple dinosaur. We're friends with you because we like you and that isn't going to change because you prefer dick."

I shook my head at him and noticed Charlie and Joshua giving him almost identical looks. He was an idiot. To me it just felt completely crazy that in the last few weeks I'd been here I'd became so incredibly close to these three boys and the girls. This was the icing on the cake for me. They now knew my deepest secret, the thing I was most scared about telling anyone and yet they were still friends with me.

"There he is," Libby said as we entered Denny's, her smile beckoning me forwards to squish into the booth next to her. She wrapped her arm around me and rested her head on my shoulder and I couldn't help but adore her. She was becoming a bit like a little sister to me. I'd always wanted one if I was honest. My whole life I'd hated being an only child. Whilst yes, at some points it had its perks, it had sucked never having someone to talk to growing up. No-one to share all those family holidays or toys with.

I placed a kiss on the top of her head and she pulled away to look at the menu.

"Shame you're gay, Lo. You two do look adorable together," October commented. I just couldn't help but notice that she had Ameliah and Libby either side of her, when normally she was adamant about sitting next to Isaac whenever we did anything as a group.

"I'm starving," Isaac moaned. "When you're all quite done petting Logan like he's a dog, can we please order, before my stomach decides to eat itself." He flounced dramatically into the end of the booth next to Joshua and sighed way louder than he needed to.

"I'm getting pancakes."

As if they were in a chorus line the whole group rolled

77

their eyes.

"Of course you are," October and Libby said together. "It's not like you've been getting them every time since you got here, Lo," October said.

"Hey, stick to what you know, right?"

"Penis and pancakes. All the P's." Libby giggled and we all just stared at her as she pushed her hair behind her ears.

Libby pinched the side of my stomach and I just laughed and laughed until I couldn't breathe properly and tears were streaming down my face.

Yep, I was content here.

Our food arrived within record-breaking time and just as everyone started to dig in, October asked. "So, if you had to choose one of the boys in the group, who would you say the best looking is?"

No matter how much I wanted to laugh about this. Wanted to finally be able to discuss good looking boys in a comfortable environment, with Isaac sitting just across from me, it didn't seem right. I glanced across the table at him and a tinge of red spread across his cheeks confirmed he felt just as awkward as I did about answering the question.

"Of course it's me," Joshua grinned, before cupping his face with his hands. "Who wouldn't want a piece of this?"

"Well, I could name a whole list of girls who haven't so far, Mr Cocky!" Charlie replied, smacking the boy lightly over the back of his head.

"That doesn't answer my question though. If you had to choose one of the boys as your ideal man, who would it be?" October repeated.

I shot her a glare, before letting my eyes drag across the other boys. If Isaac hadn't of kissed me, who would I have picked? Isaac was easily the most attractive out of all of the boys. His smoky grey eyes could hypnotize anyone. But, if I went based on who I could see myself with, who would I actually pick? Until I started spending alone time with Isaac I had no idea he had a much softer side to him. The poetry, the love for words and using them to display his emotions and frustrations.

"If I had to pick?" I all but scuppered out. "Probably Charlie."

October just stared at me and I swear I heard Libby next to me let out a little gasp.

"Don't let Beth hear you say that. She'd kill you if she thought you were trying to steal her boyfriend."

"I'm not her property."

"I'm not trying to steal him."

Charlie and I both caught each others eye as we defended ourselves, before bursting into laughter. He blew me a fake kiss and I pretended to catch it, putting it in my pocket.

It wasn't that I didn't find Charlie attractive. He was a great looking guy. I also really loved that we got on so well and for once I had things in common with another male that weren't going to lead to me having the piss taken out of me. He just wasn't Isaac. Not that I was saying Isaac was perfect because that was not the case at all. That boy had a temper like nobody else I'd ever met. He just controlled it differently to the bullies who's tempers I'd came across. He was the only boy I could think of right now, I couldn't get him off my mind at all. Despite all the complications I still longed to feel his lips on mine again and the guilt about it gnawed at my stomach.

"Why Charlie?" October was persistent. I would give her that.

"Why not me?" Charlie asked, his hand dramatically

clutching at his shirt, right over his heart.

"Yeah, October. Why not Charlie?" Isaac chimed in.

That caught me off guard. It was not Isaac's battle to fight. Why was he trying to jump in on it?

"Well no offence, Joshua. You just aren't my type that hairs doing nothing for me. Really, you could do with a trim."

The girls all oooo'ed. Isaac smiled, coyly, at me. *Touché.*

"Plus, Charlie reads good books and likes the theatre. Sounds like the perfect guy to me."

"Logan, you flatter me. Maybe in another life, we were meant to be," Charlie shot me a wink.

"Maybe. I guess we'll never know."

"At least we know what we are striving for then," Libby said as she picked at the now blotchy polish on her nails.

"What do you mean?" I asked. I knew that tone, knew that smile. That Cheshire grin that told me she was plotting again. It was the same tone all the girls had used when they were talking about trying to find another girl to set Joshua up with. I tugged at my bottom lip, playing with it between my teeth. That was the last thing I needed right now. How could I tell them that I couldn't date other people right now as my mind was just too invested in their best friends boyfriend? *Although, maybe it'd do me some good.* Maybe dating someone else was the key to forgetting about the kiss I'd shared with Isaac.

"Well, we've got to start scouting out all the talent for you on campus. For starters, there's Callum. He plays Lacrosse with Joshua, he's gay. Rather good looking if you ask me." Libby practically had heart eyes right now. So I'd take her word for it.

"You think anything with a pulse is good looking

though," October poked Libby in the shoulder in the response.

"I'm just saying. There are a decent amount of options here. Logan should start exploring them, that's all."

"Maybe I will," I replied, pushing my shoulders back, before catching Isaacs line of sight. I held his gaze as if I were daring him to comment, daring him to say anything that would stop me. *In my dreams.*

"That's my boy." Libby pulled me into a hug again, tucking my head under her chin. Part of me was actually excited for this endeavour. Was it wrong that it was more so to see how Isaac would react, than for me to really find a boyfriend?

I was still trying to work out why I was so hooked on Isaac. Not that I thought I'd be able to find an answer to that question whilst sitting at the dining table with my friends. The kissing had been great. However, the way the boy had ran out and left as soon as he realised what he was doing? Not so great.

I knew, in my heart, that I shouldn't even be contemplating anything more with the gorgeous, tan-skinned boy. Even more so with his girlfriend sitting just mere inches away from me. I just couldn't help how my mind repeatedly wandered back to this kiss. Back to me feeling that kind of affection for the first time in my life. *Lust.* That was what I was feeling.

My phone vibrated from where I was clutching it in my hands. Talk of the devil.

I'm sorry, I had no right to make this all about me. I'm proud of you.' - Isaac.

~ Chapter Nine ~

Noah looked rough. Rougher than normal.
He'd rolled in at five this morning and had
woken me up stumbling around in the dark trying to get
to his bed. I'm sure he was trying to grapple any hours of
sleep he could get before classes this morning, but this
was the third time this week he'd woken me up at the
crack of dawn. I'd turned on the main light in the end out
of frustration. His cheeks were stained with tear tracks.
Red veins spiralled around his iris's. He'd been crying. I'd
gasped a little, rubbing at my own eyes to make sure what
I was seeing was actually the truth.

"Go back to fucking sleep, Shields," Noah grumbled,
before getting into bed himself pulling his blanket over
his head. Clearly, he didn't want to talk about it at all. We
definitely weren't friendly enough for me to push at it, so
I didn't. I rolled back over, but I didn't fall back to sleep.
My brain was practically vibrating with everything that
was currently going on right now.

Why had Noah been crying? I couldn't even begin to
put the pieces together of what he did when he wasn't
here. Part of me felt as though he was living a double life.
Although, it was getting to the point where I could hardly
even class him as living here. The guys spent more time in
here studying than Noah did sleeping.

That had become our thing. Because my room was so
empty all the time, Charlie, Joshua and Isaac had decided
that this was where we would now all study together. The

common room was often too full of stressed out twelfth graders and ninth graders still trying to get to grips with the workload here. It suited me, a win-win situation for all of us. I got to spend more time getting to know the guys, they got to escape the tension of the common room and study in a more relaxed environment. Although, I felt awful for constantly having to lie to them about why my room was always so empty. However, was it really lying when I actually didn't know where Noah was?

Not that it was that, that was truly conflicting me right now.

It was the grey-eyed boy who had me contemplating everything I knew. All my morals, my dignity, my normal loyalty towards friends. I thought about all the men I'd mentally berated in my life when I watched them cheat on girls in my old school and when my favourite cousin's boyfriend had cheated on her. I'd helped a guy to cheat on his girlfriend, even if it was just a kiss. I knew it was wrong but I couldn't stop thinking about doing it again.

Noah stormed back into our room from our bathroom where he'd locked himself for half an hour this morning to shower and do who knows what, he didn't look refreshed though. Two hours sleep would do that to you. He actually looked worse now, as I saw in the light of day what I thought I'd seen this morning; red-rimmed eyes, eyelashes matted together, blotchy cheeks.

"Are you okay?" I asked before I even had the chance to think about who I was talking to. The most defensive man on this planet, closely followed by Isaac on a bad day.

"What the fuck are you talking about, Shields?" he shot back as he grabbed his hoodie and trainers from the floor, the same clothes he'd discarded at five am this morning.

"You look like you've been, uh, you know." I pointed to his face, he'd clearly tried to scrub away the tear stains in the shower, but he'd only made his skin look rawer than it did before.

"It's actually like World War Three up there," Charlie said as they entered my room on the first knock.

Noah's eyes turned as dark as the night and chilled me to the core as he scooped up his laptop, phone, and small overnight bag, before he exited the room as quickly as Charlie and Joshua had entered.

"Something we said?" Joshua asked, as he chucked the huge bags of sour cream and bacon Ruffles he had been cradling down on to my bed.

"No, not you, don't worry," I replied, my hands still trembling as I steadied myself against the desk. All I could see were fists flying and feet as they collided with my stomach, the jeers of other classmates behind them. They may as well have been in my room at that moment. With Noah's tone, they almost had.

"You okay?" Charlie asked, his hand placed on my hunched over shoulders. "What's going on?" I counted the beats of my heart and took a deep breath, I had to push through, if I gave the game away this would all come tumbling down. I wasn't ready for that.

I shot my head up, plastered on a smile and shook Charlie's hand off of my shoulder. "All good, Just Noah being his usual charming self you know. You moving in?" I asked Joshua as I tried to find space on my own bed to sit down.

"Well, with the shouting match going on up there, you never know," Joshua replied through a mouthful of chips, there was no doubt why this boy was still single.

"What do you mean?" I'd been so focused on the row that had taken place in here I hadn't even heard anything going on, on the upper floors.

"Isaac and October, they are really going at it up there and I do not mean in a fun sexy way. I'm telling you the breakup is imminent." Charlie shrugged as he grabbed a packet of cool ranch Doritos and joined me and Joshua on the bed. "I warned Isaac when he was having doubts at the start of the summer that he shouldn't invite her on his families vacation to California, did he listen? Nope and now his mom and dad think she's some psycho girl as all they did was row the whole holiday."

That had not been how I'd heard it. October had gushed non-stop about the whole trip when we'd been out at the mall the previous weekend. She'd whipped out all the pics of her and Isaac at different landmarks and even a few racier shots of her in a bikini and him in his trunks that I'm pretty sure Isaac would not have wanted me to see.

"Charlie's right. They are gonna have Julian up there if they don't quieten things down and nobody needs that level of trouble." Joshua was really going to town on the chips leaving crumbs all over my comforter, only setting my nerves on edge that little bit more than Noah had already done this morning.

"Don't talk to me about trouble," Charlie spat, the Doritos crushed under then clench of his fist "Isaacs heading towards behaviour probation. If he gets put on house arrest one more time Julian's going to take him to Dean and he'll be suspended. His parents will actually kill him at that point, but it's like he doesn't care."

That boy. He really didn't care, did he? "Julian seems nice and all, but I bet when he's actually angry that's not something you want to see?" I suggested, I thought he'd been quite lenient when he'd only given me a week's house arrest that didn't go on my permanent record, especially considering I'd broken several rules that night.

"You got that right. When he yells, he really goes for it." That sounded like he spoke from personal experience. "I just don't understand what's going on with him. Can we not just get through our final year without him making a complete shit show. I'm telling you he's planning something big, he's all over the place, missing dates with October, lying about his whereabouts, I saw him looking really suspicious as he jogged up the stairs the other day. He hasn't said anything to you has he, Lo?"

I realised I could probably attest to some of those things, but I couldn't tell them that. Even if I wanted to, that wasn't my story to tell.

"No, sorry, I don't think he would tell me anyway." I shrugged, even if he was being shifty because of what happened between us, I was still none the wiser to anything else that he was up to.

"I tell you, he sets one more foot out of line this term and I swear to hell and back that me and him are done. I can't cope with his crap anymore, Julian really went to town on me this morning about him and I'm damn near sick of it. I just wanna graduate and have him not be my problem anymore. I wanna be his friend, not his fucking babysitter." The anger slipped from his voice for his final sentence and I realised this was tearing apart their friendship, three years of friendship were about to be ruined because Isaac was out of control. I wouldn't contribute to that any more than I already had.

When I next saw him, he and I were going to have serious words.

~ Chapter Ten ~

"Can I come in?" he asked as he stood arms laden with takeaway bags that smelt like burgers, my favourite, fuck him for knowing that. His eyes scanned mine for an answer and when I couldn't resist the smell of what I was sure was the cheese fondue I caved, nodded and let him slide in past me.

There was something more sombre about him than normal as he sat down on my bed, the food now resting on my desk. He'd been in my room for more than five seconds and he hadn't made a single wise remark, his signature smirk was replaced with the thinnest line his plump, dusky pink lips could achieve.

"What's up?" I asked, as I sat down on my bed too, a considerable distance away from him. Part of me wanted to reach out and pull him close, wrap my arms around his broad shoulders and rest my head in the crook of his neck as he spilled whatever was weighing on his mind right then, but I kept my distance.

"Logan, fuck, you've been on my mind so much since we kissed and then I watched you come out and I was like damn he's brave, I should be that brave and finally do the right thing, so I did. Logan, I need to tell you…"

My phone bleeped repeatedly four times in my pocket and as I pulled it out, interrupting whatever Isaac had been saying, I was met with Charlie's name, four texts all in capital letters and a million exclamation marks.

"Are you fucking kidding me? Charlie's just told me they found CCTV of you breaking curfew again last night

87

and when they started reviewing it some more they caught you breaking house arrest too. Are you stupid or something? You're going to get yourself kicked out." Had he learned nothing from us sneaking out a few weeks ago? I'd been scared to put a foot out of line since, but no, not Isaac, he gave no fucks about authority.

"He forgot to add the fact that I'm on behaviour probation as well, turns out you can't even speak your mind in class here anymore," he sighed, he didn't sound remorseful though. He sounded like he was giving in, not apologising for what he'd done.

"You can't be for real? Do you think that's okay, like really Isaac, you're screwing all of this up for yourself? I thought you were this amazing guy, so smart and intelligent. I've looked up to you since I got here. Everyone told me stories about the riots you cause, but I thought maybe you'd mellow out as you're almost halfway through your final year, you're going to university next year Isaac, you can't do that there. I gave you my first kiss because I thought you were amazing, a great friend to Joshua and Charlie, but you aren't you're fucking Charlie's final year as a Prefect up." I thought, maybe if I bared my soul to him, bought up the kiss between us like the stupidly sacred thing I thought it had, that he'd stop being so fucking ridiculous about this. Get his act together. The way his shoulders stayed rigid, his eyes steely and locked on the spot behind me on the wall and he didn't even breathe out, I knew it hadn't had the desired effect.

"I didn't come here to get an earful, Lo. If I wanted that I'd have stuck around for the lecture Charlie just tried to give me. I came here because I thought you cared about me, that maybe you're the only person in this place that does. Because I really fucking like you Logan, like ridiculously like you. Have since the moment you walked in here last month. I thought after we kissed, maybe you liked me back. I just came here to kiss you again, to see if this could be real."

"Kiss me again? Why would I want to kiss a guy on the verge of getting kicked out? I've already given you my first kiss, I don't plan on giving anything else to someone who just wants to act like a complete loser and end up going to a behavioural school for kicked out idiots. Get out of my room." I rose from the bed, picked up the stupid takeaway he'd bought for us and went to shove the containers back at him when I heard him crack. A choked cough trapped in his throat escaped and his lip trembled, his shoulders sunk in-wards before he ran his hands roughly through his hair and locked eyes with me.

"I've been a twat, I know that. Maybe I just don't know how to change. That's why I need you, Logan. Don't you see that you bring out the best in me? Even when I don't want you to, you're sitting here forcing me to own up to my shit. You're right. Charlie must be so tired of me right now." Isaac rubbed at his neck, eyes watery, no longer the stone-cold metal they'd been since the moment he'd walked into my room. He gripped at my arm, took the bags from my hands, and dropped them to the floor. "Please Logan, don't throw me out now."

He was hurt, I was hurt and this was definitely not how I saw the evening going. Even after everything he'd said to me tonight, the look on his face was breaking my heart more than any of his vicious words. I was still scared though. Scared of being left in the dirt when Isaac chose October. I had to be real about this, this was just a bit of fun. That didn't mean I couldn't enjoy it while it lasted. It was a dumb way of thinking, but Isaac was bringing me so much happiness right now and I just wasn't ready for it to be over yet. I'd take what I could get now and figure out the rest later. Maybe it was time to just fuck it all and forget the consequences, enjoy what little good life wanted to give me.

I pulled at the collar of his shirt, crashing our lips together until we toppled over onto the bed. This kiss was a lot rougher than the playful ones before, our tongues colliding with one another, my teeth occasionally nipping at his bottom lip. I didn't care anymore. My fingers fumbled with his buttons, before I gave up, pulling it over his head tossing it to the floor. I opened my eyes, drinking in Isaacs gorgeous features. Noticing the small scar above the boy's eyebrow, making a mental note to ask about that later. My eyes flitted across the boy's face, memorizing every freckle and hollow of his face. This is what I wanted to remember when it was all over. Nothing could ruin this moment.

Chips of emerald ice. That's what caught my attention next before I pushed Isaac off from on top of me with all my mite.

"Fuck," Isaac crowed, as his body hit the floor with full force. "Why the fuck did you shove me off? You kissed me god damn it, Logan!"

My eyes darted from the figure at the door to where Isaac was now lying on the floor rubbing his elbow.

"Isaac, please stop talking," a cold voice said tiredly from the doorway. The slam of the door shaking Isaac from where he was laid on the floor. Isaac shot quickly to his feet only to be met with Noah's pissed off stare.

"Don't you have a girlfriend, Wells?" Noah asked before his eyes narrowed into crinkled slits in my direction. "Isn't she one of your closest friends?"

I dropped my gaze away from Noah's startling green eyes and starred in panic at Isaac. Two options stood in front of us; lie, dramatically, or come clean. The former was more appealing, but I knew I had to go with the latter. There was no lying our way out of this one.

"Look, Noah. You can't say anything about this to anyone else, okay? This was a mistake on both of our parts," I said, before turning to address Isaac. "You need to leave, Isaac."

"Fuck, Logan, it doesn't have to be like this. Don't push me away." His voice almost sounded like he was pleading with me. However, this definitely wasn't the right moment to engage with any underlying messages Isaac may be trying to give me. Isaac attempted to reach for my hands, but I just retracted them quickly, pushing them under the comforter.

"You have to see we've messed up, Isaac. Even I can see it and I'm not the one with the girlfriend. Maybe you should take a look at what we've just been doing." The voice in my head warned me to stop talking. "You've been cheating on the girl you're supposed to be in love with. Now get out!"

I wish I could have stopped myself from talking, but my heart was pounding so loudly I couldn't think about what I was saying. I'd retract everything I'd just said in a hot second if I could, but it was too late. It had all been said. There was now a churning in my stomach. Fuck, I'd ruined all of this. Worst of all, Noah now knew everything.

Isaac was gone before I could even blink. I was caught between wanting to chase after him or going to lie on the bathroom floor and sob whilst I threw up. But I couldn't run from this situation with Noah. I promised myself when I got here, no more running. So I did neither, unable to move from under Noah's glare.

"Didn't take you as the kind of guy who would support a man cheating on his girlfriend, Shields. Especially when said girl is supposed to be one of your gal pals."

"That's not how it is, Noah. You have no idea."

"I don't and I don't want to either. I already need a strong drink to wash out the image of your tongue rammed down Wells' throat." Noah made a fake gagging noise that definitely didn't help the churning in my stomach.

"Look I know you probably think the worst of me right now, but I need you to not tell October about this, okay? I'm begging you, Noah, it'll never happen again." If I wasn't sure I was moments away from being sick, I'd probably have gotten down on my knees to plead with the boy if that were what it would take to keep this a secret.

"You're a mess and Wells is just a prick. I can't even imagine cheating on my girlfriend. What a waste of space. You know what, I should already be halfway across the drive to Victoria right now, outing yours and Isaac's sorry asses to October. I mean, I'm sure she'd love to hear how you turned her boyfriend gay. But, right now, I need something from you more than I need to go over there and expose you."

"What do you mean?" I asked. "What could you possibly need from me?"

"What I need is for you to cover for me. No questions asked. I'm going to be here a lot less than I already am, for the foreseeable future. I have no room to get in trouble with Julian right now. Especially with the foul moods you, Wells and Havana keep leaving him in. What I'm asking you to do is if someone comes knocking and I'm not back for curfew, is to cover for me and not get me into any shit. Can you do that without fucking it up?"

"How the hell do you expect me to be able to do

that? What do you want me to tell Julian when he sees your bed is empty?"

"I said no questions asked. You'll have to come up with something creative. I'm sure you're capable of doing that if you've been able to keep your affair such a good secret till now."

I went to protest, but Noah cut me off once more.

"Or, I could just go and have a nice little chat with October. Pretty sure that would lose you all your friends."

I sighed, deeply. "Fine. Whatever. I'll cover for you." I knew when to accept defeat.

~ Chapter Eleven ~

"Your miserable face is pissing me off. What could you possibly be so sad about?" Noah asked me from across the room, where he was blasting that evening's soccer game on his laptop, even though his headphones sat beside him.

I was trying to get the Sociology homework I was still behind on done, emphasis on trying, but my head was resting on the notebook that was sprawled out in front of me, no words on the page. "Maybe, if you weren't staring at me you wouldn't be so annoyed." I lifted my head from the page to face him and funnily enough, he was staring right at me, the laptop tossed aside.

"You've groaned every minute for the last half hour, it's kind of distracting," he shot back as he pulled the laptop back in front of him so I could no longer see his face.

"Well sorry, I didn't realise it was illegal to groan in my own room." I closed the textbook and shoved it into my messenger bag, there was no way I was going to get any work done in there tonight.

"It's not, it's just pissing me off, so can you stop?" This time he didn't take his eyes off the game and it made me angrier than when he had been glaring at me.

He had been doing that a lot recently, making me angry. It was mainly little things; using my expensive moisturiser, leaving wet towels on the rug I'd bought from Home Sense, going out of his way to knock my perfume on to the floor to smash the bottle.

94

I didn't reply, I just grabbed a hoodie from my closet and slipped it over my head before I picked up my messenger bag to leave.

"Going to see your boyfriend?"

"I'd have to have a boyfriend for that." I assumed he was talking about Isaac though, even so, he hadn't been in touch since the incident the other night. I had been texting him relentlessly how Noah was holding this secret over our head, mine more specifically, to no reply. I was sort of freaking out.

I gathered up my pencil case but paused to text Isaac and ask him if we could talk, he was the only person I could talk to about this after all. When he didn't reply I wiped my sweaty palms on my sweatpants before I stood in front of the wardrobe and contemplated if I should change out of them into some jeans or pants.

"I don't think Wells is fussy about what you wear. He's not that kind of gay," Noah drawled out like he'd just said the funniest thing in the world. I hated him.

I willed myself to breathe and try to ignore the homophobic undertones to that comment, but my lips were moving before my brain could catch up. "Look, Noah, I've already bowed down to your request to cover for you when you disappear to do god knows what every night. I don't see why you then think it's okay to say shit like that."

"You have no idea what you're fucking talking about, Shields." Before I could blink he was in my face, fists crunched into balls as a storm brewed in his eyes.

Like clockwork, I ducked, almost curled up horizontally onto the floor, as he glared down at me. At that, his fists relaxed and part of me thought that maybe he could see he'd achieved the results he wanted.

"Just stay out of my business okay?" he growled

before he strode back over to his bed.

I'd had enough. I didn't even care about getting changed now, I didn't want to spend another minute in that room. I pulled open the door and slammed it shut behind me before I stomped down the stairs to the first-floor common room.

I smacked my textbook onto the table, so much so it caused the guy just down from me to jump.

Shit, it was Joshua, at least I could somewhat rant to him. "I can't even tell you how angry Noah is making me. How much trouble would I be in if I kill him?" I said, my jaw clenched

Joshua cleared his throat and as I looked up from where I was searching for a pen in my bag I noticed he was not alone. I'd seen that face before. I just couldn't put a name to it. Although, with a face like a Disney prince I'm not sure the name was important, he was like Prince Eric, but in real life. That gorgeous face was enough to banish all my problems away.

"Lo, this is Callum Croswell. We play Lacrosse together. Callum this is my friend Logan Shields, he's the new eleventh-grade transfer."

I collapsed into the chair, almost too dramatically, but I'd just had the realisation that this was that Callum, hot guy Callum. Gay Callum that the girls were going to try and set me up with. Damn Libby and her good taste in men

What a great first impression I had just provided him with. Good job me.

"Hey, Logan. Sorry to hear you have to share with Noah, he really can be a proper jerk sometimes."

I just had to play this calmly, I could do that. "Oh you know, he's just loud and annoying, ruins my faux fur rugs and uses my expensive skincare like it's some Nivea moisturiser." I almost rolled my eyes at myself, now I sounded completely whiny, even better.

"That makes me so thankful for my roommate not being a jerk. If I had to room with Noah, I'd definitely be doing a Joshua and paying a ridiculous amount of money not to have to spend more time than necessary with other human beings." Callum sent me an understanding nod and I was grateful that he didn't think I was overreacting.

"You would not want to live in those single rooms upstairs. You'd constantly have to deal with the carnage that Isaac causes up there. In my few weeks of being here, I've witnessed so much noise and destruction up there. You're definitely best to stay put. Just thank your lucky stars that you have a decent roommate," I laughed.

"Well, if Noah ever gets too annoying you're welcome to hide out in my room."

"Way to get distracted, Cal." Joshua wiggled his eyes brows, ridiculously, at Callum and I wanted to smack him. Even more so when he stood up and started packing away his textbooks. I really did not need him drawing attention to the fact that we were two gay guys having a proper conversation, that could potentially be flirting.

"In case you haven't noticed, Joshua isn't good at sharing. Don't worry Jay, we'll always have Lacrosse."

"That's why he and his besties have their own quarters on the top floor, they may as well get a gate up there, field off all us peasants on the floors below."

"So pretentious." Callum grinned and I couldn't help the giggle that escaped my lips, who knew a gorgeous guy being completely sarcastic could be so cathartic.

Joshua looked at both of us with a bemused smile that only made me laugh harder, damn him for not introducing me to this guy earlier. "Well, if you don't need me to help you pass this Algebra exam anymore, Cal, I'll be returning to my quarters." He shrugged on his backpack and turned to leave.

I shifted in my seat when I realised he was serious and I was about to be left alone with Callum, gorgeous Callum. "I mean, you don't have to leave Jay," I quickly suggested as the uneasy feeling in my stomach stewed away.

"Oh man, I think I do," he replied and when I followed his line of sight, Callum was practically glaring at him, shooting him out of the door with his eyes. "Have fun you two, don't do anything I wouldn't do," was all he said before he shut the common room door behind him.

I crossed and uncrossed my legs as I turned back to the desk, trying my best not to look up from the sociology book that remained shut on the table. I knew I should probably say something, but I needed something witty and intriguing to keep him engaged, however, my mind had gone completely blank.

Luckily, he saved me from my internal battle. "How are you finding Cherrington so far? Seems like you've settled in quite well for a mid-semester transfer."

"I guess it pays to get in with the guys upstairs, huh?" I offered up and he grinned at me, a perfect toothy smile. Progress.

"Smart move, Logan, you'll be protected up there, what could go wrong?"

"Except the house arrest?"

"Oh, this I heard about, you puked all over Charlie's slippers."

Heat flared into my cheeks and I covered my face with the textbook. Trust Joshua to have told him that. Why couldn't he have told him about my awesome sense of fashion or my singing voice? I couldn't even look at him, I would never touch alcohol again.

Callum's hands pulled at mine and I only slumped

more into the red, leather armchair, but he was stronger than me and tugged them away from my face. "I have worse drunk stories don't worry."

My ears perked up. "Go on," I gestured before I tucked my chin into my palms, elbows resting on the table.

"Well, I guess I can embarrass myself, for you. I'm surprised you haven't heard about it, to be honest. It was the first night of the Semester and me and some friends snook some alcohol in, in our luggage. We were having a bit of a gathering in my room and I thought it'd be hilarious to down a tonne of shots. Later that evening I passed out and, oh god I can't believe I'm about to tell you this." He ran his fingers through his hair, destroying what had previously been a perfect coif before he laughed at the memory he was about to tell me. "So whilst I was passed out I was dreaming that I'd spilt all the shots all over me, weird right? Nope. Not when whilst you've been passed out you've actually ended up wetting yourself."

I cackled, literally like a witch, doubled over in my chair. "Oh my god, you wet yourself? I haven't done that since I was like four and still in diapers."

"That wasn't even the worst bit."

"Hang on," I interrupted. "This gets worse?"

"My friends were still in the room, videoing me."

"I need to find these friends." Although did I really want to see a video of him wetting himself? If he didn't think I was weird already, he definitely did now.

"Over my dead body, plus the only person who still has a copy of the video is my roommate."

"Well, I know who's room I'll be breaking into tonight."

"Why can I just see you now sat at the end of my bed watching me sleep whilst you figure out where the video is." He grinned. "Well, I guess that's one way to get a guy into bed."

Oh wow, I reached into my bag for my water bag before I chugged enough to clear all the sudden dryness away. I quickly flipped open my textbook to distract from the blush that spread up my cheeks.

"Was that too much?" he asked as he pulled my attention away from the images of me in his bed, bodies twined together, his perfectly trimmed stubble rubbing against my face.

I pasted on a smile and looked up from the book. "Not at all, just completely stumped by this stupid subject."

"Ahh, the wonderful world of sociological theories. It's your lucky day, Sociology just happens to be my favourite subject."

"I'll actually give you anything for you to teach me about this Functionalism thing before the pop quiz tomorrow." I groaned at the thought of it, my grades really couldn't afford to fail this test.

"How about we make a deal? If I can teach you about Functionalism, you have to give me your number?"

There was no way I could resist the sweet smile he gave me. "Fine, I'm telling you though, you will not be getting my number any time this millennium."

"Oh, just you wait and see. I'm down to be here all night if that's what it takes. Let's move to the couch though, I've been sat at this desk for four hours doing algebra and my back hurts." He didn't really give me a choice though as he grabbed my textbook and plonked himself on the couch, patting the spot next to him.

"Oh, it's on," I replied confidently dropping down on to the couch.

Just a mere two hours later it could be said that Callum Croswell was a Sociology genius. I now knew everything there was to know about functionalism from the warm bath theory to all the crap Durkheim had to offer. He'd even rocked the couch like a slippery bath just to make it more entertaining, props to him.

"I believe you owe me your number, kind sir." He smirked as he handed me his phone with a new contact page open, ready and waiting for me.

My fingers hovered over the screen, I was tempted to stay like this for a while and really tease him, but the puppy eyes he gave me were just too much. "Wellllllllll, I guess you did earn it." I tapped my number in quickly and gave him back the phone.

"Do I really have to wait three days to text you to ask you out?" He asked as he leant into my personal space a little, his lips slightly parted as his eyes locked on mine. For a split second, I thought he was going to kiss me, but before I knew it the moment was over and he'd pulled away.

I shook my head. "Not at all." Something about him just filled me with confidence, so I slid a little closer to him and ran my tongue over my lips to moisten them.

"Good, because I can't wait that long." He sprung a kiss onto my cheek and pushed himself up the couch. "I have Lacrosse practice, but I'll text you after okay?"

I watched him clumsily trip up over the strap of my satchel and for the first time, I could see he was nervous about my reply, as his chocolate brown eyes looked down at me a little desperately.

"I'll be waiting by the phone." Everything inside of me squealed if I was alone I would probably have punched the air. I was being asked on a date by a handsome guy. I was winning at life. "Enjoy practice, say hi to Joshua for me."

"Oh, I will. He's going to be rubbing this in my face forever."

101

"What do you mean?" I asked

"Well he's been talking to me about you since you came out to him, I could tell he thought I was going to like you and now he's been proved right."

Well, this was a revelation. Joshua hadn't mentioned Callum to me. How did he think he was going to get us set up if I hardly knew he existed?

"Don't give him the satisfaction, this was all you. He sucked at trying to set us up. He didn't even talk to me about you."

"You're kidding me? He kept saying he was going to, that's how I thought you ended up here tonight."

"Nope, this was just pure coincidence." The best kind of coincidence. If I weren't still a little bit mad at him I'd probably thank Noah for pushing me out of the room tonight.

"I'm going to smack that boy over the head," he replied before he paused in the doorway. "Although, I guess it all worked out in the end. I've got to run. Talk to you later, Logan." He flashed me that dashing smile once more as he left the room and my knees almost went weak. I was going to be going on a date with a Disney prince.

I reached for my phone in my pocket and realised I hadn't touched it since entering the room. Unlocking the screen I was met with eight new texts from Isaac. I'd completely forgot that I'd sent him a tonne of panicked texts before I'd come to the common room. They ranged from *What's happening with Noah? Can you please text me back? I'm stressed Noah's going to run his mouth,* to *Where the hell have you disappeared to? I'm coming back from Victoria now, I'll meet you at your room.*

The final text was only a few minutes ago. I needed to get back to my dorm. I really didn't need Isaac and Noah having an unsupervised argument about this situation.

I exited the Common Room to see the only situation that could be worse than Noah and Isaacs conversation. Isaac and Callum stood talking on the stairs. Callum spotted me and pointed towards me, Isaac's face dropped a little, his silvery eyes almost breaking me. I couldn't hear what was being said, but if I had to guess, I'd say that Callum has just told Isaac that he'd just asked me on the date.

Well, this was awkward.

I had no desire to deal with this huge mess so I just stalked back to my room, Isaac didn't follow me.

~ Chapter Twelve ~

My nerves had been unsettled all day. Isaac was avoiding me, well he had been avoiding the whole group because of me actually. He'd skipped breakfast for the gym and completed his homework in the library to miss lunch. None of the group could work out what the hell was going on with him, even October was baffled by him doing homework overeating lunch with them. I'd just played along, acted like I was in shock at this too, texting him multiple times under the table whilst we ate to ask him what he was playing at. We'd never even said we were exclusive, not that that was even possible with him still being with October. I was doing nothing wrong by going on this date with Callum. At least that's what I was telling myself.

Callum knocked at the most perfect time, stopped me overthinking my non-existent relationship with Isaac. I opened it to see him standing there in black cord pants with a dark burgundy silk shirt tucked into them. Okay, I could work with this. The cord pants were totally in style at the moment, he just needed to swap the silk shirt for a cotton one. There were too many different textures going on right now.

"You look really good," he commented, eyes raking up my body, his smile appreciative of what he was seeing. I could get used to this compliment malarkey.

"Thank you. You don't look half bad either." I smiled and grabbed my phone and wallet off the side of my desk. "Shall we go?"

"Sounds good to me. I'm parked on the other side of campus, so we'll have to walk a little first."

"Good thing I didn't wear my heeled boots then." He raised a brow at me, his eyes wide as he tried to figure out if I was kidding or not. I was only partly kidding, I did own heeled boots, but they definitely wouldn't have worked with this outfit.

He shook his head and laughed a little, leading me to his car. I whistled lowly under my breath when I saw his car. It was a 2019 plate Audi and damn what kind of family did he come from to be able to afford that? His fashion taste may not be up to par, but if he could pick cars like that, maybe he was a keeper.

"You like what you see?" he asked as he opened the front door, resting his chin on the top of the car.

"Are you kidding me? This is a beauty." I stroked my hand down the hood of the car.

"You don't strike me as the kind of guy that knows their cars," he said as he slid into the front seat.

I followed his lead, climbing into the passenger seat. "Are you stereotyping me, Coswell?" I asked, the smell of fresh leather lingered in the air. Had he gotten a service for me?

"I wouldn't dare." He started the car and pulled out of the car park. The interiors of this car were incredible. My fingers were itching to play with the touchscreen tablet that was slowly coming out of the dashboard. I was desperate to listen to some music right now, create a nice atmosphere in this car. What were you supposed to talk about on the way to a first date? I wasn't even sure where he was taking me at this point.

We'd only just pulled off the driveway when I couldn't resist the urge to play with the tablet any longer, tapping away at the screen furiously. Damn, this tablet even had Spotify, I could hook up my own playlist and that'd probably ease my nerves.

"You're like a little child. I couldn't bear to interrupt the look of awe that's been on your face for the last few minutes. Feel free to put on whatever you want though."

"Even show tunes?"

"Even show tunes."

I quickly searched for my own playlist, pressing shuffle, beaming when Wicked's *As Long as Your Mine* came on. This was one song I'd always wanted to perform as a duet. If I actually did try and start up the choir again here this would be the first song I'd have us perform.

"I did hear you were planning to start up a singing group again. I sit on student body board with Ameliah, she bought it up at the last meeting." He looked at me from the corner of his eye as he turned out of the driveway.

"I'm... contemplating it." I replied as I turned on the seat warmer.

"If I knew the mod cons of my car would be enough to get you to like me, I'd have gotten you in here weeks ago."

Weeks ago?

"I was literally living just two floors down from you. I can't believe Joshua didn't even tell me about you."

"I've already kicked his ass at Lacrosse practice, don't you worry. Some friend he is."

I wish I'd been there to see that. I'm sure that would have been so hot. Callum going in on Joshua because he'd had to wait to be with me. That was some serious fairy-tale shit.

"To be fair to him, he has been pretty busy." Between Lacrosse practice and mediating the tension between Charlie and Isaac every day I had no idea how he had

106

time to do his homework.

"Yeah, things are pretty hectic in your friendship group aren't they? How was it moving here and becoming friends with a group like that?" He asked, switching gears quickly as we pulled onto the 406.

"You don't even know the half of it." Although I wasn't even sure if I knew the half of it just yet. Couldn't work out if I even really wanted to.

"Especially now you've added to Charlie's load. I heard you snook out to L3 with the lads. I made that mistake last year. You do know they always get caught, right? Isaac always pretends he has this master plan and it never works."

"You what?" I almost screeched, my head whipping round to look at him.

Callum laughed in return. "I can't even believe you fell for that. Isaac likes to cause trouble. I think it's in his blood."

Part of me couldn't help but agree with this. The other part knew that Isaac wasn't like that deep down. With the stress and pressure his parents put on him to be this perfect human being, it didn't surprise me that he liked to act out. "Yeah, Isaac is something else." That wasn't a lie at all.

"I'm taking us to 'The Works' is that okay?"

Is that okay? There was nowhere else, for me, that did better burgers. One point to Callum. "Definitely okay."

We were already pulling on to St-Paul's street and I was racking my brain for what I was going to say to him. Weren't these kind of things just supposed to come easy to you? I just wanted one solid topic to talk about going into this date. What had we talked about for all those hours in the common room? I couldn't even remember. That had been easy enough though, this couldn't be any harder than that. Except this dinner came with the pressure of it being a date.

He held the door open for me at the restaurant. He pulled my chair out from the table. He didn't try and order for me. So many points to Callum.

"I hope you don't think it's creepy that I've kind of been crushing on you this whole time and telling one of your friends about it. I was just working up to asking you out. I didn't want to rush into this. Especially as you're a new transfer, I know how crazy the workload is here." He was smiling at me so sweetly, there was no way on earth I could be creeped out by him.

"Not at all. A bit last century waiting so long to ask me out, but definitely not creepy." I chuckled.

His right hand rested in the middle of the table palm up and I was almost tempted to slip my hand into it. But, what if I took it and had completely misread the situation and he was just trying to stretch his arms? I'd end up humiliated and this date would be over before it had even started. I tucked my hands in my lap to avoid temptation. His hand remained like that even after we'd ordered our burgers. I scrubbed my hand over my face. All I had to do was reach down a couple of metres. I could do that. I scanned the restaurant. No-one was even sitting in any of the booths near us. We were completely isolated over here. I could definitely do this.

I flexed my fingers and before I could change my mind slipped my hand into his. His smile only grew wider, the sparkle in his eyes warmed my chest.

"What took you so long?" he leaned in, elbow resting on the table whilst I melted in those pools of chocolate brown. He must do this all the time, he was so good at sucking people in.

"Touché," I replied, squeezing his hand a little. There was something warm and safe about them.

"Heard you were basically top of your class for midterms. You've made quite an impression at Cherrington. Have you started your campaign for Charlie's job next year yet?"

"I couldn't think of anything worse than being Prefect of that madhouse." I also definitely didn't have the authority or patience to do so.

"What, even with Isaac gone?"

"That doesn't mean there wouldn't be a new Freshman Isaac next year. If I had to deal with half of the things he does, I'd have punched him by now." *Again.*

"You don't have to preach that to me. Although, not that I'm some violent guy, but me and Isaac have fought before. He used to be on the Lacrosse team. Trust me, it's a good thing he moved to the soccer team."

Now that was something I definitely didn't need to know. Wasn't I basically just making them rivals again? I needed to get over myself. It wasn't like these two would be fighting over me anytime soon. I wasn't that special.

"How are things with Noah after last night?" he asked, as our food was delivered to the table and he let go of my hand, leaving it feeling empty.

"That's an ongoing battle. If I'm honest with you, I couldn't be stuck with a worse roommate. He's so bloody arrogant. He literally goes out of his way to make any time I spend in that room with him awkward. I swear if he leaves his wet towel on my side of the room one more time I may actually scream. This morning he left it wringing wet on my expensive bed sheets. How does he have the bloody nerve?" His parted lips and wide eyes alerted me that I was shouting, I screwed my eyes shut and wished I hadn't said anything now. Even the waitress who was bringing us our drinks was staring at me a little gob smacked.

With my head bowed I massaged my temple, taking a

deep breath before looking up at Callum again. "I'm sorry," I replied softly. "He just gets under my skin. I've never had a roommate before and now I never want one again."

He was still smiling, just shaking his head a little. How was it that he still wanted to be here when I'd just ranted about my sorry roommate story to him, drawing the attention of the whole restaurant. That was enough to single handily ruin this first date.

"You're adorable. I'm kicking myself I let us get over a month into your time here before I asked you out." He dragged his foot across mine and goose bumps prickled my neck.

"I'm having a really great evening. I'm so glad you asked me out." I leant over the table and stole a fry from him. "The best part of this date so far. The fact that you got sweet potato fries and I got tater tots. Now I get the best of both worlds."

He curled his foot around my ankle. "Adorable," he commented, as he stole one of my tater tots in return.

The conversation flowed like the Niagara Falls for the rest of the night. When they took our plates away he took my hand again and my heart squealed, it pounding at more than twice the speed than it normally did. We stayed hand in hand as we walked to his car and our hands remained linked across the console as he drove us home. In my mind, I was practically running a victory lap.

When he walked me to my door I knew it was coming. He placed the softest of kisses on the corner of my lips and I tilted my head, commanding the kiss a little, so our lips could slide perfectly against each other. I threaded my arms around his waist and pulled him closer, our foreheads met as he pulled away from the kiss.

"Does this mean I get a second date?" he asked as we

stared into each other's eyes.

"Definitely," I whispered back, both of us beamed, as he kissed me again this time just a peck. With one last squeeze of my hand and whisper of a good night, he took off up the stairs to the Senior levels of the dorm, passing October on his way.

"Did I just see you kissing Callum Croswell?" she all but squealed, pulling me into the tightest of hugs, almost lifting me off the ground as she bounced up and down.

"Maybe," I said, no longer able to keep the ecstatic grin off of my face, as I squeezed her harder. Our friendship would be so much easier now I wasn't kissing her boyfriend.

"I wanna hear all of the deets tomorrow, Lo. I can't wait to tell Libby about this when I get back to our room." She placed a light kiss on my cheek and headed down the stairs back to Victoria.

I slipped quietly back into my dorm before I got caught standing contemplating my life like a weirdo in the middle of the landing, only to be met with an amused looking Noah.

"You move on quickly, Shields," he commented, smugly.

Oh, fuck off, Noah!

~ Chapter Thirteen ~

"I need something else from you," Noah said as he sidled up next to where I was sat on the floor. My mirror propped up against the wall as I performed my vigorous skincare routine trying to muster up some excitement to head out with the boys that afternoon. Having another one of these little blackmail chats with Noah definitely wouldn't help with that agenda.

I placed the cap on the bottle of serum and pushed myself up off the ground, I was not going to have that conversation with him looking down on me. "What else could you possibly need from me?" I asked as I returned my skincare tray to my night table. I made the annoyance in my voice clear, but I didn't look at him, I was tired of his judgmental gaze.

"I'm going away for a few days." That explained the case being out again. "I'm not going to be here for classes or in the dorm at all. I need you to tell Julian and my teachers that I'm sick. Got it?"

He was hardly asking, more like telling me that this was how it was going to be. Like it was that simple. He really was something else. "What do I say if he comes to check? Or if he sends the school nurse here? Have you thought about that?"

He waved me off like he'd just asked me to pass the salt, not to lie for him for days and days. "That's your responsibility to figure out, not mine. Just do it, okay?" He started throwing a variety of clothes into his case and

I knew that meant I should concede, it was happening whether I liked it or not, but instead it just made my blood boil even more.

"You're asking to get caught. A few nights spread out across the week isn't that bad, especially when you're still showing up for class, but going off the grid is not what I agreed to." I stood my ground, shoulders back, arms crossed in front of me. He just continued packing.

"I think you'll find you'll do whatever I want, Shields, you don't want your little secret getting out." He dropped his wash bag into his suitcase and zipped it up. "Just do what you're told." He practically wagged his finger at me like a disapproving parent. Well, I've had enough of them for one life.

"And what if I don't? Nothing is going on between me and Isaac anymore, I'm dating Callum, no-one is going to believe you if you out us," I all but shrieked at him as I stomped my feet and like someone who doesn't fight back a lot I yelled louder like it was going to help me get my own way. "You don't get to boss me around anymore."

He pounded his fists into the top of his case and squeezed his eyes shut. "Logan, I'm not asking for much," he gritted out, his jaw tight. "These next few days are just really fucking important okay? Please, just do it," his voice quivered as he pleaded with me and I couldn't move anymore, couldn't even open my mouth to fight back. There was no way I could raise my voice again when the torture in his eyes looked like he was at breaking point.

"Can you just tell me where you're going?" I whispered. "It would make this lying business so much easier."

Those cracks in his outer exterior began to seal as he dropped the case to the floor and pulled the handle up. "I told you from the very beginning I was going to Hamilton. What more do you need to know?"

"I don't know? How about who you're meeting? Why you're going? Where in Hamilton you're actually going? Any kind of information would be helpful, Noah. Especially as you're asking me to cover for you." I crossed my arms firmly in front of my chest. I really wasn't asking for a lot from him.

"Look. Fuck. Logan. I just have to be there. I can't tell you why. That's it okay. I'm done fucking talking about this." He ran his fingers through his floppy blonde hair, exasperatedly. Sighing the loudest sigh I'd ever heard, he was starting to sound as defeated as I was.

"Fine. Fine. Whatever, I'll cover for you, but this is the last time." He nodded somewhat gratefully as he stacked his jacket on top of his case. "Now if you don't mind I need to go meet the boys to go to Niagara Falls."

"Have fun. Get some cute couatery photos with your boyfriend. Wait, which one is actually going, Coswell or Wells?" That small grateful smile faded. If you'd have blinked you'd have missed the fact that it had been there in the first place. He replaced it with an evil Cheshire grin. God, I hated him. I grabbed my camera from inside my top drawer and pocketed my wallet before I took off and slammed the door behind me.

I raced off up the stairs and it was only when I reached the top step I realised we weren't meeting till eleven am because Charlie and Joshua had their prefect/deputy prefect meeting till then. This left me with no other option than to see Isaac, alone, or I could have sat on the stairs like a loser and waited the half-hour for my other friends.

I needed to talk about bloody Noah and Isaac would really understand my anger, so I took the plunge and wrapped my knuckles on his door.

He opened the door shirtless, eyes rimmed with deep purple circles. "Late night?" I asked as I slid into his room.

"Climbed over the back fence at 5am, was absolutely fucked," he commented as he pulled on the shirt he had strung over his shoulder.

"Well, at least you didn't get caught." I rolled my eyes, I hadn't realised that we weren't on good enough terms for him to even invite me on a night out.

"I've got the sneaking out down now don't you worry," he grinned as he rummaged in his drawer for a pair of socks.

I couldn't help but notice how tidy it was in there for once. The last couple of times I'd been up here there had been textbooks everywhere, notebooks scattered across his desk, bed, and floor. He was the type of studier I didn't aim to be, sporadic, unorganised, messy. This was all gone now, books were stacked neatly on the shelves, pens organised in their pots, a stack of assignments done and in plastic wallets ready to hand in. I was impressed.

We stood in an awkward silence, he stared at me and I stared down at the floor as I tried to muster up something to say.

"Did you enjoy your date with Coswell?" he asked like that was the best thing we could possibly talk about right now.

"It was nice, thank you. Sorry, I didn't get the chance to tell you and you had to hear it from him. We're okay though right?" It had been on my mind since I'd seen him on the stairs a few nights ago, there had been something in his eyes that made him look completely devastated. It had kind of crushed me if I was being honest with myself.

"Totally fine, don't you worry about it." He smiled, his lips tight, no sign of his signature smirk.

Just then my phone buzzed and alerted me that Charlie and Joshua were ready to leave downstairs. "We should go, Charlie's just driving the car round from the parking lot to come and get us."

We walked down in complete silence and drove in almost complete silence as me and Isaac ended up in the back together. The only noise came from the front seat where Joshua and Charlie chatted aimlessly over the sound of the radio.

The excitement of getting there was almost ruined as Isaac dragged his feet behind him like a sulking child, whilst me, Charlie and Joshua talked animatedly about Clifton Hill and all of the crazy that came with it. It was almost like a tackier version of LA if that was even possible. There was a gloomy look on his face every time I turned around to check he was still with us, deep concentration between his storm cloud grey eyes.

I tried to push away the worry I felt, but no matter what I still cared about him, so I dragged my feet as well. Charlie and Joshua hardly even noticed as I pulled out of the conversation whilst they decided whether we should go play mini-golf or bowling after the Falls and I fell into line next to Isaac.

"You okay?" I asked as I nudged my elbow into his. He looked over at me and the thunder only rumbled harder within his eyes, like deep black holes.

"What do you want?" he asked in return as he slowed down his pace. I had an inkling he didn't want to have this conversation overheard by his best friends, not after his mass panic of texts when he thought Noah was going to expose us.

"Wow, why did you bother coming if you're just going to be a complete grump?" I sighed. I'd been looking forward to this trip since the moment I decided

116

to come to Cherrington. At that point, I didn't even realise I'd actually have friends to see it with, which only made this ten times better and I really didn't want mardy pants here to ruin it.

He shrugged and went back to watching every tiny step his feet took, I wanted to walk away and leave him to it, enjoy the day with Charlie and Joshua, but there was a mood radiating from him that made me think I'd done something wrong.

"Spit it out, Isaac. I'm not a mind reader, what's the problem here?" My tone was bitter and I hated that that's what it had come to. He'd got his way and I'd got mine, I guess. I really did have a good time with Callum last night and I wanted to give it a go with him, but I didn't particularly want storm Isaac following me around.

"Leave it, Logan. Walk away, I'm not in the mood to have this conversation." He slipped his sunglasses back down over his eyes and thought that was it, conversation over, but this had become an itch I needed to scratch.

"If I've done something, Isaac, I'd like to know. I have a right to know why you're skulking around like someone's kicked your puppy. You're ruining the day." I scowled at him, not that he noticed because his eyes were fixated on anything that wasn't me, I could see it even through his coloured shades.

"Fuck off, Logan. Do you really need to do this anymore? Haven't you got better things to be caring about? Like Coswell." The bitterness of his tone soured my mood even more. There was absolutely no need for him to bring Callum into this.

"What's going on?" Charlie asked, halted at the bottom of the hill. "I'm not going to spend the day here if you two are just going to bitch at each other like this." The sound of the falls gushed in the background and I was sure if we just turned the corner we'd be able to see

117

them, but Charlie looked so stern right then, he literally had the face of a headteacher as they reprimanded a naughty kid. It meant that we weren't going anywhere until this was sorted.

"Nothing," I muttered. "It's fine, it's done. Let's just enjoy the rest of the day?" I tried to walk away, but Charlie just grabbed my arm and glared at me with his prefect stare, he really had that mastered.

"Me and October broke up." Isaac finally caved, his voice plummeted as I studied his face for some kind of emotion, but his eyes weren't watery and his lips stayed pulled together tightly.

"What?" Joshua exclaimed, as if he'd only really just tuned into the conversation, which was probably true, to be honest. He loved the drama. "When? Why?"

"Does it matter? I don't want to talk about it, I just want to move on, can we please just get back to our day."

Joshua went to speak, but as Isaac went to walk away Charlie waved his arms in protest to not push anymore. I wish he hadn't though. I'd like an explanation as well, why had he done this? When did he do this? I didn't get a chance though as Isaac breezed around the corner and the three of us were left to stare at where he once stood and then at each other.

"I know I said it was imminent, but I thought they would sort it. It's the first time in the two years they've been together it's ever been rocky, I thought they'd be able to work past it," Charlie said and I could see the worry in the crinkles on his forehead.

I felt it too, but I also couldn't help the niggling feeling of responsibility that ate at my insides. That I may be played a little bit of a part in their breakup, it was a selfish thought, but the timing couldn't just be purely coincidental. "He'll be okay, Char, we just have to give

118

him time," I tried to reassure, but Charlie didn't look convinced, his worry lines only deepened.

No-one said anything for the next ten minutes, we walked peacefully to the best vantage point of the Falls and then I was rendered completely speechless. It was more magnificent than I could have even prepared myself for. The photos didn't do it justice, not the way the water spilled off the edge of the rocks or how it crashed at the bottom and bled into the turquoise river that parted the two countries.

My marvel wasn't ignored as Charlie and Joshua both snapped pictures of my reaction and then we took a bunch of group selfies in front of the falls like every tourist around us.

Isaac however, sat a few metres up the way, elbows rested on the rocks, eyes hypnotised by the two falls that straddle the Canadian/American border. Even with all the awe I had been feeling, I couldn't ignore his shaded eyes and the way he bit his lip like I normally did when I tried to stop myself from crying. I would have lost it if I'd seen any of those tears spill down his face, my heart wasn't made to take in a sight like that.

119

~ Chapter Fourteen ~

"It feels so good to be done with exams." I sighed as me and Joshua walked out the exam hall, his twelfth-grade math exam and my English exam had been in the same place, it was nice to have someone to talk to about this the second we left.

I'd hardly seen anyone over the last few weeks since the Falls trip, we'd spent meal times together which had been awkward because either Isaac or October didn't turn up each time like they had it scheduled, and we all felt that big gaping hole in the group as we sat and ate. It was strange, I'd gotten so used to it being the seven of us over the last eight weeks or so, now one person was missing and it was like the whole group had been blown apart. Ameliah and Libby twitched when it was just the two of them sat with us guys without October. Ameliah was better than Libby at keeping up appearances because me and her had become such close friends after we set up the choir, but it wasn't like that for Libby, October was her best friend and it must be so weird for her to be with us and not her. It wasn't my problem to solve though, I was already way more involved than I wished to be. I wouldn't try and fix things between Isaac and October, they had to do that themselves.

"Tell me about it, final ever set of Christmas exams at this place completed." He grinned back at me, but there was a tone to his voice that told me he'd miss it. "Any plans to celebrate this evening?" He asked like he didn't already know, like I hadn't already told the group at breakfast this morning I wouldn't be joining them for dinner.

"You know I'm going out with Callum. We are going to Niagara on the Lake for dinner and then we are going to walk out to the lake for sunset." It sounded like the perfect date. The nights were starting to draw in earlier so if we ate just after four and then strolled to the front we'd hit the sun setting at the perfect time. I was excited about the food, I'd found this beautiful little restaurant for us to eat in called Zees Grill and I'd packed my big camera to get some snaps of the beautiful views. Maybe I'd even put my fake ID to use and buy Ice Wine for the first time, as Niagara was known for producing it. It was just a shame I wasn't as excited for the guy I was going to be sharing the views and the food with. Fuck Isaac Wells for springing his stupid break up on me and making me question everything all over again, just as I'd pushed him into the unattainable box.

"I know it's only been like three weeks." I sighed as Joshua started his sentence, because I knew exactly what he was going to say and it killed me that Joshua was more excited for mine and Callum's date than I was. "I know, I know, I'm too excited and it's too early, but you guys could be perfect together and I'm just you know so happy that I finally introduced you to him." He beamed at me as we arrived outside Edwards dormitory.

I cleared my throat and cocked my head to look at him, eyes narrowed. "You introduced him? Are you kidding me? He told me that he'd been asking you since day one to introduce us?" I laughed. "It took me storming in and making a dick of myself to finally properly meet him, I will not let you take the credit for us finally dating."

"Hey, I was going to, I just kept forgetting and then you and Isaac were constantly spending time together. He was going through a rough time with October so me and

Charlie just thought it was good to let him talk to someone that wasn't us about it, someone that was a little less biased as you hadn't seen their whole relationship form like we had. It didn't seem the right time to introduce you to a new guy when we all knew Isaac needed someone to talk to."

If only he knew that it wasn't just talking going on in those little sessions. That maybe if he'd have introduced me to Callum straight away I wouldn't have ended up shacking up with his best friend. That was wishful thinking. I think I'd fancied Isaac from the moment I locked eyes with him in Charlie's doorway.

"Look I know your heart is in the right place, but you need to just chill okay? Give us a chance to get to know each other," I replied as we parted ways on the second floor and I headed back to my room, only to find the one and only grey-eyed boy, Mr Isaac Wells stood at my door. Exactly what I needed when I was supposed to be getting ready to go out with Callum.

"Can I help you?" I nudged him out of the way just to get to my room, as per usual Noah wasn't here, who knows when he'd be back or if he would be as we broke for Christmas break tomorrow.

He slipped past me as I opened the door and stood awkwardly in the middle of my floor. I opened the closet and pulled out the outfit I'd prepared for tonight, something simple and warm. "Look, I haven't come to cause trouble or anything. I've come to give you my blessing or whatever it is that people do when the person they kissed moves on with someone else. I'm really happy for you and Coswell. I hope you live a long and wonderful life together," he smiled, not grinned, but there was a layer of sarcasm to his voice like the happiness wasn't wholehearted.

"Thank you, Isaac, that really means a lot. I'm sorry about you and October by the way, how is she taking it?" I slipped off my blazer and re-hung it on the hanger I'd taken it off that morning before I started to undo the buttons on my shirt. My mind questioned whether it was right to do this in front of Isaac, but I turned my back to him and I was just going to slip a shirt off and pull another, nicer shit back on.

"Not great, but it's been coming for a while. She knew that I knew that. We'll get through it, we were friends before we got together and eventually, we will sort things out and be friends again I hope." As I did the buttons up on the second shirt, I turned just in time to see his smile falter and slip, his eyes more glossed over than when he'd first told us all about the breakup. Whether he'd fallen out of love or not with October a breakup after two years was still hard, no matter the circumstances. We all had to remember that.

"You guys will get through this, I'm sure of it. Can you avert your eyes a second, I just need to put these jeans on?" I dangled the skinny black jeans in front of his face, the identical pair to the ones I recommended him to get on his little family shopping trip. He grinned in recognition and turned his back to me so I could quickly switch out my school trousers.

I looked great, I eyed myself in the mirror and couldn't help but tip my head at my choice of a silky emerald shirt that complimented my auburn curls and how good my ass looked with this shirt tucked into my skinny jeans. He let out a low wolf whistle, which stopped me in my admiration tracks and I raked my eyes back over to the boy in question.

"You look great, you're going to knock him dead." He stroked his hand across my cheek and I had to turn my head away from his hand to get him to move. "I'm sorry, I'm sorry, just have a good night, okay?" He added as he went to leave, his voice dropped to a whisper and it damn near broke my heart.

"Hang on a second. It's okay, we both need to move on from the kiss right?" I replied as I pulled him into a strong hug. "We can do that right?" He nodded into my shoulder and I didn't want to let go, of him or the kiss, but we had to, we *really* had to.

A throat cleared behind me and we shot apart like a chemical reaction. I turned to see Callum, looking gorgeous in a navy shirt and dark jeans, but with a face like thunder as his eyes flitted between the pair of us, like he knew he'd just walked in on a moment.

"Sorry, am I interrupting something?" he asked as we took another couple of steps apart.

I shook my head desperately, as did Isaac, but I could feel my cheeks as they started to flush with colour. "No, Isaacs just having a bit of a bad day after his breakup with October, needed a hug." I offered him a small smile and for a while, it was enough to get him off my back.

Isaac left swiftly and Callum drove us almost silently to Niagara on the Lake, just the sound of the radio to keep the silence from drowning us. We'd walked to Zees hand in hand offering up small talk about the day and exams being over, but the second we sat down in the big plush chairs around the candlelit table his eyes were quizzing me without him even having to say anything. Like if he looked me up and down for long enough he could figure out what he'd seen between me and Isaac, but that was impossible, not even I was sure about what had happened there.

We ordered swiftly, him a beer which caused me to raise an eyebrow because we had to drive tonight, but he assured me one wouldn't hurt. It didn't reassure me though, because the second our plates arrived at the table he ordered another one.

"Seriously?" I asked as he swigged the second beer. "You know I can't drive your car right? I only have my G." I wanted him to stop, but he just waved me off with a flick of his hand.

"It's just a fifteen-minute drive I'm sure you can handle that." He may as well have spat in my face with that tone, but he didn't, he just added a smile at the end of the sentence. I hated that I'd done this, I'd made Disney Prince Callum angry, something I didn't think was possible.

"You wanna talk about what's making you mad or should I just get an Uber home?" I asked before I sipped from my water to try and calm my nerves before we talked about the inevitability that was Isaac Wells.

"It just looked like I was interrupting a moment between you and Isaac back there and I'm trying to work out what the fuck that was, because I thought things were good between us." He looked more scared than anything, like what I was about to say next would break his heart.

I just shook my head. "Are you crazy? Nothing's going on. I told you he was upset about October and he needed someone to talk to. Charlie and Joshua were busy with prefect stuff, so he came to me. Its Isaac, come on, how could you think that?" How had anyone missed it? Now I thought about it he'd made his attraction to me obvious since day one, but everyone had just dismissed it to Isaac having found a new friend.

"You guys were hugging though?"

"Friends hug, would you not hug Joshua if he was going through a hard time?" I shot back and I hated that I was getting so defensive about all of this. It just made me look so much more guilty.

He nodded and his face softened, as he placed down the half-empty beer bottle which made me feel a little more relieved. "As long as you're sure, Lo? I really like you and seeing you two together like that, like I know it's only been a few weeks but I have such a good feeling about us. I know we are about to leave for Christmas, but I hope we can pick up where we left off here when you come back." He smiled the sickliest sweet smile and took both my hands across the table and squeezed.

My heart dropped and I left Niagara on the Lake feeling ten times more guilty than I did when I first arrived. I hated myself.

~ Chapter Fifteen ~

From the moment the plane touched down in Calgary, I'd felt a tinge of regret about being so happy to leave St-Catharine's. As I'd stood alone at the airport, waiting for the Uber to pick me up rather than my parents, it struck me why I hadn't come home for the long weekend.

Having been away from my parents for almost two months I'd completely forgotten how soul-destroying it could be spending lengthy periods of time with them. On the first night, they'd quizzed me for hours about the new male friends I'd mentioned, pushed me on the nature of my relationship with all of them.

If these had been the parents I longed for I'd have gushed for hours about how amazing my friends were and about the guy I'd enjoyed spending endless hours with and wished to be my boyfriend. But, they weren't. So I'd answered all their questions with yes/no answers, denying any other relationship than friendship with any of the guys I'd mentioned.

This, however, had backfired. The fact that I'd not started dating any guys resulted in them thinking I was straight again. So I'd spent more nights than I wished to fielding questions about potential girlfriends. This time answering them with firm 'No's' reminding my parents, more times than I should have had to, that I was in fact gay. Homosexual. Only interested in boys. Only interested in Isaac. Even when I really should have only been interested in Callum. Wonderful Callum.

The moment I stepped off the plane I felt nothing but

relief to be back on Ontario ground, just a couple of hours from School, with the knowledge that I wouldn't have to see my parents for another six months, maybe more if I could convince Julian to let me stay at Cherrington over the Summer. I hoped I could just find a job down here and not have to return home to anything of the likes of how Christmas had been. If I had it my way I'd never go back. Make life easier for both me and my parents.

As I dragged my carry-on case through security and turned my phone off aeroplane mode, it bleeped almost instantly.

When are you back? - Isaac

His timing, as ever, was spot on.

Just landed. - Logan

You need a lift from the airport? - Isaac.

That I did, I'd thought about it on the way to the airport and was about to book an airbus when I remembered that I had an Aunt and Uncle in Central Toronto. So I thought I'd head up there and see them before class on Monday, but this would make life easier.

Please. Terminal three - Logan

I'll be there in an hour, you wanna get food on the way back there's a Tex-Mex place just up the road from the airport. - Isaac

Sounds good, see you soon. - Logan

By the time I'd waited about ten years for my suitcase to be the last one off the conveyor belt, Isaac had already pulled up in the short-term pick-up section. He revved the engine on his obnoxious sports car as he spotted me in the distance, before hopping out to load my case into the trunk.

"Callum not here to pick you up?" he asked as he pulled out of the parking space with a Cheshire grin on his face.

"Don't start, Isaac." He knew Callum wouldn't have driven all the way from Leamington to come and get me.

"Just saying. Have you ever been to Lonestar Texas Grill?" He'd already got the address typed into the Satnav, ready for us to go. He knew me too well. I'd live off Mexican takeaway if I could, that and burgers. They rotated around my top two types of food. Right now it was definitely Mexican at the top

"Just drive." I shook my head and sank into the leather seat. Obnoxious or not, this car was like luxurious levels of comfort. Heated seats, plush interior, a touchscreen sound system that looked like something from the future - my favourite Spotify playlist on the screen. Damn it was a bad idea sharing my username with him.

It was just a short drive to the restaurant he'd been talking about and as he pulled into the parking lot I snuck my first proper look at him since before Christmas. Fuck those beautiful grey eyes and the way they controlled my mind to think about nothing more than kissing him.

Not that I would. I still really wanted to give things a go with Callum. He'd really made the effort over the Christmas break to stay in touch with me. We'd even managed to FaceTime a few times, which was lovely as I got to see a friendly face whilst being trapped at home. Part of me wished I'd been eager for more or overexcited

129

to see his gorgeous face rather than just an escape from my parents. I wasn't though, not like how my stomach churned when I saw Isaac parked up waiting for me or how my heart lurched at the sight of my favourite song ready to play as we pulled away.

I pushed the dull ache in my chest down as we were seated at our table, menus placed in front of us and I couldn't lie, Isaac did so well, the place smelled amazing. We quickly ordered some food, a big old burrito for me and tacos for Isaac, plus a huge sharer plate of nachos for the both of us. When the waitress left an air lingered around us, it wasn't awkward per se, just thick and murky, like I could see in the very distance what I wanted but I'd have to battle through the fog to get there.

"You okay?" he asked, pulling me out of my long stare at the beauty of his sun-kissed skin and piercing grey eyes, thick brown hair pushed back across his head in the most stylish way.

I wanted to snap my gaze away from him but I'd been caught, there was no way I could hide from that, part of me didn't even want to look away.

"Yeah, just thinking sorry, it's been a weird three weeks and I'm so glad to be back here, but I guess it's a lot to process. Also, the flight was awful, we were late taking off and then because we were late taking off we missed our slot to land and we had to circle Toronto for an hour before we could touch down and I feel crappy. Like I could do with a good face mask and massage just to feel that little bit more human right now." My skin felt like dried out crap, craving a good injection of moisture right now. That would be the first thing on my agenda when I got back to Cherrington, thank the lord Noah wouldn't be back till tomorrow night.

"You'd never know you just stepped off a delayed

flight," he said, his lips curled up into a small smirk.

Screw him. "But I get it, I know life at home isn't great for you. Guessing your parents still aren't happy with the fact you like men?"

Typical Isaac, never one to tread carefully around a difficult topic. "Nope, still perfectly homophobic. Definitely didn't mention the fact that I'm dating a guy the whole time I was home. So much joy at Christmas when you can't even discuss your loved ones with the people who are supposed to love you unconditionally," I laughed bitterly, but a year ago the fact would have probably made me cry, so it felt good to be able to finally laugh about it. Especially with someone, I'd told most of the ins and outs of mine and my parent's relationship too.

The air thickened even more around us as he turned his head away and pulled at his lip between his teeth, his eyes no longer able to meet mine. They searched the restaurant as though he was looking for our waitress with our food, but I knew it was because I'd mentioned Callum. Even with his blessing I knew it wasn't a great topic between us, Callum was like Voldemort and as soon as I'd said his name I'd regretted it.

"So you two are still dating or whatever then?" He finally turned himself back inwards to our table, but his eyes focused on the menu, the cutlery, anything but me.

I nodded in reply, I didn't trust any of the words I could possibly say right now. All over Christmas, I'd thought about Isaacs breakup, I didn't want to be vain or self-centred, but I couldn't help but wonder if it was because of me, because of us and what had happened. I'd let my mind wander to all kinds of places, whether he'd caught feelings for me and decided to break up with October to be with me, which was completely crazy, because Isaac could and already had done so much better. Or whether our kiss had made him think *okay maybe I'm*

131

bisexual or gay and he wanted the chance to experiment and figure himself out and what he liked. To be quite honest the thoughts had plagued my mind more than I wished to admit. I'd thought about Isaac more than I wished to admit.

"Well what I'm about to say is about to make things so much more fucking awkward between us, but you know I'm completely reckless so fuck it. I miss you, Logan and I really crazily, stupidly have this thing for you. This isn't like me at all, but you've fucked my brain up with just a few kisses and now here I am making a complete idiot of myself because I didn't do this properly. I'm sorry I pushed you away and into Coswell's arms, but I really do like you and I thought maybe you'd have broken up or something over Christmas and we could give this a go. Which is why I bought this, well not really, I want you to have it regardless of whether you like me back or not because it's for you." He reached into his backpack and pulled out a slim package wrapped in the most perfect, but ironic navy and white pinstripe wrapping paper with a gold gleaming bow and slid it across the table to me.

"Isaac, you didn't have to get me a Christmas present. I didn't get you anything." I sighed as I fingered across the slips of the paper and pulled the wrapping open carefully, it was too beautiful and somewhat meaningful to ruin. "No way!" I practically screeched, before I remembered we were in public in the middle of a packed-out restaurant. "How the heck did you get this?" I said as I grinned like a six-year-old on Christmas day at the sheet music in front of me. Not just any sheet music, my all-time favourite song *As Long as You're Mine* from Wicked, but no it didn't just stop there, somehow Isaac had managed to get his hands on a signed version from

Kristen Chenoweth and Idina Menzel. If there was any reason to fall in love it would be this.

Isaac looked like the cat that got the cream with his Cheshire grin as he watched me light up animatedly at the gift, "You're so very welcome, by the way." He added and I just shook my head at him, because I couldn't be more thankful for such a beautiful gift. "I trolled the Internet for this, all different Broadway forums, which I'm now signed up to and I can't figure out how to unsubscribe to. I keep getting emails from Wicked123 and MadForBroadway, if anyone looks at my emails they are going to think I've completely lost it."

I wanted to cry, was this how getting a gift from a loved one made you feel? Like you could never be more grateful for anything, even something as simple, but completely thoughtful, as signed sheet music of your favourite song. To have someone look so pleased with themselves as you react with glee to their gift. To want to reach out over the table and take their hands and squeeze them to show how thankful you are and pull them into the sweetest of kisses and think of all the things you are thankful for about that person. Because Isaac, right now, made me feel that crazy whirlwind of emotions.

But there was a fence between us, a huge fucking fence. I was seeing someone and me and Isaac had started seeing each other under such bad circumstances whilst he was still seeing someone, someone who was my friend - that still completely ate me up - I couldn't do that to Callum. Part of me wasn't sure I should do it even if I was completely unattached. If Isaac could do that to someone he'd been with for two years, there would be nothing stopping him from doing it to me, especially with him only just discovering he liked guys. I didn't want to be a guinea pig or his next steppingstone.

Not even the way his silver eyes had looked at me

right then could stop that worrying thought buzzing in my head. I had Callum; safe, Disney Prince Callum who in the future could be perfect for me. I had to give him a chance, it was the right thing to do.

"Isaac," I started, hesitantly, and his grin died at my words, my tone enough to ruin anyone's mood. "I'm with Callum and I don't want to mess that up. I don't know if he's a forever person, but right now I'm enjoying getting to know him and don't want to stop that. You will never understand how glad I am that I became friends with you and I don't regret that we kissed or that there was something starting between us last year, but the circumstances we did it in were wrong. We never should have gone behind October and the whole of the gangs back and I just can't look past that. I'm sorry."

The food came out perfectly on time as I finished my ramble and we sat and ate in complete silence until Isaac shook his head at me. "We can still be friends, this will pass and I will move on. I don't want this to come between us. Please just say that I haven't ruined everything between us?"

"Don't be silly." I forced a smile. "That's not the case at all. We'll always be friends Isaac, all of us regardless of what happens. I can't imagine any of us ever falling out." I had to insert the rest of the gang into this, it had to be about all of us, not just me and him because I couldn't promise we'd always be friends, I knew part of me may always want more.

The prickled around eased us and after we paid the check and drove back to Cherrington, I forced myself to believe that we could be friends. That these feelings between us wouldn't always be there, but part of me realised I had started to fall for him and nothing was ever going to be the same as those feelings hit home.

~ Chapter Sixteen ~

I'd made a crazy decision and asked Callum to sit with me and the gang for lunch just mere days after me and Isaac agreed to be friends. I couldn't decide who'd been more excited when I'd asked the group if they'd be okay with him spending lunch with us, Joshua, or the girls. Joshua was ecstatic. Partly because I was happy, which was nice, but also because his friend was getting to get to sit with us. The girls were overjoyed. They all thought Callum was gorgeous, plus, it gave them someone else to coo over.

Isaac hadn't been there when I'd asked the group the night before if Callum could sit with us, he'd been stuck in detention and stupidly it didn't cross my mind that night to message him and check he'd be okay with it.

That was why I was now stood tugging at my sleeve as I waited for Callum to meet me outside the dining hall before we went in. As I shuffled from heel to heel, I spotted Callum above the crowd coming straight towards me. His handsome smile beamed like a beacon of light through the flurry of students that scuttled between classes. I felt part of the tension ease in the back of my neck and when he took my hand and led me into the dining hall, I almost forgot why I'd been so worried in the first place.

Until we'd grabbed our food and headed to the table. I spotted Isaac before I'd even noticed who else was already sitting at our table. His eyes searched mine in confusion as me and Callum plopped ourselves across from him on the bench. Clearly no-one had informed him that Callum would be joining us today.

I couldn't let that distract me right now. Callum was already iffy about what was going on between me and Isaac. The conversation he'd walked in on before our last date had been brought up a handful of times in the last few weeks. Every time I'd shut it down. I really didn't need him digging around in mine and Isaac's past. I was still thanking the universe that he hadn't walked in moments before and heard Isaac giving his approval for us to be together, that he really would have questioned.

Focus. I let Callum drape his arm around my shoulders as we settled in at the table. So many pairs of expectant eyes now stared at us. I couldn't help but roll my eyes. These people were the best friends I could ask for, even if they were about to be super embarrassing. Just at that thought, Libby let out the most indiscreet squeal, clapping her hands like a seal, as she grinned from where she was sat beside Isaac.

"I did warn you about this," I half-whispered to Callum, he just rubbed at my shoulder in reply. I felt a burst of pride run through me, the small gesture reminding me that I wasn't having to hide this and that no-one was about to beat me up for being happy and content.

"You guys know Callum," I said to the whole table, as Joshua joined us, scooting up next to Callum.

"We love Callum," Joshua commented before Callum even had the chance to speak for himself. "We one hundred percent approve of this relationship."

I bristled under Callum's touch, my spine rigid at that word. That word was heavy and came with commitments and emotions and feelings that I wasn't sure I was quite ready to feel just yet. From the look of confusion on

Charlie's face, he'd clearly spotted my reaction. My face was an open book after all. Charlie had no trouble reading me.

"Are you guys, you know? A couple?" Joshua asked, the question sliding out awkwardly. "I don't mean to pry. Logan's just a bit of a secretive creature."

"I mean, it isn't a conversation we've had yet." Thank god Callum was handling this so easily, so I wouldn't have to find some awkward reason for why we hadn't had this conversation yet. "But." Oh god, there was a 'but'. "I'd really like us to be a couple," he said like it was just an easy breezy statement and he hadn't just basically asked me to be his boyfriend.

My hands felt clammy from where I was clutching them together under the table. Was he expecting me to give him an answer right here in front of all of my friends? I felt myself shrink into the bench, like a tortoise retreating back into its shell.

The silence was deafening as him and all of my friends waited for me to reply. They must have known if I was going to say yes that I would have done so by now. The longer I waited to say no, the more awkward this was going to get.

It wasn't that I didn't like Callum, I did. It was like there was a blockade between us moving onto the next stage of our relationship. Like I had to defeat the big, bad villain at the end of the game to progress to the next level. Only it wasn't a big, bad villain that I needed to defeat. It was the grey-eyed boy who was looking at me so pleadingly across the table. I couldn't say no to those eyes when they looked at me with such real emotion. This wasn't like that night when he was trying to stop me going on that second date. This was real desperation.

I needed to say something. Callum's arm had dropped from my shoulder minutes ago and I could feel Joshua bouncing in his seat next to Callum. Everyone around the table was waiting for my answer. I locked eyes with Isaac and he gave me the smallest smile that smashed my heart into tiny fragments. Some were waiting more than others.

How could I agree to this when the boy I was falling for, wasn't the one asking the question?

I pushed a little distance in between me and Callum before I turned to look at him. The way he tugged at his lip confirmed to me that he already knew what my reply was about to be. "I'm sorry, Callum. I'm just not ready to be in a relationship yet." I heard a small gasp in the distance that I knew had come from Libby, but I couldn't bring myself to glare at her for being so inconsiderate right now. I couldn't tear my eyes away from Callum as he forced a smile and nodded.

"You're right," he agreed. "It's too soon." His arm wrapped around my waist, pulling me closer to him again. I let out a silent breath as I pulled away from him.

"I can't do this. Callum, I just can't. I don't wanna hurt you. I'm sorry. I don't want to be with you." I looked him in the eyes only to see pure heartbreak. Both of us trapped in between my friends, nowhere to run, both of us left to soak up the humiliation of our very public break up.

October cleared her throat, drawing everyone's attention away from us. "So, applications for Prefect of Victoria for next year are open and me and Ameliah have some news. We are both running. Against each other."

I was done. I had no desire to hear about becoming a prefect. I felt him slip from beside me out of the seat, my eyes trailed him out the door. No one said anything, they just tried to carry on like it hadn't just happened.

It was the only thing I thought about all day. It

distracted me in class to the point I couldn't hear the teacher over my own thoughts, even when I got back to my room and flopped on my bed I couldn't see anything but Callum's face, Isaac, the group. How much damage had already been done by me falling for Isaac?

This had to end. I couldn't keep doing this. I was hurting so many people right now and they didn't even know about it. I snatched up the sweatpants from my floor and donned my 'Cherrington Academy' sweatshirt.

I took the stairs two at a time until I made it to the top floor. I didn't even bother knocking. However, when I stopped in the centre of his room, him staring up at me from where he was sat cross-legged on his bed notebook resting in his lap, I had no idea what I'd actually come up here to say.

"What the fuck?" He swore as the door slammed into the wall and then banged shut again.

I just gaped at him. I really had barged my way in here and for once I wasn't even sorry about it. This conversation was needed. "What was that about at lunch?" I asked arms folded tightly in front of my chest.

"What when your almost, but not, boyfriend asked you out? Yeah, that was pretty damned awkward. Think everyone was quite glad when you two didn't return for dinner."

I could punch him. His tone was so bloody cocky. It was like he was genuinely pleased that I'd turned Callum down. I just couldn't work out if it was because he found that entertaining or if he was actually really happy I'd said no. Part of me, the part I wish I could stamp into the floor, was hoping for the latter reason. "I'm talking about how you were looking at me. You wanted me to say no. You were practically urging me to say no."

"You're imaging things," he said, rolling his eyes at me as if I'd just said the craziest thing on the planet.

139

I took a step closer to where he was now sat bolt up straight in his bed, so I could look him fully in the eye and see if he would still lie to me like that. "Don't lie. I thought you were going to cry if I said yes." I held his eye line, it was getting to the point of it being an awkward length of eye contact, but I didn't care. I needed him to admit this to me. I needed the validation that I'd made the right decision by saying no to Callum.

"Why are you doing this, Lo?" he asked as I stepped closer to him. "We can't do this, you told me we had to stop this, that it wasn't right."

I knew he was right. I knew it so bad. I felt like I was repeating everything he'd said a few weeks ago that had made me so angry. I stepped forward again, my skin tingling with a mix of desire and anxiety, I clutched my hands at his face and all but whispered. "But, what if we could?" His eyes softened, I'd almost forgotten what it felt like when he looked at me with those cotton grey eyes. I couldn't help but run my thumb along his jawbone, his cheek leaning into my touch as I did.

"I gave you that option, you didn't take it," he whispered back. My grip fell to his wrists, holding them so tightly to stop my hands from trembling. I could feel the tremors up my arm, as my heart pounded so loudly I couldn't hear any thoughts that would stop this from happening.

It happened all at once. I'd been repressing the thought for weeks, pleading with my brain and heart to stop thinking about it. Not even contemplating what it could mean or how it would truly feel to open myself up fully to that possibility. As I gazed into his eyes, his thumb tracing a soft circle onto my wrist. I just knew. What I wanted was sitting right in front of me. I'd come to conclude that it wasn't because he was unattainable or just one of the most gorgeous guys I'd ever seen. It was because I wasn't scared around him, I could be exactly who I wanted to be, no holding back. It'd been like that since the day we met three months ago. I felt a little bit crazy because I'd started to wonder if maybe he could even be the one.

It was like leaping off a building. I slid myself into his lap, my legs straggling his. He looked up at me as I nestled myself down, eyes wide and gaping. "What are you doing?" He asked, but his voice wasn't willing me to get up, it was almost as if he was checking to make sure I was sure about this.

I shushed him, cradling his cheek once more, before leaning in to kiss him. His lips immediately captured mine, sliding his tongue past my slightly parted lips before I'd even had a chance to wind my arms around his neck. And if I hadn't already leapt off a tall enough building, I had now. I pushed him backwards, his head hitting the pillow. I felt empowered as I hovered on top of him, slotting my leg perfectly between his as we continued to kiss fiercely, teeth and tongue clashing together.

His eyes quizzed mine as I rapidly unbuttoned his shirt, my hands roaming across his chest. His abs tensed under my touch, but as I kissed down his neck the tension slipped away and he whipped my t-shirt over my head. I didn't even hesitate as my hand slipped beyond his waistband. I was so caught up in devouring every part of his body I didn't even feel him remove my pants. It was only when our naked bodies collided did I realise that this was happening. In the back of my mind, I prayed I'd remembered to lock the door.

Shirts were strewn across the floor and sweatpants discarded across the room, the sheets were tangled around us and just like that, it was gone. I'd given it to Isaac. That sacred part of me that I knew I couldn't get back. I was more than okay with it though because I, Logan Shields, was in love with Isaac Wells.

As Isaac fell asleep, I slipped out of his grip. I didn't want to get caught in here. In his bed. Both of us naked.

That would be completely unexplainable. I slipped back into my clothes and hoped that I didn't run into anyone as I flew down the stairs back to my room.

"How do you do it?" Noah slurred from within the darkness of our room.

I practically leapt out of my skin, not expecting him to be here right now. The room was only lit by Noah's dim desk light, the light barely highlighting his face. After everything that had happened this evening, I didn't have the energy for this right now.

"I just don't get how you or Wells do it?" he stumbled over his words, as he asked the damned question again. Was he drunk?

I fumbled for the light switch on the wall, not wishing to have this conversation with Noah's face being lit up like he was about to interrogate me. "Do what, Noah?" I asked as the bright, white light filled the room. I could now see the bottle of dark liquor he had clutched to his chest. It looked like whiskey, but I couldn't be sure.

"Cheat. Both of you are as bad as each other. I saw you. Sneak up there after dinner. I was going to see Charlie and I saw you slip into his room. How can you do it? Doesn't the guilt eat you up." He was beginning to sound like someone who actually had morals. He wasn't wrong though. The guilt had been eating me up for the last two months and half of the time I hadn't been cheating on anyone. Even now that we were both single, it still felt weird, like we were going behind the backs of so many people. I really wasn't any better than Isaac. Even more so now we'd slept together.

142

"I don't know," I muttered in reply, as I searched my dresser for a clean pair of pyjamas. Part of me wished I'd just slept in Isaacs room.

"When you love someone…" I turned around at this so quickly, I felt dizzy. Who was he to start talking about love? I observed him, his vacant eyes staring wistfully into the distance. "You wouldn't hurt them. You couldn't. I definitely couldn't hurt her." He was so drunk at this point he was hardly coherent.

I did the only sensible thing I could think to do and pried the almost empty bottle of whiskey from his arms. He hardly protested, his limbs felt limp as I pulled at them to access the bottle. "You need to go to bed, Noah," I commanded. He didn't respond, just climbed out of the chair, pulled his shirt over his head, and fell onto his bed.

I pulled the comforter from underneath him and tucked it over his half-naked body. He'd thank me for this in the morning if he was any half-decent person. If I weren't, I'd have just let him freeze to death. He passed out before the comforter even touched his body.

I stared down at him, soft snores escaping from his lips. How had the two of us lived together for three months and I hardly knew anything except his name, age, and the fact that he played soccer. What had he been talking about tonight, who was this girl? He'd never even mentioned dating or anything like that. Not that he mentioned anything like that to me at all.

What had really intrigued me was why he'd been in Charlie's room? Now that was curious.

~ Chapter Seventeen ~

Dr Bellard's nostrils flared as he yelled my name. That wasn't a good sign. It probably didn't help that this was the fourth time during class that he'd caught me not listening. Everything was just so complicated right now. The guilt of everything that happened last night with Isaac was eating me up. How had he managed to cope with the guilt when he'd been cheating on October with me? The more people that had gotten involved the more this situation had spiralled.

"Mr Shields, I'm not going to ask you again." I hadn't even heard the question, so he was definitely going to have to ask me again.

"I'm sorry sir, can you repeat the question?" I tried to sound as polite as I possibly could, as I'd watched him kick one too many students out of this classroom for not listening

"I asked you, how many hours does the moon Lo take to orbit Jupiter?" the teacher replied through gritted teeth.

"Forty-three hours sir, sorry." At least I'd known the answer. Maybe it was time for me to admit defeat and ask to be moved back down to eleventh-grade physics.

"Whilst that is correct, in future I'd ask you to please pay more attention, Mr Shields. I'd have thought you'd have learned that by now. We aren't like your old state school. Only the intelligent thrive in this school."

I merely nodded in response. I couldn't muster up the

energy to respond to the humiliation. I ducked my head, staring at the blank page below me.

I was just beginning to focus again when my phone vibrated from where I had it tucked in my lap. My head flopped back and I let out a small sigh. I almost couldn't bring myself to look. I couldn't decide who's name it would be worse to see on my screen right now. Isaac? Callum? October? Why did it matter, I was lying and hurting all of them?

I glanced down at the phone quickly and spotted Charlie's name. *Phew.* He was a lot better than the alternatives.

What's wrong? – Charlie.

Or maybe not when he was asking questions like that. I shook my head and quickly shot back a reply to him to tell him *nothing.* In all honesty, I'd completely forgotten that Charlie was in this class.

I've never heard a bigger lie. You've been distracted for weeks now. Bernard isn't the kind of teacher you want to not be paying attention to. I'll wait for you after class. We'll go get lunch and you can tell me what's going on with you. - Charlie.

I bit back the urge to laugh. I forgot how forceful Charlie could be when he slipped into his Prefect mindset. Whilst I knew the boy had good intentions asking this question, I couldn't talk to him right now. I couldn't lie to him more than I already was.

Despite my protests, I found Charlie with his signature messenger bag waiting right next to my desk before I'd even had the chance to put away my pencil case.

"Canteen or Denny's?" Charlie asked, his smile way

too energetic for the conversation we were about to have.

I was already struggling to keep up this facade, so best to be as far away from anyone else we may know right now. "Denny's."

Charlie nodded in reply and led us down the driveway to the edge of campus. We took our seats in our regular booth and Charlie quickly ordered us our usual, strawberry cheesecake pancakes to share.

He spoke first, breaking the silence. "This is starting to get ridiculous. Over the last few weeks, I've seen you nauseatingly happy and then down in the dumps. Then you and Callum started dating and you just seemed so good together and then you broke up and you just look sad again. What's going on? Is someone giving you shit? Is it Noah? Your parents?"

The concern in his eyes was killing me. I was so conflicted. The secret was already out to one person, I just couldn't work out whether it would be sensible to tell another? Although, I knew Charlie finding out would be nothing like when Noah discovered us kissing in my bed. There would be no threats of exposure, but there would still be judgment and much worse than that there would be disappointment. My internal battle must have been obvious as Charlie continued to talk before I could even begin to start explaining.

"Look, you don't have to tell me exactly what's wrong. I'm just concerned, Logan. Especially after what happened at your old school." There it was. The sucker punch to my guilty heart.

I winced. "No need for that, Charlie, I'm not being bullied. God, just promise me you won't judge me, okay?"

Charlie nodded. "I won't."

"I have well and truly fucked up." I sighed heavily, covering my face with my hands exasperatedly. "I've been seeing someone for a while."

"I think we all know that. You and Callum were looking so loved up before lunch the other day. Why is that so fucked up?"

"It's not Callum." I couldn't even look at him right now. I didn't want to see how disgusted he was by me.

"I'm sorry, what?" Charlie's chair slid back a little across the floor. "So you were cheating on Callum or you're cheating on the other guy? Jesus, Logan. What the hell? Why are you only just telling me this?"

"Because the other person was already in a relationship too, well at the start he was."

"Damn, just when I didn't think it could get any worse."

"Just stop, okay? I already know how bad this is." I pulled at clumps of my hair as I ran my fingers through it, roughly. I couldn't believe I'd done this, to October, to Callum. I was no better than the guy I cussed out last Christmas when he cheated on my favourite cousin.

"Shit, Logan." Charlie's eyes widened. "I'm sorry. I just did not expect that at all. Wow. What? Is it someone at this school? Do I know him?"

I pursed my lips together. This was it. The pinnacle moment. I could lie, could tell him it was someone from another school or back home in Calgary. However, Charlie would never fall for that bullshit. So, regrettably, I just nodded. Drawing a deep breath in, I clasped my hands in front of me to keep them from trembling. "It's Isaac," I said, the damaging words almost inaudible.

"I must have heard wrong, because for a moment there I could have sworn you said Isaac. Our very straight friend who's just come out of a relationship with the love of his life and our dear friend, October." Charlie was shaking his head so much, I thought I was about to be sick. This was a mistake.

147

"Look, Charlie, you can't make me feel any more guilty than I already do, okay?" I could feel the bile collecting in the back of my throat, as I said the words. I wished I hadn't started this conversation in the first place

"You're being serious?" Charlie deadpanned. "Wow, alright. I *really* do not know my best friend at all. Are you telling me he's gay? I'm so confused right now." Charlie slumped over, his head falling into his hands.

"I have no idea. I mean he must be bi or something. I mean it was him kissing me, he started all of this. I wanted to be with Callum, I really was trying to be with him and Isaac came back to me and tried to get me to break up with him."

"Christ, October is going to be heartbroken. You know how much she adored Isaac. How could you two do this to her?" Charlie's voice was rising and if he weren't currently so angry I'd be trying to shush him before he told the whole bloody campus.

"I wanted to call it off. I tried when we first kissed a couple of months ago and then I tried again when Noah caught us and again when he tried to kiss me when I got with Callum." I couldn't stop myself, the filter between my brain and my mouth wasn't communicating. It was all just spilling out everywhere.

Charlie raised his hand in my face. "Wait a hot second. This has been going on for months? Plural? Fuck, how did I not notice? Have you slept with him?"

I shook my head, this was already too much, I couldn't tell him that me and Isaac had now had sex, that would only make this ten times worse.

"Well, at least that's something," Charlie concluded. "I mean, it's just a fling right? You've kissed, what a couple of times? This isn't a big deal at all, maybe October doesn't even need to find out. It's harmless.

Isaac is probably just confused, what teenager doesn't question his sexuality every now and again, right?" Charlie shrugged and I just sank into my seat. Charlie raised his eyebrow. "Unless it's more than that?" His voice was softening and damn it I was caving again. "Do you actually like him?"

I nodded, tears bristling the corners of my eyes. I balled my fists, pressing at my eyes in an attempt to stop the tears from falling "I did tell you I'd screwed up, Charlie." I stabbed the pancake in front of me and shoved a forkful into my mouth. The pancakes just tasted salty as the tears dribbled down my face. All I'd wanted to do for weeks was to tell Charlie about all of this. He was easily my best friend here and I wanted to be honest. I just didn't want to see him so disappointed in me.

"What are you going to do?" Charlie asked after a few moments.

"I honestly don't know. I've tried to stop thinking about him, but it's Isaac. I really do like him, Charlie." I forked in another mouthful. "It's not something I've ever experienced before. I've never had a relationship and now look at me, I've hurt a great guy to be selfish with Isaac. It's so freaking messed up. This could all blow up. Noah could literally drop the bomb at any minute."

"Bloody hell, Noah knows? How is it that October doesn't know yet?" Charlie replied as he let out the most bitter laugh I'd ever heard.

"Just because he told Beth about you and Becca being lab partners last year, doesn't mean he's going to blab about this. Maybe he's a changed man?" I lied. I was pretty sure there wasn't a clause in mine and Noah's blackmail agreement that allowed me to tell Charlie, our prefect, that he was sneaking out multiple times a week in the blackest hours of the night to get up to whatever he got up to.

"Logan, look, just be careful okay? I don't want you to get burned by him. I'm going to give you some advice, as your prefect and as your best friend. Tell October sooner, rather than later. The longer you leave it the more upset she is going to be. But, if she hears it from someone else, she's going to hate you and you don't want to ruin that friendship any more than you already have and for heaven's sake, don't kiss Isaac again and definitely don't sleep with him," he sighed, shaking his head, before he pulled out his phone and began typing furiously.

"What are you doing?" I asked, staring as his fingers flew across the touch screen.

Charlie finally set his phone down on the table and replied "Right. Me and you, we are going to go and have a talk to Isaac about this. I want to hear both sides of the story." Charlie shoved a couple of bills on the table to cover the half-eaten pancakes and had his coat on before I could even process what was about to go down. "Come on, up! No time like the present," Charlie pressured, willing me to move from where I remained seated.

I knew this probably wasn't the best time to object to Charlie's requests. I already couldn't figure out if Charlie was mad or just disappointed. With shaky hands, I pushed my chair out-wards, before following the boys lead back into the dormitory and up to the top floor.

~ Chapter Eighteen ~

Charlie entered the room first, cheeks flushed and breathless after sprinting up the stairs as he stalked over to his best friend. "You're an actual idiot," he shrieked. "How could you do that to October? How could you do this to Logan? You knew he was still vulnerable coming here from his own school. Or was that the attraction of this? Was he just an easy target, someone you could take advantage of?" Charlie jabbed a finger into Isaac's chest, as Isaac rose to his feet.

"Hey. I'm not some fragile doll I'll have you know. I wanted to kiss him," I yelled before Isaac could get a word in edgeways.

Isaac's face dropped as he realised that Charlie now knew about our situation. He sized up to his best friend, pushing out his chest, but he didn't do anything. He just stood there and let the prefect continue to scream at him, his fists balled by his side. I could do nothing but watch, part of me knew that Charlie just needed to get all of this out of his system.

"I just thought you were better than that Isaac, I really did. Same for you, Logan." Charlie shrugged his messenger bag to the floor, before perching on the end of Isaac's bed, putting some distance between the two. "I just don't understand," he sighed as he glanced back and forth between me and Isaac.

I didn't really understand either, so I couldn't help him there. How had this even started? When did it begin? Because the more I'd thought about it, Isaac had been flirting with me from day one.

"Did he tell you?" Isaac asked, gesturing towards me. He answered his own question before Charlie even had the chance to respond. "Of course it was him if it had been Noah I'd have October banging down my door right now."

"Yes, he told me." Charlie nodded. "I can't believe I had to hear it from him. Yes, he's one of my best friends, but you, Isaac, we've been friends from the very beginning of high school. Do those three and a half years mean nothing to you?" Charlie palmed at his eyes, if he started crying I'd lose my shit right here, right now.

I wished I hadn't pulled Charlie into this mess. This was not the kind of devastation I wished to see take place between these two boys.

"Are you going to tell October?" Isaac asked, his voice as quiet as a mouse, eyes pleading with Charlie.

"Is that really all you care about?" Charlie stood up from where he'd sat on the bed, storming over to where Isaac was leaning against his desk. "Not how much damage you've done, but whether I'm going to tell her about how you kissed him repeatedly before you two broke up?" He shook his head staring down at the other boy. "God, I don't even know who you are right now."

I could see the flashes of guilt I felt mirrored on Isaac's face. If we hadn't screwed up before, we had now.

"Of course it isn't," Isaac replied, sighing deeply, before grabbing onto Charlie's arm. "Don't you think I feel guilty about all of this? Please don't be mad at me. I'm already so fucking sorry for all this. I know how much of a mess I've made."

"I'm glad you know that, Isaac."

We all whirled around in sync, to where the door was now wide open.

"Charlie said it, you're an idiot Isaac. A real stupid idiot. He has every right to be yelling in your face right now. You're lucky I'm not screaming at you too."

Brilliant. Why not just shout it from the balcony. Joshua's lacrosse bag was already on the floor next to him. How long had he actually been standing there for? How hadn't we noticed?

"Oh great. Would you look at that, Charlie? Now he knows," Isaac yelled, as he gripped at Charlie's collar. "You may as well just post it on Facebook."

The more people who knew, the closer this secret was to getting out to October. It only took one slip of the tongue from the multiple people who already knew and that would be it. Exposed.

"I was going to find out sooner or later, just like October is. These things only stay secret for so long," Joshua retorted, from where he was now stood next to our prefect peeling Isaac's hands off of Charlie's shirt.

"So, what are you saying? You're going to tell her?" Isaac jeered, as he slammed his fist down on the desk.

"No," Charlie chimed in. "But, you should and soon. Castle already knows and you can bet your life that he won't keep it secret for long."

"You're well and truly fucked if Noah knows. I'm shocked he hasn't already told her," Joshua added.

"Noah isn't going to be a problem. I've already told you that. I've spoken to him." I locked eyes with Isaac. Part of me wanting to reassure him, the other part of me hoping, dangerously, that this meant that things may be able to carry on as normal.

"Look, I have to go to lacrosse practice," Joshua said as he recovered his bag from the floor, glaring between Charlie and Isaac. "I only came in here because I was worried you two were going to end up having a blazing row and spilling this affair to the whole damn dorm." He moved towards the door once more. "I know what both of you are like when things get too heated in these arguments." This piqued my interest, I'd never seen the pair fight like this before. "You think you can have this argument a little bit quieter?" Isaac rolled his eyes at his best friend, as the door shut behind him. Leaving me, Isaac and Charlie to the deafening silence that had swallowed the room's atmosphere.

Charlie just glared at Isaac. "I've heard his side of things, I want to hear yours."

I took this as my cue to leave. The other two boys were so caught up trying to see who could look angrier, so they probably wouldn't even notice if I left. I made my way to the nook by the stairs, where a love seat sat. I dropped myself into the chair, not quite yet ready to go back down and face more shit from Noah. Unfortunately, I could still hear the commotion going on inside Isaac's room. As much as I didn't want to hear the pair continue to argue, I *was* intrigued to hear Isaac's side of things. I closed my eyes, slumped in the chair as I tuned myself back into their conversation.

"I'm sure he's told you how it happened."

"Just get on with it, Wells."

"Look there isn't much to tell. I go over there after detentions, after meeting with Julian, after arguments with October or my parents. At least I used to all the time before him and Callum got involved. He's easy to talk to. He listens."

Was that really all I was for Isaac? I couldn't believe that. I wouldn't. Not after he practically begged me to end things with Callum. He wouldn't do that just to keep venting to me. Would he?

"That doesn't explain to me how you've ended up sucking his face." That's exactly what I was thinking,

154

Charlie. Even I couldn't really fathom how we'd ended up kissing. "Do you kiss everybody who gives you a chance to vent?"

That made me wonder. Had anyone ever really given Isaac a chance to vent? The boy was constantly getting in trouble. Never major trouble, but enough that it would be scarring his record. All I'd seen since being here was people constantly berating him. Had anyone given him a chance to explain? Maybe then we'd get to see why he was really like this.

"So now you're going to make me out to be some kind of serial cheat? You wanted to hear this Charlie, so let me finish."

Silence engrossed the room again. It was eating at me and I wasn't even in the room. I hated hearing the boy I'd started to fall for attacking his best friend like this. I couldn't bear the regret that was consuming me. So much regret for all the damage that would come about from what had started with us just getting caught up in the heat of the moment.

"We'd been bantering back and forth for what felt like hours. I was worked up over something or other and rather than completely berating me like you do, like my parents have always done. He challenged me. He challenged me to think about how I was behaving."

That was pretty much correct. Whilst I'd given him a sharp telling off, I'd also questioned why he did this. I'd pushed him to carry on with his poetry, to put his anger into that, rather than taking it out on his class teachers.

"He made me realise that I'm lucky to still be here. He pushed me to think about my future, both here and at university. I don't know how it happened, but before I could think about it I was kissing him. I made the first move, so don't be mad at him, okay?"

"I'm not going to apologise for doing my job, Isaac."

Right here comes prefect Charlie. This was his ultimate defence. He'd put on his prefect hat and read out the riot act.

"You seem to forget sometimes that your actions have consequences for me too. Every time you get chewed out by Julian, I get it ten times worse. What goes on in this house is my responsibility. You just don't ever seem to think about that when you sneak out at night or harass the freshmen in the middle of the night with your paranormal experiments."

Those pranks had died down a little. Part of me wanted to put that down to the fact that I was helping to calm him down, rather than causing chaos in the house.

"I get it in the ass from Julian more than you can imagine."

If this weren't a serious situation I probably would have snorted at that. I really hoped that Isaac was keeping a straight face right now. He probably wasn't.

"After you, J and Logan snook out to that club, he wanted to strip me of my title. I worked hard to earn this title, to be chosen three years in a row and all you ever do is go out of your way to destroy that. I've had enough, Isaac."

I knew that Julian had been giving Charlie some shit about the pranks and the sneaking out, but I hadn't even begun to think that Julian would strip Charlie of his prefect status.

"Fuck, Charlie, I'm sor-."

"It's too late to be sorry Isaac. So, you kissed him? That doesn't explain why you're still trying to see him. Wasn't cheating on October enough? You wanted him to stoop to your level and cheat on Callum too?"

"I can't explain it, Char. It just happened. Before I knew it, I wanted to spend every evening in his room. I was taking him dinner, coffee, we were doing homework together and talking about anything and everything."

"Sounds like you were dating him. Had you forgotten you'd already got a girlfriend?"

"Maybe I was just thanking him. Thanking him because he wasn't always so mad at me. He was disappointed in me in a different way, in a way where he wanted me to improve myself, not just tear me down. He had so much belief in me Charlie, no-one's ever believed in me."

My heart was clenching. I couldn't handle hearing Isaac talk like this. This is why I was falling for him. I wasn't scared to admit that to myself anymore. This side of him was just so beautiful. He'd made himself so vulnerable to me, more than he had to anyone else. That thought alone made all the pain we'd caused, worth it. That was really messed up.

"I was in too deep. I still am. I stopped showing up with the motive of homework or venting. I'd kiss him before he even had the chance to talk. Then one day it just, you know, went too far."

"You slept with him?" Charlie broke the silence. Isaac must have nodded as Charlie continued. "Jesus, Isaac, why? Why would you want to do that?"

"Hey, what the hell is that supposed to mean? The last person I expected to be judgmental about this was you. What are you trying to say, that I wouldn't want to sleep with him because he's a guy? Newsflash! I find him attractive. What's wrong with that?" Isaac sounded so defensive and that made me grin like a stupid idiot. These were the compliments I'd been craving from him.

"The problem is," Charlie screamed. "That you had a girlfriend and since when did you even start liking boys? In the three and a half years I've known you you've never once mentioned being attracted to a guy." Charlie's tone was as bitter as a lemon.

When I thought about it, I knew Charlie had every right to feel bitter in this moment. It wasn't nice to find out something like this when you thought you knew everything about your best friend.

"I didn't know I had to tell you any time I found someone to be attractive. Plus, I've been with October for two of those years we've been friends, so it's not like I've had anyone else really to tell you about."

"Like I could ever believe that now!" Charlie all but growled at Isaac. "You cheated on her, you can no longer use that as your excuse." Charlie was yelling again, his tone spiteful and malicious. He clearly no longer cared about the reasoning behind the affair, too mad to see that Isaac was basically telling him that he was struggling right now. Had probably been struggling for a while with how he felt about himself, about his sexuality.

"Look, Charlie." I heard a body slam up against the wall, my body half rising from the chair prepared to go in and break up the fight. "You can make me feel like shit all you want. I already hate myself for doing this to Toby, but it isn't actually any of your business. So, get the fuck out of my face before I do something I'll regret."

"You don't get to play the victim in all of this Isaac. You've done this to yourself. Now, this is my business, because when all this blow up I'm going to be the one picking up the pieces, for Toby, for Logan and for the rest of the group. It'll be me trying to repair the group. All because you couldn't be a one-woman man," Charlie spat, his words like venom. "I feel sorry for Logan; the boy doesn't even realise you're using him."

"I'm not using him," he cried. This wasn't a new thought for me. I'd thought many a time that maybe Isaac was using me to experiment. A wave of relief washed over me when Isaac quickly shot back.

"You're a liar, Isaac. You don't even know the meaning of the word honesty," Charlie jibbed.

"Fuck you, Charlie."

"Oh here comes the martyr again. Why do you always have to fuck up like this?"

"Shut your mouth, Montgomery or I'll shut it for you."

"What does Logan even see in you?"

Charlie was really pushing all of Isaac's buttons, this wasn't going to end well. I couldn't decide whether to go in and end this row or just leave them to scream it all out at each other.

"I'm serious, Char. Don't push me."

"You don't scare me, Issy. You're just a user and a cheat."

"I'm not a fucking user. I think…"

I didn't catch the final part of what Isaac was about to say, all I heard was a body crash into a piece of the furniture and a cry of pain echo throughout the hall. Bodies scrambled on the floor and it sounded as though fists were hitting bare skin in there.

"Why him?" Charlie finally asked, panting between words.

I breathed out in relief, at least Charlie wasn't in too much pain to speak and continue this fight.

"What makes him so special?" Charlie screamed.

"Why does it matter, Char?" Isaac sounded choked and it was then my heart broke at the fact that I was part of the reason that these two best friends were tearing chunks out of each other right now.

"Just tell me," he pleaded. His tone was so broken and desperate that goose bumps rose up my arms.

"You see him, right? He's beautiful."

Why was Isaac only saying this to Charlie? Why

couldn't he just say that to me?

"Maybe not in the traditional way, but he is. God, Char. He's made me want to try to be a better person. Try to reign in the anger and aggression. He's made me work harder in class and actually want to achieve something in my life. He believes in me when I don't believe in myself. He actually thinks I've got a shot at getting into McGill, even though I'm not sure I can do it. He's proud of me when I succeed. For once I'm at ease. I'm no longer this constant disappointment when I'm with him. He doesn't need me to be this perfect human like October did. I can just be myself and as long as I'm trying in life he doesn't have a problem with that. He likes me just the way I am and I'll be damned if I'm giving up on that."

Before I knew it, I could hear someone exiting the room, slamming the door so hard behind him that I felt the ground shake beneath my chair. I curled my legs into my body and prayed that Charlie wouldn't see that I was still up here and had been listening this whole time.

I poked my head around the corner, slightly. All I could see was Joshua stood outside the door with open arms, Charlie falling into them. "I'm so sorry, Char," Joshua whispered to him, his lacrosse gear dropping to the floor as he pulled him closer. "I'm sorry it wasn't you."

~ Chapter Nineteen ~

A jab to my shoulder drew me from my slumber. My body cried out for at least another five minutes sleep, but it seemed that that wasn't going to happen. I grumbled as I opened my eyes, my head flat out on some uncomfortable surface. Had I really been that tired?

When the next jab poked between my shoulder blades I'd had enough. I couldn't for the life of me work out why Noah was trying to force me to wake up. I shot my head up, feeling that my body wasn't being comforted by anything other than a wooden chair, a crick in my neck now irritating me. I surveyed my surroundings noting this was indeed not my room and actually the common room. My sociology textbook was splayed open in front of me and I was sure there was probably an imprint of the page now on my face.

My head turned to look for the person responsible for the poking. "What the hell, Joshua?" I rubbed at my eyes, he was standing in front of the open curtains, the sunlight streaming through almost blinding me.

"You are in the common room, you know? Not your bedroom," Joshua remarked, his tone was steady, yet it still made me feel wary of him. I wasn't quite sure where we stood after yesterday.

"Tell me about it, my necks killing." I rubbed my fingers around the back of my neck, twisting it side to side in the hope that I'd be able to iron out some of the knots that had formed.

"Or, maybe, it's just that giant hickey, just under your

ear."

He reached out to poke it and I swatted his hand away, silently relieved that he was joking around about this. "I have no idea how you and Isaac managed to keep this a secret for the last couple of months."

I shushed at him. "Why don't you just say that a bit louder, Jay? Not sure the people on the other side of campus heard you."

"Relax, Lo. No-ones about, everyone's in the assembly the Dean called. Which is where both you and I should be." He dropped into the chair next to me.

"It slipped my mind. Didn't sleep well at all." A yawned followed that. I hadn't slept well, my mind overwhelmed by everything going on and the fact that I had a quiz this morning I hadn't prepared for.

"I know, I heard you sneaking into Isaac's room last night." My cheeks flushed to a deep shade of red, the heat travelling far down my neck. I'd been trying desperately hard not to alert anyone I was up there.

Ignoring his response, I asked quietly. "Can I ask you something?" Joshua nodded, something about his movement clearly cautious about what I was going to ask. "Is Charlie in love with Isaac?" I didn't really need an answer, just confirmation. Although, part of me didn't want to know. I knew it would only make things more difficult than they already were. Nobody else needed to be caught up in the middle of a love pentagon.

"What makes you ask?" His arms were crossed in front of him, resting on the table. He narrowed his eyes in at me, clearly trying to work out what my motives were for asking this.

"Just, please, answer the question."

Joshua, for a few moments pursed his lips together as he considered what his reply would be. He was obviously unsure as to whether he should make this revelation to Logan, but then he nodded his head, his pursed lips turning to a frown. "Yeah, yeah he is."

I let out a shaky breath. This was all I needed.

Before I could ask any more about this, Joshua was already continuing. "So, I'm sure you can understand why this is so hard for him, seeing Isaac like you, choose you. When he never once looked at Charlie that way, even before Beth and October came along."

I looked at him, sympathetically. I could understand that pain. "I never intended for this to happen, Jay. I definitely didn't do this to spite Charlie, not one bit."

"I don't doubt that." Joshua nodded at me, I was grateful for that.

"I really did have no idea there were feelings there. All I've seen is Charlie with Beth and despite what anyone tells me about their relationship and her crazy personality, they've always looked perfectly happy to me. So this has come as a bit of a shock to me."

"Regardless of Charlie's feelings, you still knew that Isaac had a girlfriend. Plus, you had Callum. He's my friend Logan. You and Isaac have put us all in this hugely awkward position." He sighed frustratedly, his fingers almost tearing into his afro.

"Jay, I'm sorry you're caught up in all of this, I'm sorry Char and Isaac aren't speaking, but I don't know how to fix this." I wanted to slam my fists on the table. Hurl the textbook across the room. For the last two months, there had been this guilt gnawing at my insides and now it'd turned to rage. Mainly towards myself. I felt my nails painfully digging into my palms as I clenched my fists. "I knew it was bad, I didn't realise it was that bad. Charlie really does love him, huh?" There was a dryness at the back of my throat, my words almost sounded choked.

"Charlie fell for him in the first few weeks of ninth

grade. I still remember him telling me, but he knew nothing was ever going to come of it."

I could almost feel my nails piercing my skin. This was the pain I'd been causing for everyone else. I'd been so selfish. I'd been taking everything I could get and hardly even thinking about the consequences. "It's really been that long?" I rasped out.

"Charlie never even tried to pursue him. Had we not ever found out about you two, we'd still be thinking he was the same straight guy we've known for the last three years." He chuckled a little bit and that almost made me angrier. He should have been so much madder at me than he is. If this were someone else hurting my best friends, I'd definitely not be laughing with them.

"I get that." I nodded. I was exhausted. I desperately wanted this conversation to end so I could go back to my room and sleep for the rest of the day. I'd play sick and get out of classes. This was karma for spending another night in Isaac's room. Although, even when Isaac had finally fallen asleep, my mind remained ablaze.

"Then Charlie started seeing Beth and the following year Isaac and October got together. Part of me thought that was it."

"But it wasn't?" I asked.

"What you have to understand is, Charlie really does love Beth. So I assumed, for a while, that this meant he was over Isaac. But, then I'd catch him staring at Isaac when he thought no-one else was looking. He looked like he'd been hit with a car when he first found out Isaac and October were official." This just made me feel worse, I was almost hugging myself at this point, hands clutching at my elbows. Who had given me the right to fuck up this bad? "I still had to watch him longing for our best friend and it was damn right heart-breaking." His eyes were glossy as he spoke and then he paused for a second, taking a breath to collect himself. "What made it easier was he didn't think he ever stood a chance, so he was happy to settle for putting his efforts into other things; being a prefect, all his clubs and into loving Beth."

"So he loves them both? I don't understand." I was really confused. All of this was just so messed up.

"It bothers you, doesn't it? That he has feelings for Isaac?" His head was tilted towards me. I felt like I was in a therapists office. Although I was questioning if that's where I actually should be right now.

I really had to think about that though. Did it bother me? Should it when Isaac so clearly has never reciprocated those feelings. Up until me, Isaac had never shown any inclination he liked men. Part of that made me feel special. But, then again, he'd never had the chance to know about Charlie's feelings. That could change things.

"Should it bother me?" I asked.

"I don't think we'll ever know the answer to that. Charlie's never going to tell Isaac, especially after this. Can I give you some advice though, Lo?" I merely nodded my head; I'd take any kind of guidance I could get at this point. "Stop seeing him. Don't let this get too deep for you. If he can cheat on October and ask you to cheat on Callum, he can do the same to you."

I didn't even have to think about that, I was already shaking my head. "I can't promise that, J. I'm sorry." The tears were falling now, even though I'd tried so hard to bite them back.

Joshua placed his hand on my shoulder and squeezed a little. I looked up at him as the tears stained my cheeks. "Do you really like him that much that you're willing to risk ruining so many people's lives? Octobers, Charlie's, his, your own?" He asked, his hand still on my shoulder. I knew he wasn't asking in a pretentious way and that he actually cared and wanted to help, so I nodded.

"This is too much crazy for me if I'm honest. I like you, Lo, it's been refreshing having you come in and shake up the dynamic of our little group. As a three, I've always had to play the middleman. It's been nice for Isaac to have someone else to cause trouble with and maybe, just maybe you *have* played a part in mellowing him out a bit. I mean he's definitely gotten in a lot less trouble in the last few weeks than he has in previous semesters. I've also been happy that you've got so much in common with Charlie, all the theatre and reading shit, me and Isaac have never managed to vibe with him on that."

"What are you actually saying, Jay? I can't tell if you're about to evict me from the group or if you're allowing me to stay, even if that does involve still being with Isaac." I asked, my voice sounding more choked than ever as a fresh wave of tears fell.

"I'm saying I'm taking a step back. Maybe you guys just need to duke this out amongst yourselves. We're all graduating this year and you'll be before you know it. You're old enough not to need me fixing all the problems." He was standing up again, he had classes to get to, so did I. Not that I planned on going to them looking like this.

I agreed with him though. We did all need to sort this out amongst ourselves. "Would you recommend me talking to Charlie? I won't tell him you told me he has feelings for Isaac."

"That's for you to decide," he replied simply. It was true. I had to make this decision for myself.

"I think, more than anyone, I understand how he's feeling."

"Do you though?" Joshua shot back. "The feelings you have for Isaac are at least somewhat reciprocated. It's never been that way for Charlie."

"I guess you're right." It was in that moment I'd already decided I was going to go and speak to Charlie. I owed him that at least.

I spent all day drifting in and out of sleep. I'd emailed my teachers to say I felt unwell and that if I didn't feel better tomorrow I'd go see the school nurse. That had worked and it'd allowed me to build up the energy and courage to go and see Charlie.

In the periods between sleep, I'd racked my brain about what I was going to say to him. How I was going to bring up his feelings for Isaac. There was already an uneasiness in my stomach as I climbed the stairs to his room. A restlessness running through my body as I raked over every which way this conversation could end. My skin was almost tingling as I hovered outside the door. I felt like that scared boy that had arrived on the first day. This time that fear was real. I was about to confront one of my best friends about being in love with his other best friend, the guy I was in love with.

I didn't have to knock though. The door was opening as I stood frozen to the spot.

Charlie was clearly trying to leave, his coat zipped up over his chin and a duffel bag slung over his shoulder. There was a thick layer of stubble coursing across his jawline and the bags under his eyes were enough to carry mine and the girls whole shopping trip. He cleared his throat and I hadn't even realised I was in his exit path.

"Are you going somewhere?" I asked, so timidly, I couldn't even look him in the eye.

"Home," he replied, his voice clipped.

"What about classes?" He just looked at me like he couldn't give a crap about classes. That was completely fair after everything that'd happened this week. "Can we talk please?" I asked, hoping we could just go into his room and talk for a bit. I didn't want to be having this conversation on the doorstep.

He didn't budge, his arms just folded in front of his chest. His glare told me I should probably just get out of his way. "Please," I pleaded. He just shook his head.

"What is there to talk about, Lo? Didn't we already do this? Look at where that got us. Now if you don't mind I'm trying to rest. I don't want to be sick for classes on Monday. If you need the advice of a prefect or anything like that, go talk to Joshua, he's acting prefect for this next few days whilst I get better.

"I know, Charlie," I said simply. Hoping that he'd catch on and I wouldn't have to actually say what I was talking about.

"You know what, Lo?" he pulled at the straps of his duffel bag that was falling to the floor, hoisting it over his shoulder once more. His feet shuffling, impatiently.

"I know that you're in love with Isaac," I whispered, not wanting to shout this for everyone to hear. Charlie didn't deserve that.

He grabbed at my shirt, pulling me into his room, slamming the door behind us both. "What the fuck," he all but growled. "How?"

"I just know, Char. I'm sorry."

"Oh Logan, you're becoming so much like him and you don't even know it. You aren't the victim in this situation. You may have been one at your old school, but not anymore. You don't get to play the martyr right now." I couldn't take the disappointment his eyes. My head bowed so I didn't have to look at him.

"I don't think I'm the victim," I replied honestly, my leg shaking so much I had to lean on the wall to steady myself. "I know how much pain I've caused. I'm sorry that I did this. I really am. I didn't know you had feelings for him."

"What and now you do you're going to leave him alone?" Was that what he expected? I looked up at him, gawking at him in response. "Yeah, I didn't think so. You don't care, Logan. You don't care that I loved him first and that you swooped in and stole my best friend. I trusted you, Lo. I thought you were an incredible guy, that had come out the other side of something so horrific. You're no different from all of them. You've bulldozed your way into this group and you haven't cared about the wreckage you're leaving behind."

I didn't want to cry again. He was right, I wasn't the victim in all of this. I didn't get to cry. I gritted my teeth and swallowed repeatedly, sinking the urge to cry. "Charlie, please," I pleaded. "I don't want this to ruin our friendship. I love you guys and I just want to make this right."

"If you wanted to make this right you'd leave him. You'd stop seeing him. You'd go back to Callum and stop ruining everything."

"I love him, Charlie."

"Join the freaking club, Logan. Been there, done that, worn the t-shirt for the last three years. You aren't the first and you won't be the last to be drawn in by Isaac."

"You can hardly comment, Char. You've been in love with someone else, whilst being 'in love' with your girlfriend for the last three years." I wanted to scream at him, but this just dribbled out as a high-pitched whisper.

He stepped towards me and I immediately brought my hands to my face, ducking down to avoid the blow. But, it never came. He just stepped around me, opening the door.

"I think you should leave Logan. Continuing this conversation isn't really beneficial to either of us. Isaac is never going to love either of us. I've accepted that, it's time you do too," he replied, his voice unnervingly calm.

I wanted to tell him that he was wrong, that we needed to talk. But, I couldn't. Despite his calm tone, his eyes were glossy and his fists were scrunched up. We'd both already hurt each other enough for one day, I couldn't push that anymore, I wanted to be able to redeem this eventually. So, I accepted defeat. Turning to head out of the door.

"Enjoy your break, Char," I replied sincerely, reaching for the handle to shut the door behind me.

He said nothing. There was just silence as I closed the door, my movements slow hoping to hear any kind of reassurance from Charlie. It didn't come and I was left standing awkwardly on the prefect landing once more.

~ Chapter Twenty ~

Charlie practically jumped up from the table almost the moment I sat down. If that didn't make it obvious that something was up, I didn't know what would. It was the first time I'd seen him since his mental health break. He looked awful, had the break not helped?

No-one seemed to notice though, everyone else was consumed in the conversation that Libby and October were currently having. The track team were having a meet this weekend and Libby and the cheer team were supposed to be going out to support them, but the school had double booked them for the Lacrosse game that was taking place at exactly the same time. Libby being the good friend that she was to October was trying to convince her that they could do both. To me, it just seemed inevitable that Libby would have to choose to take her squad to either one of the events.

"Look, I'm talking to the rest of the girls and we are sorting it. The Lacrosse game is at one and your meet is a two, we can definitely do both." Libby reassured what looked to be a pissed off October. I was trying not to get involved. October was already pissed at me because I was going to the Lacrosse game to support Joshua, over her meet. The simple facts of it were, Joshua's meet was an away game and I'd had to purchase a bus ticket for it to travel to the rival school way before I even knew about Octobers meet.

"But, the Lacrosse team are playing in Mississauga, it's going to take you at least an hour on the bus to get back from there and by the time the Lacrosse game is finished and you've travelled back, our meet will be over." She was stabbing at the salad on her plate with her fork, not even looking Libby in the eye right now.

"Toby, I'm trying here. It isn't my fault you guys were so late booking us. The Lacrosse team booked us for this meet months ago, if you'd have come to me before then we obviously would have cheered for you."

"Oh thanks for that, Libs," Joshua remarked sarcastically, shuffling his tray off the table as he made to leave the dining room. "If it really means that much to you Toby, the cheer team can be there for you instead of us. But we have a big game this weekend and you're just racing some school down the road, so it would be more exposure and press for the cheer team if they are there for us." With that he made for the exit, scraping off the remainders of his jacket potato into the bin, before leaving the dining room, heading in the direction that no-one had noticed Charlie had left in except me. Or well that's what I thought.

"As riveting as this little argument has been for the rest of this lunchtime, I have math homework to be getting on with. You just going to be eating that sandwich, Lo? Yes, great you can come and help me in the library." It definitely wasn't a question, she was summoning me and I knew better than to refuse a summons from Ameliah. The way she'd outlined her eyes in the deepest black eyeliner today only made me want to oblige more to this command, it made her deep brown eyes look more devilish than normal.

"Sure, I've already done the homework for this week so I can help." I pulled my satchel up over my shoulder, putting the packaged sandwich into my bag, I hadn't even had a chance to open it yet.

"Great, let's go. See you at dinner guys." With that we were heading out of the dining hall and out onto the driveway, but we weren't heading towards the library, more like in completely the opposite direction towards the sports fields.

"Where are we going?" I asked, the last time she'd led me away from the group like this was when she'd been suspicious of the bruising on Isaac's face. I hadn't done anything to raise suspicions recently, so I couldn't work out why I was being dragged to a solitude spot to have this conversation right now. All the worse kind of thoughts were shooting through my mind. What could she possibly know? Had she seen something between me and Isaac? Had Charlie or Joshua told her something they weren't supposed to? No, they wouldn't do that and if they had, she'd have told October by now.

"What's going on with you and Charlie?" You couldn't fault her, she was blunt and straight to the point consistently. She showed no mercy, it was one of the reasons we had such a good friendship even though we didn't spend every day together like I had when I was close friends with Joshua, Charlie, and Isaac.

"What do you mean?" I asked dryly. Where would I even start with that question? There were so many things going on with me and Charlie, but at the same time right now there was nothing at all going on between us.

"I saw him shoot up when you arrived at lunch, it was like you'd burnt his ass or something when you sat down on the bench. I'm asking what's going on between you two?"

"I honestly don't know what you mean. You know what he's like, probably running off to put out another fire in Edwards. Prefect life, ey?" I don't know why I tried to play this game with her. She always saw straight through me and my lies.

"So something *is* going on between you two? I knew it. Wow. Beth will kill you, you know? She is more brutal than me, she'll kick your ass into next week when she finds out her boyfriend is cheating on her, especially with a man. She's always been super sensitive about that whole bisexual thing."

Oh wow. She had read into this completely wrong if she thought that me and Charlie were having some kind of an affair. That couldn't be further from the truth right now, he wouldn't even talk to me. "Oh god, Ameliah, no. There's absolutely nothing going on between me and Charlie like that. We are just friends."

"You sure? I've seen him like this before, when he's liked another guy, but hasn't told anyone. Not that he'd ever acted on it, because he was with Beth and he really does love her before you start thinking otherwise." Did she know? About Charlie's feelings towards Isaac? How would she know that? I couldn't believe that Charlie would have told her, he didn't want anyone to know, he was excruciatingly angry with Joshua when he found out that it was him who told me that Charlie had been in love with Isaac for years, he definitely wouldn't have told Ameliah just willy nilly.

"I'm sure. I don't even see Charlie like that, we are just friends. That's all it's ever been and definitely all it ever will be between us."

She exhaled a little bit. "That's good to know, that isn't information I'd like to know right now. Beth would chew me up and spit me out if she knew I knew about her boyfriend having an affair before she did."

"You don't need to worry about that. No affair going on here."

"Okay, well if you two aren't hooking up behind everyone's back, why has he got his knickers in a twist

174

about you? You've clearly done something to piss him off." She wasn't going to stop pushing about this. I just didn't have an answer for her right now and I really didn't have the energy to try and make something up.

"We just had a bit of a disagreement that's all, me and Isaac got in a bit of trouble with Julian and Joshua tried to cover it up from Char and yeah everyone's a little bit pissed at each other right now. We'll be fine, don't worry yourself about it," I lied, even I wasn't sure we'd be fine again.

"Okay, if that's all it is, I'll leave it be. But, you can talk to me you know, Lo. I've said it a million times I'm here for you if there is something more going on I wanna hear about it and be there for you."

"I know, I know and I promised you before that I would if there was a problem." There was an itching in the back of my throat as I lied to her. As I kept things from her yet again, I was such a fake in this friendship group and I hated it.

"What was the disagreement about?"

"I think it was just a bit of cabin fever you know? We've all been spending so much time together and towards the Christmas break, after exams, Isaac was a bit out of hand and you know how Char gets when Isaac goes off the rails. I thought he was going to hang him out to dry over the top floor bannister after the stunt he pulled before Christmas."

She was looking at me with knowing eyes. She definitely knew about Charlie's feelings towards Isaac. She must know as much as Joshua did, knew that sometimes it just got a bit too much for Charlie when he spent too much time around Isaac. Now that I knew about his feelings, I saw it too. There were days when Charlie would just sit in his room all day and not want to be disturbed. I used to think it was because he was busy with homework or prefect business, but now I could see that after we'd spent days together as a group all packed into one room watching films or tv for hours upon hours. He needed a break from him, a break from his feelings towards Isaac.

I couldn't imagine that, needing a break from Isaac, but then I was the one who got him, not Charlie. Or maybe I could, sometimes Isaac did get a little bit too much, but it was like any regular person could be annoying and you needed a little time away from them. Charlie needed this break because he was overwhelmed by how he felt for Isaac, how he'd felt for three whole years. How did you avoid that for three years? I couldn't for the life of me work out how Isaac didn't know.

She nodded at me as I zoned out into my thoughts and I knew she got me, it was a relief that I didn't have to try and make up anything else to convince her. This lie was enough.

"You guys will be fine. Don't stress about it, a little bit of time apart wouldn't hurt any of you guys. You spend so much time together it's actually ridiculous, way more time than me and the girls do. You're practically up each other's asses." That was definitely not a funny joke. If only she knew.

"Very funny." I forced out a fake laugh. "We don't, you girls spend more time together, you guys literally live in each other's rooms."

"You guys have your own quarters in Edwards, you're definitely worse than us."

"Correction, Isaac, Joshua and Charlie live up there. I live in my humble abode on the second floor with the lovely Noah."

"How are things between you two? I'm surprised you've lasted this long sharing a room with him. The guy he lived with in Sophomore year paid to move to his own single room to get away from that boy's sharp tongue." I was surprised in myself really, the Logan who lived in Calgary would have one hundred percent thrown in the towel by now having to put up with how Noah treated me. Part of me sometimes still wanted to storm into Julian's office and plead with him to find me another bed to sleep in when things got bad with Noah. I'd rather sleep anywhere than in our suffocating room.

"Don't tell anyone I've told you this, but I actually think that boy has a heart. Shocking I know." She looked more confused than shocked, although I hadn't given her any context for my revelation.

"You've been spending too much time with him to think that. You know what he does to people, he wouldn't help you if you were drowning." Now that I did believe that boy only cared about himself and covering his own ass.

"Oh for sure." Although the cracks had definitely been showing recently, I just wish I knew what he was doing when he wasn't in our room. "So, the library?" I suggested.

"You're still so sweet and naive little Logan, I did the homework last night." She patted my shoulder and I rolled my eyes, I definitely should have seen that coming.

"Of course you have." She kissed my cheek and strode away from me in the direction of the English block. She was way too good at getting information out of me.

~ Chapter Twenty-One ~

I'd never been a fan of birthdays. Last year when I turned sixteen I took myself to the cinema to see the late night showing of *Les Mis*, alone. I'd cried into my popcorn in the mostly empty theatre as Eddie Redmayne sang *Empty Chairs at Empty Tables* and then bought myself dinner at Kelsey's to celebrate. I'd come home to a small stack of presents from my parents, not that they'd stuck around to watch me open them. I'd treated myself to an overpriced cupcake but had eaten it without even sticking a candle in it. I hadn't exactly been hopeful about any wishes coming true at that point in my life.

The years before hadn't been much better. I'd spent most of my teen birthdays celebrating alone. My parents more often than not being out of town on business with their law firm. Always sending a small stack of expensive presents to replace them. By age fourteen I was used to it. More so, I didn't mind it, I'd gotten used to at that point. Alone at school, alone at home. That was my life.

Not anymore, I knew even with lack of harmony currently in the group that they'd been planning something for my birthday. I'd spotted them all sneaking around together, somehow even managed to get Isaac, Charlie, and October in the same room.

Even with that thought in mind, I had not been prepared for the eruption that took place as the clock struck midnight on the 30th of January and my 17th birthday began.

I'd been sound asleep when the most out of tune

version of *Happy Birthday* began in my room. I sat up, with disorientated eyes that soon turned into puddles of tears as I sat surrounded by the best friends I could possibly ask for. Libby held out a cake in front of my eyes, covered in what looked to be seventeen candles roaring with flames that I prayed wouldn't set off the fire alarm.

As the song finished, my friends jested for me to make a wish. The last few months, despite being a little rocky, had been fairly good. I couldn't think about how the conditions could really improve. Except for the tension between the four of us boys.

I smiled up at the expectant faces, our prefect's eyes catching mine, I knew what I'd be wishing for as I quickly blew out the candles, whoops and cheers echoing in my room.

When the bleariness left my eyes I finally got a true look at the cake. "Is that a red velvet cake with strawberry buttercream icing?" I surveyed the cake and grinned so wide the corners of my eyes crinkled up. The cake looked exactly like my favourite breakfast dish.

"You can damn right bet your ass it is. We got the chef at Denny's to make it with the buttercream they normally put on your pancakes." Libby looked so incredibly pleased with herself as she placed the cake down on my dresser and clapped with glee. However, it was Isaac and Charlie who I was glancing between. I'd bet my ass on it that it was one of those two who had come up with the idea, they knew me better than anyone.

"Okay, Libs. Try not to get drool on the cake," Isaac joked, rolling his eyes at me as Libby continued to stare at the cake, her hands almost pawing at it.

Out of the corner of my eye, I could see Charlie watching mine and Isaac's every movement. It was almost unnerving. Eventually, he cleared his throat, drawing my gaze away from Isaac's. "So, presents?" Charlie suggested.

"This one is from all of us," October said as she pushed the envelope towards me. I pushed down my covers a little, taking the envelope from her grip.

I went to slide my fingers through the envelope, pulling back a little to think through how I was going to react. I hated having to open presents in front of people. I didn't want to be disappointed. Not that I could be with all of their faces beaming down at me. "Guys, you didn't have to d-."

"We always do this," Ameliah interrupted as she slid onto the bed to sit next to me.

"She's right. Every birthday since us girls have been friends we have this tradition of staying in the persons room that night and eating cake whilst opening presents at midnight." October was grinning at me as she pulled herself some duvet.

It was only then I noticed they were all in their pyjamas and for once Isaac actually had some on. I admired the grey pyjama shirt and bottoms. They were one hundred percent, not his.

Slowly, the rest of them followed Ameliah and October's lead, until they were packed into my bed like a tin of sardines. Regardless of what was in this envelope, this was already the best birthday ever.

I slid my fingers under the fold of the envelope, tearing it open. Splashes of green and purple littered the card and caught my attention, whilst goose bumps coated my arms. "Oh no you didn't," I cried, my voice high pitched and screechy. "This is too much." I glared at them all as they waved their hands in protest, clutching the two tickets to see *Wicked* at the Gershwin Theatre on Broadway in my palms. I looked between the groups, tears glossing over my eyes as I whispered almost silently.

"Thank you."

"It really is no bother," Charlie replied. This was the first time I'd heard his voice since before his break and hearing him speak to me, that alone, was all the gift I needed from him. "You can take whoever you want by the way. You still have a plus one for our New York graduation trip, so maybe someone special," he suggested. "I mean, I'll only be mildly offended if you don't choose me to go with you." He shot me a small smile and I relaxed into my pillow. I hoped this meant that he was over the cold shoulder he'd been giving me since he found out about everything that had been going on between me and Isaac.

"I couldn't think of anyone else to go and see it with," I replied, beaming at him, before pulling him into the tightest of hugs. I hoped that if I clung on forever we'd never fall out again. I couldn't bear the thought of him being angry at me like that for a second time.

"Plus, you'd have to pay the rest of us to go with you," Isaac teased from where he was sat at the opposite end of the bed, leaning up against Joshua.

"Well, if I wasn't excited about your guy's graduation trip, I am now." If I had been alone right then I'd have been dancing around the room in glee. On my first trip to New York not only would I be going with the greatest of people, but I was also getting to see a show that had been on the top of my bucket since I'd been old enough to know what *Wicked* was.

"Well, we've got to graduate first, let's get through the rest of this semester before we start to think about celebrating," Joshua groaned.

"You guys have nothing to worry about," October replied. "You're all smashing it. When do you guys start to hear back from universities?"

All three of the boys groaned in sync, Charlie

groaning the loudest of the group. "I definitely don't want to be thinking about that right now," Joshua said, pushing Isaac off of where he'd been trying to get comfy on his shoulder.

"No school talk. Let's plan the party for tonight." Libby clapped, excitedly, pulling out a notebook from her backpack.

"Party?" I asked, the thought alone sent chills down my spine. For too many birthdays, even in infant school, I'd handed out invites, with no-one showing up. I couldn't remember the last time I had a birthday party I enjoyed. Although, would I enjoy this party? If Isaac and Joshua were going to have anything to do with planning this party it was probably going to get way out of hand.

The worry must have been evident on my face as Joshua shook his head at me. "Don't worry. I've already reigned this one in," he said elbowing Isaac lightly in the ribs. "I've already confiscated the ridiculous amount of liquor he was planning to bring with him. For some reason, he'd bought like eight bottles of Disaronno."

Me and Isaac shared a knowing smirk, before bursting into laughter. Everyone around us looks confused, but my heart was contracting at a rate that definitely wasn't healthy about the fact he'd remembered from that night out many moons ago.

We'd all fallen asleep not long after that, a mass of bodies wound together. It wasn't even as uncomfortable as it sounded, even if Libby was curled up exceptionally close to me. Not even Noah walking in at seven am to see us all wrapped up around each other could ruin the great mood I'd started my seventeenth birthday in. The exhausted part of my mind even thought I heard him mumble 'happy birthday' as he spotted the ridiculous number of balloons and wrapping paper that was taking up a large amount of our carpet space. The best thing was he didn't even seem that annoyed that the mess had begun to clutter his side of the room.

After I'd finally managed to get rid of everyone, in a bid to get ready for classes, it truly began to sink in what they'd done for me. Only a small part of me being slightly disturbed that they'd snook in and done all of it whilst I was sleeping. There were 'happy birthday' banners strewn across the room, an amount of balloons I couldn't even begin to count bobbing in every corner. The big bag of breakfast pastries that one of them must have slyly gone out to raid from the dining room early this morning, now demolished on my dressing table. If I hadn't just spent over half an hour really giving my skin some love I'd probably have allowed myself to get quite teary.

With breakfast already being consumed at 7:30 this morning I had a little bit of extra time to get ready for class and wow was I thankful for it. It was my birthday after all. I planned to spend all the extra time I could grapple at choosing between the Alexander McQueen or Versace cufflinks when there was a knock at the door. The decision would have to wait.

I swooped over to the door, the toothbrush I was using balancing in the corner of my mouth as I pulled open the door, revealing that Cheshire grin that I truly adored.

"Happy Birthday," Isaac said, sidling in past me, pushing the door behind him.

"You already said that at midnight and then again when we all woke up this morning." I chuckled, as he wrapped his arms around my waist, pulling me right up against him. He kissed my lips softly around the toothbrush before spinning me around to see the large box on my bed. When the hell had he put that there?

"And what's this? Another gift for me?" I faked a gasp

183

and he tickled my ribs.

"My present to you," he said placing multiple kisses up and down my neck. If there wasn't a beautifully wrapped gift box waiting for me on my bed, I'd definitely allow myself to get caught up in him.

I pulled myself out of his arms, grabbing at the large, rectangular hamper, stroking the dark, navy ribbon. I undid the bow, gently, discarding it on to my bed and the box practically fell open in my lap. The gift inside of it revealing itself to me. Or should I say gifts? It was perfect. He was perfect. His hand covered mine, twining our fingers together and I cupped his cheeks pulling him into a messy kiss. "You are wonderful," I whispered against his lips, before crushing them with mine.

As I pulled back from him, I grabbed at the box so I could get a better look at it. "So, I did good?" He asked, a gentle smirk stretching across almost the entirety of his face.

"You did very good," I purred back at him, shuffling back the straw box into my lap. It was like I was cradling my baby as I looked down at it. It was like a hamper of everything I could possibly desire. I hadn't even had a proper chance to scan everything that filled the hamper box to the brim. But what had caught my eye first was the one-hundred-dollar gift card for The Works. I wasn't sure what I wanted to squeal about more; the fact that I now had one hundred dollars of free money to spend there or the fact that he knew me so well.

Then it caught my eye. The biggest mug I'd ever seen. "You know me way too well, it's actually quite disturbing," I said squeezing his hand.

"Look at the bottom," He replied, turning the mug over so I could get a better look. *You put up with my childish behaviour and I put up with your caffeine addiction. Let's put up with each other forever. - Isaac x.*

Tears brimmed at the corner of my eyes, this was something else. Something more than us sharing sneaky kisses and longing looks. This felt like a commitment and if it weren't the steely-eyed boy staring at me, eyes expectant and waiting for an answer, I'd probably be freaking out about the fact that this was someone offering themselves forever to me.

Nothing else in the hamper really mattered after this. Nothing else that could happen today could top this. I pushed the hamper off of my lap, pushing it to the end of my bed, before turning to Isaac and practically pouncing on him, his head hitting the pillow before he could even realise what was happening. I kissed him, long and hard. I didn't even care about breathing right now, I just wanted to be wrapped up with this boy. Lost in his arms and his kisses.

Of course only to be disturbed by our favourite person clearing his throat. "Hadn't realised you two were back on again. Broken up with your girlfriend yet, Wells?" Noah asked as he returned from the bathroom, damp hair flopping over his face. Well, at least he'd gotten dressed in the bathroom for once. With Isaac's gift being sprung upon me like that I'd completely forgotten the blonde showering in our bathroom.

Isaac let out a growl in his throat and I was convinced he was going to go for Noah. If I didn't know what I knew I'd probably be attacking him too, but we didn't need to be causing more tension between the three of us. Instead, I kept my hands pinned to Isaac's shoulders, saving him from whatever fight he was about to start. "Leave it, Isaac," I muttered to him, as I peeled myself away from the boy, brushing down my blazer to straighten it out.

I didn't even look at Noah, determined to not let him

185

ruin today. "Class?" I suggested to Isaac as he pushed himself up off the bed, collecting his bag from the floor.

"Class," he agreed and with that we left the room, leaving a silent Noah to stand in the middle of his room on his own, the fight he wanted to pick denied from him.

Classes flew by in a blur of textbooks and pop quizzes. We weren't deep enough into the semester to expect proper tests yet, but these pop quizzes were beginning to get challenging enough for me.

Before I knew it I was being guided to my own party. I was utterly amazed when Libby threw open the door to the common room revealing what they'd been working on since the moment they left classes that afternoon. A beautifully decorated room. All the decorations in scarlet and gold, my Harry Potter house colours. Balloons filling almost every inch of the floor and metallic spirals draped from corner to corner.

When these girls went big, they went really big. It was amazing. I hugged them all hard, thanking them endlessly for all the effort they'd put in. Minutes later guests began to arrive, I recognised every faced as they pulled me into hugs, high fived me and handed me presents that I hadn't been expecting. It was so wonderful to see so many of the boys I'd become friends with from Edwards over the last few months, I couldn't believe I knew enough people to fill the common room. Never mind considering so many of them to be friends.

Even as Callum passed me I felt a sense of pride that we'd managed to stay somewhat friendly even after our very awkward ending. He pulled me into a small hug as he entered the room, sliding a card into my hand as he went to join the rest of the boys from our dorm.

"Whys it so quiet?" Isaac asked as he entered the room. He was right there was no music playing, even though it was clear the girls had pushed all of the tables to the side to create a mini dance floor.

"I knew there was something I forgot, I left the boom-box in your room this morning. I'll run back and get it, don't worry," October said and I passed her the key so she'd be able to get into my room. This wasn't going to be a party without a sound system. I still couldn't believe all the trouble they'd gone to, I definitely didn't think they would be able to top how they'd decorated my room in the darkness of the night, but the streamers dangling from the ceiling and the canvasses of photos of us and our memories hung on the wall said otherwise.

I was staring at the photos that me and the guys had taken at the falls the first time we'd visited, lost in thought about how different it had been back then even though it wasn't that long ago. I'd just started to date Callum and me and Isaac were fighting like crazy, but we all still looked so happy, the tension and somewhat animosity between the four of us hadn't developed yet. I was glad we'd been able to put aside whatever hurt there was still nestled between us, even if it were only completely put away for one day.

The door to the common room came flying open, slamming so hard off the wall that it definitely would have left a dent. It pulled me from the memory of the photo and the shriek that followed the slam caused me to turn to see who it had just erupted out of. *October.* Her tear-stricken face was the first thing that caught my eye before my eyes travelled down to what was causing the tears.

The room was silent, except for the raging sobs that were leaking out of her. My whole body was trembling, but my feet felt as though they were rooted to the ground with cement, unable to move to her and do or say anything. What would I do even if I could move? This wasn't explainable. This was a crater heading to Earth

187

with nothing to stop the crash that was about to happen.

"What's going on, Toby?" Libby said, as she bounced up from the sofa rushing to her side, her voice laced with concern.

October said nothing, just held out the mug to Libby so she could inspect it. Libby surveyed the mug but didn't even think to flip it over and look at the bottom. Part of me wanted to run to her, snatch it out of her hand so she wouldn't have to see. But I knew it was too late at this point. The secret was out.

"I'm so sorry, October," I began to grovel, rushing to her side, grabbing onto her arm, and squeezing it soothingly. Everyone at the party was now staring at us. Our friends, people I'd befriended in classes, my companions from the choir I'd worked so hard to become a leader of. I spotted Callum amongst the crowd, the way his confused face looked at me pushed me to the verge of tears. I didn't want him to have to find out about Isaac like this.

I couldn't cry though, I wasn't the victim in all of this. I realised that now more than ever as October pulled her arm out of my grip like my palm had burned her, backing right away from me. "Don't you dare talk to me, Lo." She mustered up between her cries, black tear tracks smudging all down her face.

"Can someone just tell us what's happening?" Libby yelled from where she was standing next to us. "What have you done to her?" She asked. I'd never seen her so angry, she was practically staring daggers into my soul right now.

"I'll tell you what he's done to me," October bellowed, causing me to almost jump out of my skin. I searched the crowd and watched as Isaac weaved his way to the front to stand opposite me and October. "He stole my boyfriend, that's why Isaac broke up with me." Her face crumbled again as she sank down against the side of the door frame.

The once silent room was filled with gasps and people muttering amongst themselves. Uncomfortable looking faces not sure where to look or what to do in response to this outburst. Charlie was staring at the mug, Joshua at his side looking equally as disappointed. This was awkward for me, but it must be just as awkward for them having known about this for the last month and having kept it from the girls.

Libby laughed and I shot her a look that told her 'now wasn't the time for laughing'. She immediately stopped. "What do you mean he stole your boyfriend?" She asked as if it was the most ludicrous thing on this plant. For most people in this room, it probably was.

"Read the bottom of the mug," October said, grabbing it from Libby's grip and flipping it over. "Actually, whilst we have a crowd I'll let you all see the most disgusting thing I've ever had to see in my life.." Angry tears were flowing from her now red raw eyes, as she held the bottom of the mug up for everyone to see. Part of my heart was breaking as a message that was only meant for my eyes was revealed to dozens and dozens of my friends. I couldn't even begin to think of what they were all thinking of me right now.

"He was the guy who you couldn't stop thinking of?" Callum asked in the smallest of voices from where he was now stood next to Charlie and Joshua.

I nodded at him and Callum pushed past the crowd, sliding past where October was blocking the exit and out the door within a blink of an eye. As I watched him leave I heard the choked sobs he took with him. Just one more person I'd hurt in this mess.

"Is this true?" Libby asked. "Is this true?" She asked

again, this time turning to look at Isaac. We both just looked at each other, we were defenceless there was no way at all we could try and deny this. October was holding all the proof she needed in her hands.

"Yes," I said, loud enough for everyone to hear, may as well squash these rumours myself rather than have everyone speculate about what had been going on. "It's true."

"Let's not do this here. Not everybody needs to hear all the dirty details of what you two have been doing for the last couple of months," Charlie said, as he started to herd the party attendees out of the room.

"Months?" She screamed, her face red raw and voice hoarse. "What are you talking about, Charlie?" October asked.

"October don't do this right now. Let us get everyone out of here and then they can explain this to you," Ameliah said as he took October by the hand and moving her out of the way of the door frame.

"Did everybody know but me?" October yelled across the room, the coffee cup grasped in her fist, tightening every time she re-read the engraving on the bottom of the mug. Before she released it from her grasp at full force. The mug smashed up against the wall, exploding into hundreds of fragments. Charlie gasped. Joshua froze and my hands trembled as I surveyed the damage, both to the mug and to everyone who stood around me.

No matter how strong I wanted to be right then, I couldn't stand it. I couldn't watch one of my best friends be heartbroken by my actions. So, instead, I did what I did best. I ran.

~ Chapter Twenty-Two ~

I went into hiding. I turned my phone off. Only left my room for classes and hid in the back row of any classes I shared with the rest of the gang. I dug out the supply of protein bars I had stashed under my bed and made the decision to live on them for the foreseeable future.

I ran back to my dorm between my classes, not risking bumping into anyone who was going to give me any shit. Today I was fuelled by the B- philosophy paper I clutched in my fist, the paper completely crumpled at this point. I'd spent weeks and weeks over the Christmas holiday working on this paper, I couldn't fathom that it'd only be worth a B-. I stormed up the stairs of the dormitory to the second floor ready to empty a whole bottle of expensive shower gel onto my body and scrub away the overwhelming disappointment I was currently feeling.

As I fumbled around in my pocket for my room key, I was distracted by the small sobs that were escaping through the crack in the door. They were so quiet I was practically having to strain to hear them at this point. I began to prepare for the worst, October waiting in my room crying in the bed I'd kissed her boyfriend on, ready to rip into me. I almost wanted to turn around and leave, but I had nowhere else to run to.

I opened the door slowly, peering into the room to survey what I was about to deal with, but my side of the room remained empty. The room was completely clear except for a small figure curled up into a ball in his bed, his comforter wrapped around him, his face planted in the plush pillows, muffling the sobs.

I walked over to his bed, taking small steps, racking my brain for what I was going to say to him. It's not like I could just ignore his tears. "Are you okay?" I asked, my voice hushed and gentle. The body of the figure under the covers quivering a little as he sobbed into his pillow.

He didn't even move as he muttered his reply into the pillow. "She's gone." Was all I heard, before he lifted his face out of the pillow and rolled over to look at me, his face an angry shade of red and blotchy from the salty wetness. "She's gone and I wasn't even there to say goodbye." I was almost crying too at the way his face crumpled, as he screwed his eyes shut trying to stop any further tears from falling. "Why didn't I spend longer with her last week when I had the chance? I knew she didn't have long left, but she told me to come back here and sleep properly. Four days. Four days I was gone and now *she's* gone." He wiped his tears away furiously, as they poured down his face.

Stunned, I found myself perching next to him at the end of his bed. Almost tempted to reach out and hug the boy. "Who's gone?" I asked tentatively, I'd never seen him properly shed a tear, never mind act this hysterical. I wasn't exactly sure how to handle this situation.

Through choked tears, Noah whimpered out the name Jessie. "She was my girlfriend." The past tense of their relationship crushed my heart, multiple tears now streaming from my own eyes. "And now she's gone and I'm not quite sure how this goes on, how do I go on?" He asked rhetorically, there was no answer for that right now. I knew he would just want to cry angrily, cursing out the world for causing the pain he was currently feeling. He explained to me how it was anaplastic thyroid cancer, that

192

had killed her. It had been too late when the doctors had discovered it, the prognosis giving her a year, but the doctor telling Noah and Jessie's mom that the cancer was already incredibly aggressive and that a year was a rough estimate. It had been eight months, eight months and thirteen days since the diagnosis and that was it, she was gone. The rarest, but deadliest of thyroid cancers had consumed her.

Noah curled his fists around the comforter so tight his knuckles blanched white, his now red nose snuffling as the tears continued to fall quicker than he could wipe them away. "Noah," I mumbled, grabbing onto his shoulders trying to stop him shaking, his pleading eyes looking up at me as I soothingly rubbed his shoulders. "I'm so sorry for your loss. I had no idea," I said, immediately regretting my dreadful excuse for sympathy and comforting words. "What am I even saying? How can I help? Is there anything I can possibly do for you right now?" I spluttered out, even after all the abuse he'd given me over the last five months all I wanted to do was be there for him. "Just name it and I'll do it."

"Leave. Please," the boy retorted simply, pulling the comforter up over his chin, tears leaking onto the bedsheets.

I nodded and realised there was nothing I could possibly do to comfort the blonde boy, not right now. This day, the first of March, would be one he'd never be able to forget. I took one last look at Noah and frowned, he looked so small curled up in the foetus position under his blankets. You'd never have known that the boy was six foot two with the way his limbs were so tightly pressed against his stomach, his chin tucked deeply into his chest.

I gathered up my bag, sliding my laptop and charger into it before exiting the room. As soon as I let the door close behind me I opened up WhatsApp on my phone, punching out a short message to all the boys I thought could help right now. It read *Emergency dorm meeting, common room now*. I pressed send and hoped that no matter how the boys currently felt about me that they'd meet me there.

The boys quickly piled into the common room around me, Charlie had his worried prefect look on his face, no doubt because it was so unlike me to call a house meeting. Normally, I didn't even speak in the house meetings he arranged himself. He watched me closely as I stood at the front of the room trying to command the attention of the thirty boys I'd managed to get a hold of.

"Look," I began, a shaky breath escaping my lips as I exhaled. "I know some of you are pretty angry with me right now, maybe even a little disappointed." Charlie's frown was piercing in my peripheral vision. "But, this isn't about me." Some of the Freshman were glaring at me now, perplexed. "Many of you know my roommate, Noah Castle. Probably because you've lived with him or you're on the soccer team together. Maybe even because you've been burnt by his honest and relentless personality in the past." Some understanding faces glanced up at me in agreement. "Who you don't know, is the Noah Castle who's been suffering, suffering as his girlfriend slowly lost her battle to cancer." I kneaded at my eyes as they glazed over, willing myself not to cry as I looked out at the sombre faces in the audience, some of the boys now sporting a shocked appearance, others willing me to go on. "I'm not asking you to like him if that's what you're thinking. I'm asking you to be there for him. We need to show him he's not alone through this."

Charlie was the first to speak, his voice low and withdrawn. "I had no idea. How did I have no idea? I'm supposed to be your prefect. I'm supposed to make sure you guys are okay and I didn't even spot that one of us was hurting so badly." He slumped over, resting his head in his hands.

I couldn't let him take the fall for this. Noah had done an incredible job of hiding his emotions. "It's partly my fault too," I replied. "He blackmailed me into not telling you he was sneaking out most nights to go to Hamilton. I just assumed he was working there and whatever. I didn't realise he was spending all his time at the hospital with her."

"What were you thinking we could do to help?" Isaac piped up, his eyes locking with mine for the first time since my birthday party.

I studied the fatigue engraved under the older boys eyes, his usually styled hair hanging around his face. There was a field of overgrown stubble shielding his chiselled jaw. I shook my head, lowering my eyes, now wasn't time to open that can of worms. "A show of support. I haven't quite thought of what exactly, but between us, we must be able to come up with something."

A flitter of boys nodded before Joshua suggested. "What about a song?" Marcus, another senior went to protest, but Joshua held up his hand, sternly. "Let me finish. When I was in tenth grade and Noah ninth, shockingly we were in the choir before they disbanded and gave all the money to the sports teams. But, although he'd never admit it, Noah actually enjoyed being part of the group before he made any enemies here. I think a song would show sentiment."

Most were in agreement and it didn't take much to convince the boys that they just had to be there and that they didn't have to participate in the singing.

That's how we found ourselves the next morning scattered up and down the floors of Edwards, as Oscar, a

tenth grader began to strum his guitar a slower version of
Starley's *Call On Me* echoing up to the high, beamed
ceilings that covered the six floors of the Edwards
dormitory. The partly dimmed lighting created a
makeshift spotlight on the boy playing the guitar.

I gently wrapped my knuckles on the door to the
room me and Noah shared. As Noah hadn't moved from
the foetal position in the last eighteen hours I was still
pretty worried that this whole stunt wouldn't work. I
hoped so much that this would draw him out of the room
or even just out of his bed. No-one should have to be
alone during a time like this.

Noah opened the door, wearily rubbing at his red,
blotchy eyes. His jaw moved for him to speak, but before
he even had a chance to question what the hell was going
on, Charlie had already begun to sing softly from where
he was positioned on the third floor. Joshua and Isaac
were stood beside him, trying their best to makeshift
some kind of harmony. I watched as Noah's eyes shot up
to them in confusion as the first few lines of the song
travelled down to him.

Another boy, Lewis, took over the second half of the
first verse. He was a junior like myself and Noah, but he
was also a defender on the soccer team. He'd told a story
to the group of us gathered in the common room, that
once during a game he experienced a nasty tackle against
the rival school from Burlington. Noah had been the boy
to hold him back from punching the causer of the injury,
stopped him being sent off and suspended from playing
for the rest of the season.

As the bridge began I joined the boys who were
singing on the second floor, breaking away from where
I'd been standing next to Noah. We'd shared a room for a
whole semester and I'd never once seen anything but a

smirk or playful smile on his face, but as I watched his lip tremble and his eyes gloss over it pushed me to sing with all of my might.

The house broke out into the chorus, the more uplifting beat ringing through the corridors and down the stairs. Even the boys who had protested in joining in with the performance for Noah, no longer resisted the urge to sing, now lining the balconies and stairwells, voices joining together as one.

The boys repeated *you know you can call on me* for four more beats until the second verse began and the crowds on the stairs from the third floor parted and one boy broke from the ranks. He stepped down the stairs, sporting a blazer that was way too short on the arms as he took lead on the second verse. Wyatt Castle smiled down at his younger brother and the first, fresh tear crept out of Noah's eyes, the rest following in an unbroken stream. Warmth flooded my heart, knowing that the brother had just driven eight hours from where he was studying at McGill University to be here for his brother. Wyatt's voice rose as he raced down the stairs, the melody carried by the humming on the third floor. He made his way to Noah's side, wrapping an arm protectively around his brother's broad shoulders.

I observed the pride glazing over Noah's face, as someone from our year picked up from where Wyatt had left off in the verse. Noah's eyes continued to leak relentlessly as he nodded in thanks to Landon. A boy who, the rest of Edwards had come to learn, was buddied with Noah when Landon was in ninth grade and Noah was in tenth. Landon had told us all about how during the second semester of his first year at Cherrington, Noah had been there for him and filled him with strength and hope when his mom had passed away from cancer. I hoped that Noah could seek some form of comfort in

Landon now being there for him after everything they had been through together last academic year.

The chorus began again, the line *call on me* distributed amongst the boys who had taken solos throughout the song including Noah's ex-mentor and my ex Callum. They were joined in harmony by many of Noah's fellow housemates and soccer teammates. The pain wasn't forgone, but appreciation shone out of the boy, his shirt drenched, and his hands still trembling a little, but his wide eyes displayed how beyond thankful for the display of support he was. Clutching his shaky hands into Wyatt's blazer he let fierce tears fall, as the song came to a close.

I watched the scene unfold, my own face wet and stinging. So many of the Edward boys now settled on the third-floor balcony, a sign written in Latin carried between them. *Viribus,* it read, the same word that shone from above the entryway outside. Strength was exactly what Noah needed right now, it was what all of us needed at this point. Edwards had become my home, my family, and to see all the boys come together like this for Noah, one of their own, embodying exactly what the founding fathers of Edwards had valued most, I couldn't be prouder to be an Edwards boy. I grinned, through the tears, up at the boys above him, for a few moments, I forgot about all the animosity currently between them, about all the problems that we were facing together. I smiled harder as I watched Landon run down the stairs to hug Noah before Wyatt pulled the boy into our room, what I'd learned today had once been his room too.

I looked up again, most of the boys had dispersed amongst the floors again, some returning to their respective rooms, others heading to the common room. I, however, couldn't see past Charlie, Isaac, and Joshua, standing still looking over the bannister of where they resided on the top floor. I briefly caught Charlie's eye, but he just shook his head at me. The words I'd heard him telling Joshua about his feelings for Isaac ringing in my head once more. As I watched Charlie push off of the bannister, to head back to his room. Joshua still looked completely disappointed in me and what I'd done, and Isaac wouldn't even look at me, choosing to stare at anything that wasn't me. It wasn't that I'd expected that after this performance we'd all just fall back into being best friends again, but I'd still been holding out hope.

I sighed deeply to myself, not wanting to interrupt the brotherly moment that was probably currently taking place in mine and Noah's shared room. Instead, I took off down the stairs and out the front doors, plonking myself on the bench that stood lonely on the patio. Alone, I thought to myself about everything that had happened over the last few months, how many mistakes I'd made, how many people I'd hurt, how I'd ruined their group's relationships and friendships. It was then, that it truly hit me how badly I'd screwed up. I didn't even recognise the nasty person I'd become. I didn't know that I could even be this guy, the kind of guy who stole someone else's boyfriend, breaking more than just one heart in the process. But, I had. I'd become the worst version of myself. This wasn't how it was supposed to be. I didn't come all this way to hate myself more than ever.

I dropped my head into my hands, the tears falling once more. I stayed like this for hours, it was only when the cold got too much that I decided to return to my room, my pity party over. I had to be there for Noah now.

~ Chapter Twenty-Three ~

He hadn't been there when I'd arrived back. I must have been sat on that bench for hours and hours because there wasn't a scrap of evidence that Noah Castle once resided here. All that was left was the school provided furniture. It was almost as if I'd imagined living with Noah for the last five months and now nothing.

He was gone and now I had to deal with everything on my own, not that he'd be any help, but I'd always be coming back to the cold, empty other half of the room, to nobody and no one. That thought sent my anxiety into overdrive, my spine crippled at the idea of being alone again at school, no one to talk to. It made my stomach churn to the point I had to grab Noah's bin and hurl into it. He wouldn't be needing it for now and I'd clean it eventually.

I laid in bed for twelve hours, from seven in the evening till seven in the morning wide awake. I tossed and turned all night to get comfortable to the point I'd moved my stuff over to Noah's bed to see if it would help. I even tried the floor to see if I could maybe get comfortable there, but I couldn't. The thoughts in my mind pulsed around my body, kept me restless and on edge and in the end I got up and got dressed at eight am and sat on my bed with my laptop and logged into Facebook.

That was a huge freaking mistake. My wall was jam-packed with posts from the girls I was, emphasis on was, friends with from Victoria, all slagging me off for what I'd done with Isaac and to October. I knew it was wrong, I'd known all along from the first moment we'd shared that night as he helped me unpack, to the night we danced together in the club and to our very first kiss. I hated myself for what I'd done. I'd tried so hard to stop my feelings, to make things work with Callum and to get over Isaac, but I couldn't. I loved him, I fell for him on day one and the more I got to know him I couldn't stop falling harder and harder. It ate me up carrying those feelings around whilst I was still with Callum, that I lived for seeing Isaac in the corridor and spending time with him at lunch even though we couldn't be together.

I'd ruined everything by going after what I wanted and being selfish. I deserved to be alone, this is what you got for hurting all the people around you that had welcomed you to their school, to their group and made you feel like you'd found a home for yourself and a family you'd never had. That's what happened when you stomped on everyone's heart and feelings just to kiss one gorgeous, grey-eyed boy.

I deserved how everyone eyed me when I went down to breakfast the next day, how people whispered and pointed at me in the hallway between classes. Word travelled fast when everyone lived together and the affair had been screamed about in the middle of the boy's dormitory.

I sat down in my physics class, Charlie nowhere to be seen which made me feel even more unsettled and my normal physics partner, Robert, turned away from me when I tried to work with him on our normal project. The girl, Chelsea, on the other side of him, told me that they'd be working together now. Turns out when I got back to my room for lunch and I looked up Chelsea on Facebook she was on the track team with October, should have seen that one coming. It was probably what I could expect from all of the girls on the track team. Probably all of the girls to be fair, I'd helped October's boyfriend cheat, broken every rule of girl code along the way. They had a right to hate me. Everyone should.

I ate a protein bar for lunch curled up on the top of my bed, laptop open playing old episodes of Keeping up with the Kardashians. I wished I didn't have to go back to class and when my eyes reopened at four PM I realised I didn't. I'd wrote out an email to my class teachers for that afternoon and told them I was sick and thankfully, since I'd missed hardly any time here, they accepted it no questions asked. They just told me if I was going to miss tomorrow to get a note from the nurse.

I fell quickly back to sleep and when my alarm went off the next morning I contemplated doing just that. I looked sick, I was as pale as a ghost and the bags around my eyes made me look just as awful as I felt. I didn't though, I wouldn't behave like the victim in all of this, I wasn't and it wasn't fair to everyone I'd hurt through my actions.

Instead, I washed my face with cold water, pushed my hair out of my eyes threw on my uniform and went down for breakfast. The second I walked through the dining hall doors I was overwhelmed by the whispers. It had been two weeks since the affair was revealed, yet it was still the hot topic of gossip. I heard my name and Isaacs name and the words *fucking* and *hooking up* being thrown about on every other table as I weaved between them to get to the food queue.

It was hard not to blanch at every word or to want to cry at the names they called me and the way the story had spiralled into so much more than what it was. That they were now saying I'd cheated on Callum as well, when I hadn't, not physically anyway, but I knew in my mind emotionally and mentally I had. My feelings for Isaac had never stopped when I'd been with him, I never should have strung him along like that.

This only got worse when I joined the queue for the toaster to get a bagel and October and Libby were directly in front of me, like the next people in line. October turned around, her red-rimmed eyes stared me down and it was all it took for me to turn straight back around and bolt for the double doors I'd just entered through. That wasn't possible. A gang of girls lined the door they saw me headed for, all dressed in their cheer uniforms, of course, morning practice had just ended.

"What the fuck is wrong with you?" A girl with short black hair screamed in my face, so close her breath ghosted over my nose and lips. "Who gave you the right to steal someone else's boyfriend and turn him gay, huh?"

Another girl, someone I recognised from my year, I wanted to call her Kayla, but I couldn't place her name as her hands pushed at my shoulders and sent me flying to the floor. "You fucking hurt one of us girls again and a bump to the ass won't be the only thing you get," she spat down at me as the girls circled me and laughed as I laid helpless on the floor.

In that second I was back in Calgary, back at my old school and all of the pain of the beatings hit me like they were happening to me in that moment. I felt every sharp kick to the stomach, every blow to the face and I wanted the ground to sink beneath me and never open back up. I clenched my eyes shut and tried to count to ten calmly, but my breaths turned to wheezes and I knew if I didn't get myself up off the ground I was going to have full-blown panic attack in front of everyone.

When my eyes flicked open no one was there, the girls were gone and whilst people still stared from their places at the tables, no one was coming for me. So I pushed up off the floor and ran straight to my room, straight back under the covers where I vowed not to move from again until this had died down.

I was a hostage in my own room, but I deserved this.

~ Chapter Twenty-Four ~

The hammering bang to my door woke me from my slumbers. I stared up at the clock through bleary eyes and noted that it was two in the afternoon. Although I had no desire to find out who was behind the hammering, I knew if I did not attempt to answer the door the thumping would not stop.

I pulled up the comforter around my shoulder and padded to the door, squinting through the looking glass. I jumped back a little as I saw Julian and Dean Withers starring back at me. I was doomed.

Every morning I'd woken up with this pit of dread forming in my stomach, as I continued to miss more and more class every day, but as it got to the end of the second week of not going to class I couldn't bring myself to start going again. I feared I would have missed too much at this point, that I'd been gone too long and wouldn't be able to catch up. That and I'd had a complete lack of energy to drag myself to class, every time I woke up I'd felt more tired, I definitely wouldn't be capable of producing coherent notes at this point of my exhaustion.

I surveyed the damage to my room before I opened the door. Food containers littered every surface, protein bar wrappers coated the carpet that once surrounded the trash can. If I weren't so tired I'd probably be disgusted in myself. I opened the door wide enough to present myself to the authority figures, but not enough to showcase the state of the room.

"Good afternoon, Mr Shields," Julian said, his words filling me with fear as he looked me dead in the eye. I was well and truly screwed. I wanted to shrivel up under the glare I was currently receiving. "Will you come downstairs and join us in my office, I think we need to have a little chat. You can leave the comforter behind, it won't be necessary for this conversation," He said, dryly.

I nodded before I slipped back into my room to discard the comforter and pull on my *Cherrington Academy* sweatshirt over my vest. I didn't bother to change out of my two-week-old sweatpants, because who were they to judge me? I followed the pair down the stairs to the ground floor and into Julian's office. I'd been here a few times before after sneaking out and some of the pranks I'd witnessed from Isaac. Normally I was surrounded by Joshua and Isaac, Charlie standing over us sighing disapprovingly every now and then as we were reprimanded for what seemed to him like the millionth time. I took a seat at the desk, not even looking up as the two men took the seats opposite me.

"Logan, it's become tireless seeing you in here." Julian began, as he tugged his fingers through his already greying hair. "I mean you've been here what, five months now? This is not acceptable." It was as if I could hear him berating me, but my brain couldn't process it, as I sat there not moving. I couldn't even compose my thoughts on what was happening right now.

"I have to agree with Julian on this, Mr Shields," Dean Withers chimed in. "Although the residential problems are hardly ever brought to my attention, over the last fortnight I have received endless reports from your teachers that you have not shown up for any of your classes or handed in any of the assignments that have been due." He picked up a thickish looking folder off the table and flicked through it, peering down over his glasses at the words in front of him. "Following this, I took a look at your record and noticed that despite often getting into trouble in residence with Mr Havana and Mr Wells, your academic record *was* spotless. Until the start of February when it began to slip and now with multiple non-submission grades it's getting much worse. With your attendance grade plummeting too, it's brought me great concern about what is going on with you, Mr Shields." He closed the folder, placing it on the table once more. I couldn't believe I'd managed to put together a folder that thick in the short time I'd been here. I was sure at my old school a folder like that for me didn't even exist.

"Logan, this is your chance to jump in and defend yourself. I watched you in here the first few times hiding behind your friends and getting away with more than you should. However, at the end of the last semester, I thought we'd made progress, you were owning your mistakes and you'd become an incredible part of this community. Especially when you restarted our choir I thought you were set to do amazing things at this school. So, tell us what's been going on?" Some of Julian's sternness had faded away at this point, his eyes softening as he waited expectantly to hear any kind of excuse come out of my mouth.

Nothing came. Not one single word. I sat there silently, twining my hands in front of me to keep myself from tapping any surface I could get my hands on. What were the pair expecting to hear? I'm so sorry that I haven't left my room for the last fourteen days, except to collect my takeout's of course. But, I recently had an affair with one of my best friends, who also happened to be one of my closest friend's boyfriends. Whilst I was seeing one of my other best friends teammates and that

207

recently just exploded in my face. Because that would most definitely work with our head of house and the Dean of the entire school. Instead, I just stuck with saying nothing.

"Mr Shields," Dean Withers probed. "I'm telling you now really isn't the time to go silent on us. You aren't helping your case by refusing to speak. You're already looking at academic suspension right now. I'm going to have to call your parents and I can't imagine they would be happy to travel all the way here to meet with me about your behaviour." If I weren't in so much trouble, I'd have laughed in his face. My parents wouldn't go to the school five minutes down the road to deal with my bullies, never mind travel two thousand miles to hear how badly behaved I was. "Are you listening, Logan? You're already so lucky that the pranks and sneaking out have been kept off your record, but this we really can't. This is two weeks' worth of unexplained absences and unsubmitted work, that is definitely *not* okay."

A knock at the door disturbed whatever else the Dean had to say to me and before I could even acknowledge what was said, Julian was gesturing for whoever it was to come in.

"I thought maybe you wouldn't be comfortable talking to me and Dean Withers, so we called down your prefect." Charlie entered the room and hovered at the door. If I was to be frank with them he was the last person I wanted to see and I'm sure he didn't want to be dealing with me and my problems right now. However, as he moved to stand behind me and placed a soft hand on my shoulder, I felt like I was about to melt and that all the truths would come spilling out. As his thumb rubbed at my shoulder I was grateful that he was here for me, maybe he'd just get them off my back and I could crawl back into my bed and not leave for another two weeks.

"Hey man," Charlie said as he perched on the desk in front of my chair, leaning down to try and get my attention. "You wanna have a chat?" He asked, his tone not pushy, but his eyes pleading with me as he observed my appearance, probably in disgust. I hadn't showered in a while and the last time I looked in a mirror my skin was grey and my eyes rimmed with black circles.

I caught, in the corner of my eye, how he looked up at the Dean and Julian and frowned a little. Me and him we shared that physics class together, so he must have been a little bit aware that I wasn't going to class. Or maybe he just thought I was avoiding him. But, I'd been skipping all my meals too, so he must have noticed my lack of presence in the dining hall.

"Can we have the room for a few minutes?" Charlie asked. Maybe he thought with the authority figures outside I'd talk. He was wrong.

Both Julian and the Dean looked at him questionably, as if they weren't sure if that would be a wise decision right this moment. I knew I was currently in a lot of trouble and they probably didn't want Charlie to have the chance to feed me lies on how to get out of this situation.

"Just give me a chance to talk to him. See if I can get to the bottom of this. If not, you can follow procedure and call his parents and punish him however you see fit," Charlie appealed to them with earnest eyes, talking almost as if I was no longer in the room. I wished I weren't.

The pair of them nodded and exited the room. Casting a sceptical gaze over me and Charlie, as they closed the door behind themselves.

Charlie hoisted himself properly onto the desk, elbows resting on his knees, chin tucked into the palm of his hands. "You need to tell me what's going on, Logan. I can't help you if you don't let me in on what's happening." My mind was swirling, I couldn't work out why he'd even want to help me after everything I'd done to him. "Logan. Focus. Dean Withers is about to hang you out to dry if you don't start making excuses. I'm not talking house arrest, Lo. I'm talking suspension, maybe even expulsion. Do you want to go back to Calgary?"

I snapped my head up at the mention of my hometown. It wouldn't come to that right? I couldn't go back there. I wouldn't. I'd have to go back to my old school and I couldn't face it. I rubbed at my eyes, almost in disbelief. They felt scratchy and raw from the long nights I'd spent staring at the ceiling and crying in intermissions. Despite spending the last two weeks tucked up in bed, I'd slept very little, merely two to three hours a night if that. The events of the last few months repeating constantly in my head. My body was a tomb of exhaustion, but my mind was relentless to its wishes to sleep. The clips of the last few months played like a film on repeat in my mind, before turning into clips of the unremitting bullying I'd experienced in tenth grade. It was when the faces had begun to blur that it truly haunted me and kept me awake. I was no longer sure who the bullies were anymore, the memories intertwining. From Isaac kissing me, to me kissing my bullies. Until a few nights ago when they'd changed completely. All I could see now was October cowering, sobbing, begging me to stop, begging me to let her and Isaac be happy.

The vision flashed in front of my eyes again and I blinked repeatedly, desperate for it to go away. It had scared me how I'd hurt October, hurt her in ways I couldn't even imagine. I'd taken something from her that wasn't mine to take. Just like how the bullies had taken my happiness and my right to be a proud gay man. I was just as bad as them and that stung more than anything.

"Logan, is this about Isaac?" Charlie asked as he watched me benevolently, observed me with concerned eyes.

His name stirred a pit in my stomach which I'd had on lockdown for the last few weeks. I'd tried hard not to think about him, shoved any thoughts of the boy to the back of my mind. The replacement mug he'd sent me still sat outside my room. I didn't want it anymore and I definitely didn't deserve it. I'd only touched it once when it had first appeared, the words no longer engraved to the bottom of the mug. That told me everything I needed to know. There had been a note attached to the mug, it had just said a single word, *sorry*. Sorry for what?

I shook my head to get rid of the thought, my mind was set now on the conviction that I'd forget about Isaac, let go of everything that had happened between us. I would move on with my life, no matter how hard it would be. Besides, Isaac was never mine, to begin with.

I glanced up at Charlie, our eyes meeting and I spoke for the first time since I entered this office, intent on making my intentions as assertive as possible "This has nothing to do with him, Charlie," I replied, my teeth gritted, my tongue struggling to form his name.

"Then what, Lo? Give me something to work with. Anything at this point. I can get you out of this trouble, you know I can. I just need a reason. Have you been ill? We can get you a doctor's note if that's the case. I'll bribe the nurse if I have to."

"I'm not going to tell them I was sick, Charlie. I don't need you to do this for me. You've done enough to protect me and look how that turned out. Just tell them I wouldn't talk to you and leave it at that. I'll take the suspension, they can call my parents. You and I both know they won't defend me and they definitely won't be rushing here to be by my side."

211

Charlie looked dumbfounded. I was probably the first boy to refuse his help in this office during his three years as prefect. I'd seen it every time I'd been in here, neither Joshua nor Isaac had ever been reluctant to his help. Normally they were begging for him to dig them out of the trouble. His eyes were sad as if he were struggling to admit defeat. But, finally, he nodded sombrely at my request, before leaving the room to bring back in Julian and the Dean. I heard Julian thank him for trying, as the door to the office reopened and they seated themselves behind the desk opposite me once more

"This afternoon we will contact your parents and explain the situation, but for now you should know that you are looking at a week's suspension, which will go on your academic record that we give to potential colleges and universities that you apply to next year," Dean Withers said, his voice clipped as he searched the metal draws in front of him. I watched him blankly as he pulled out some forms and began to fill them in with my details.

"We've considered your living situation and know it would be unpractical for you to be sent off campus for your suspension. So, on this occasion we will allow you to stay in Edwards. However, you will be under strict house arrest and me and Charlie will be watching." Julian stood up across the desk as if he were getting ready to escort me back to my room. It was as he rose that Dean Withers handed him a binder full of papers and a stack of books.

"During this time, Mr Shields, you will reflect upon your actions and complete the catch-up work for the two weeks missed by yourself and the week you will miss because of your suspension." It was then when the Dean looked up from where he was filling in my academic suspension forms. "We are done here, for now," he said finally before Julian plonked the folder of work and books into my unexpecting arms. "I'll get Julian to come talk to you when I've gotten in touch with your parents and discussed the suspension as they may want you to serve the suspension at home, but I will let them know you have the option to stay here."

I wanted to scoff, there was no doubt in my mind that my parents would agree to me staying here. I'd hardly heard from them since I moved back after Christmas break. Instead, I just nodded and stood up from my seat, tugging my sweatshirt down from where it had risen up from being sat for so long. I moved to the door, I longed for the solitude of my room right now. Before I could even step a foot outside the office, the Dean was calling out to me again.

"Can I give you a piece of advice, Mr Shields? As a guy who once upon a time lived in this very dormitory, with a prefect as protective and family orientated as Charlie is to you and the rest of the Edwards boys, talk to him. He *will* listen, there is a reason why he's been a prefect since tenth grade, something I'm sure you've been able to see since arriving at this school and engaging in a friendship with him. He's as trustworthy and empathetic as they come."

I blinked, it had been unbeknown to me that Dean Withers had previously been a student here and had shared the same sentiment towards his Edwards family that I had come to hold in the last six months. A shiver splintered my spine, before I turned away from the Dean, pulling the door behind me slowly, before sprinting up the stairs, back into my room before I could be intercepted by the prefect waiting outside the office.

I was back under the duvet before the tears could even begin to fall. I scrambled for my phone that I'd discarded onto the floor days ago, my thumb scrolling through the contact list desperately, eyes skimming every name until I reached the letter Z. The realisation hitting me like a ton of bricks. I had no one to call, no one to tell me how deep in shit I was right now. I'd burnt my bridges with my friends here, lost touch with the few friends I had at home and my parents were a complete no go. So, what did that leave? Nothing. Nobody. It's not like I hadn't thought about what I would do following the fallout, about the lack of friends I'd be left with, but until now it hadn't quite sunk in. Not until I really needed them and they weren't there. I felt selfish all over again. Maybe if I'd have treated them right in the first place I wouldn't be in this position. Even my own mind was sharp and relentless towards the pain I was currently feeling.

The phone slipped from my fingers, back on to the floor, I had no use for it anymore. I curled myself inward, knees tucked into my chest, silently crying, trying to regulate my breathing as the pressure in my chest pushed harder. The clenching around my heart throwing off my count of how many breaths I was currently taking. My fingers shot to my wrist in sign of a pulse. I wasn't even reassured by my heart palpitating, the sound of it beating against my ribcage loud and heavy in my head. I'd tried to take a count of the beats of my heart as it pushed the blood around my body, but my breathing turned shallow and I gasped for air, clutching the sheets. Clutching for life. Trying to inhale deeply, trying to catch my breath, but it stuck at the back of my throat, choked. Tears dripped onto the comforter that I hugged to my body, my version blurry as I hyperventilated. My mind blank of the breathing techniques I'd taught myself over the years, the panic too much to overcome. I let it consume me, I was too tired from the lack of sleep to fight back. Sweaty palms released the comforter, my wheezing breaths high and audible, until they weren't. Suddenly, the world went black.

**

He was the last person I expected to see as my eyes fluttered open. I rubbed at my eyes just to be really sure it was actually Noah hovering over me at my bedside. I hadn't seen him in weeks and weeks since Jessie died, he'd been absent, grieving. We'd not even had the chance to talk about what the boys had done for him, how they'd comforted him. I hadn't pushed though, I didn't want to stir up any feelings, Noah was already hurt and heartbroken enough.

The emerald eyes looking down at me were the brightest I'd seen them in months, a soft hue of yellow lighting Noah's pupils, they caused tears to prickle my own eyes once more. I stared back at him for a few moments more, before I pulled my gaze away, even though I could still feel him watching me, cautiously.

"I was already on the way back to school when Charlie called me." Of course Charlie would call him, it was like he was trying to torture me even more. "Said you were in the office with the Dean and Julian. Didn't tell me much, but I could tell he was worried about you. What's going on? You, J and Isaac been sneaking out again?" His normally light and sarcastic tone was forced, the softness in his eyes depicting a slight worry about my sorry state.

My tears retreated and I laughed bitterly. Not only did I not have any friends anymore, but because of this Charlie had contacted the one person I wasn't even sure I could class as an acquaintance, never mind a friend, to come to my rescue. Comedy gold. What was Noah expecting me to do? Open up to him, spill everything that

215

had happened? Could I do that? Could I bare the pain I'd been feeling over the last few weeks? I wanted to. I was so desperate to that I was sat here contemplating talking to Noah – the boy who'd blackmailed me over Isaac for months. So he could continue to sneak out and see his dying girlfriend. I reminded myself.

"If only it was that simple," I forced out, my voice shaky, almost trembling as much as my hands were under the covers.

"It can't be that bad?" Noah questioned, eyebrow raised, eyes as inquisitive as they had been on the first day they'd met.

"Well, I've been suspended," I offered up. "Does it get much worse than that?" I laughed, bitterly, again, tears burning my eyes and threatening to fall. "Fuck," I swore to myself, feeling the bed move as Noah got himself comfy at the end of my bed.

"Fuck indeed," Noah replied. "How have you managed that? I've not even been gone that long. What the heck has been going on?" It almost sounded like a demand and coming from Noah it probably was. But, when I engaged in his line of sight again, pushing up on my elbows to an upright position, I could see a glint of concern in his eyes. I'd never seen him like this. It wasn't like we'd been warm and loving towards each other during our six-month period as roommates.

"Where would I even start? The fact that October found out about me and Isaac? Or that I haven't been to class since. Or that everyone now hates me because I broke Octobers heart and ruined her relationship with the boy she's been in love with almost her whole time whilst at this stupid bloody school."

"Well, when you put it like that it really does sound messed up."

216

"You aren't helping," I quickly retorted. I knew he was only trying to make me feel better like I had him just a month ago, but that didn't stop me from wanting to throw a pillow at him right now

"Right, sorry," Noah apologised, quickly. "Just so you know, I never told October. I know I was a shitty person when I first found out about and Isaac, but I would never have gone as far as to tell her. I couldn't ruin her relationship like that."

"What, like I did?" I shot back.

"Well, you can't lie to yourself and say that you didn't. You knew Isaac was her boyfriend when you first started seeing him."

"I know that I really do, but I didn't do it on purpose. I didn't mean to fall for him. I pushed him away so many times and I was constantly reminding him about his girlfriend." Was I trying to reason with him or was I just trying to make myself more of a victim?

"So, are you saying it's all his fault? Because it definitely didn't look like that to me," his tone wasn't aggressive, just forceful. Forcing me to see how truly awful this looked from an outsiders point of view. I could only begin to think about how much more awful it looked from October's point of view.

"Okay, I get the fucking message. I fucked up," I yelled, my hands flailing in the space between us. "Why on God's green Earth did Charlie think calling you was a good idea. He's already tried to talk to me about this and failed. Hence the suspension."

"I have no idea, maybe he thought you actually needed a good bout of brutal honesty to snap yourself out of this, to realise that life can't continue like this." He gestured to the empty take away containers and dirty clothing that littered the floor and the surfaces of both mine and his side of the room "First of all, this room stinks like something died in here. Secondly, you look like you died, and someone resurrected you five minutes ago, and last, but, by no means least, you can still fix this. I'm not saying it's going to be easy, but I don't think you actually want to lose all of that lot as friends. Especially those girls, I see how you look at them, how you cherish their friendship, how you see them as your sisters."

I nodded along, everything Noah was saying was true. Right now, though, I couldn't see how it would be possible to repair the damage I'd done. "But, where would I even start?" I asked Noah, in an almost pleading manner.

"First of all, you need to get some help, if I have to go to a grief counsellor you need to go and get some therapy for your anxiety and depression. Then, you need to talk to them, all of them. It doesn't need to be all at once, one at a time if it'll make you feel less anxious, but you need to start with October, she deserves to understand. She needs to know why you did this and how you feel. Do you love him?" Noah asked even though I was fairly sure he already knew the answer.

"Of course I do, do you think I'd have caused all this destruction on a whim?"

"Then you should be fighting for him, and for your friendship. As I said, it isn't going to be easy, but you can't let someone you love just slip away from you like this, trust me."

I almost wanted to cry again, especially when I saw tears pool in Noah's eyes before he viciously swept them away. "Okay. I understand. I really do. Thank you, Noah."

"Don't thank me. Just go and do it. It's time to get up, but please before you do anything else, shower! You absolutely stink!"

~ Chapter Twenty-Five ~

I felt like I was about to jump out of a plane. This was the vulnerability of putting your life in someone else's hands. The vulnerability of exposing all your fears to this one person who would help guide you to the ground. I found the door open and shuffled into the room bypassing the certificates that acknowledged Dr Gwyneth's achievements as a therapist, the rush of the wind hitting my face. I was about to plummet face first from twenty thousand feet, the exhilaration coursing through my veins faster than the blood pumping round. The fear had me crippled on the edge of the plane, but I knew without that fear I wouldn't be here. It wouldn't be pushing me to jump. It wouldn't be forcing me to face everything that had happened. I knew that when I hit the ground safely, it would be worth it. I just had to take that leap.

Dr Gwyneth was nothing but nice, she sat and listened as I projectile vomited the last six months of my life all over her. She didn't flinch or frown as I told her about the affair, about how many people I'd hurt along the way or how I'd been suspended. She sat almost frighteningly still, only breaking stance now and then to tuck a falling grey hair back behind her ear.

"So, Isaac? Is he still in the picture? How have you left things with him?" She asked.

I didn't have an answer to that. We hadn't spoken since my birthday. I wasn't even sure if he knew about my breakdown. If Charlie had told him, he hadn't come running to see how I was doing. I shrugged in response.

"Not really, I guess. I've only really seen Charlie from the group since it all came out. He was so disappointed in me when he found out, you should have seen his face it almost killed me." I wasn't going to tell her any more than that. It wasn't my business to be exposing Charlie's feelings too, I was just about managing to spill my own.

"You care about his opinion that much?" She wasn't asking it like it was completely ludicrous, more a little surprising if anything. She'd tilted her head softly to look at me as if she were trying to analyse me from every angle she could reach.

"I do. That's the thing about Charlie. You do care about his opinion. I've never met anyone like him. You see even with all of this going on, even when he knew and was harbouring my secret, he still kept it together. He carried on being the best prefect, putting out fires whenever they came about. He even helped me and we weren't in the best of places. He was still debate captain, fencing star and acing all his classes. Not just anyone is capable of all of that. Charlie is spectacular."

Then it dawned on me. As I sat in the chair telling her how many times he'd supported me, saved me from Julian, pushed me to do good things like start the choir back up and listened to me complain about Noah. That it had been Charlie all along that had, had my back. Even when he found out about me and Isaac, he still hadn't blown our cover. He'd kept my secret even though he didn't want to. What had I done in return? Treated him like shit, repeatedly put him in a bad position, ruined his friendship with one of his best friends and been completely ungrateful when all he ever wanted was the best for me. After October, he was the one person I'd truly hurt and he was the one person I really wanted to fix

220

things with. I didn't want him to graduate and leave this place with us on bad terms. I wouldn't do that. I couldn't.

"I know where I need to start," I said to her firmly, as I began to shove the pamphlets and worksheets she'd given me into my messenger bag. "Thank you, so much. Honestly, this has been such a big help."

"Same time next week please, Logan. We still have a lot of work to do." Her smile was warm and motherly and I almost wanted to sit back down and bathe in a sight I hadn't seen in so many years, but this was important. More important than my parent problems.

I nodded, as I slung the bag over my shoulder. There was still a long way to go. I wasn't going to be fixed overnight. I just had to try with Charlie right now, whilst I was fired up and didn't feel like I wanted to run back to my bed and hide. It was now or never. "I'll be back Dr Gwyneth, I promise," I reassured, as I headed for the door. "Thank you, again," I said as I exited the room, pulling the door behind me.

I'd taken these steps to the top floor way too many times, literally. I'd felt every single emotion going up them, fear, excitement, anxiety, joy. But, never this. Never this determination. Never the feeling of do or die. I wanted to fix this more than anything, I didn't want to lose my best friend.

I didn't even hesitate as I wrapped my knuckles repeatedly across the door, not stopping even as I heard the footsteps on the other side of the door coming closer.

"I'm coming," he cried as he pulled it open clearly expecting to see some kind of mass panic with the rate I'd been pounding on his door.

I stumbled back a little and realised I hadn't really thought through what I was about to say to him, but I couldn't let that deter me. I realised this had to be from the heart, it had to be gut-wrenchingly honest. No matter how much it hurt. "First of all, hi. Second of all, can I come in?" I asked, the words pouring out of my mouth before my brain could even compute them.

He just stared at me. His eyes narrowing in on me. It was painful as the seconds turned to minutes before he spoke. Each second almost pushing me to run back down those stairs to dive under my covers. Eventually, he just nodded, moving out of the way to let me enter his room. I unclenched my fists, my nails mere seconds from piercing the skin of my palms. "Thank you," I replied as I crossed the threshold into his room.

"Spit it out, Logan. I don't have time for your shit today. So, just say what you have to say and leave." I'd never heard that tone from him before. I'd heard him annoyed at me when I'd first got caught sneaking out. I'd heard his disappointed tone when I first told him about this affair. But this, this was different. This was anger. Full-on rage. Bitter, snake venom rage.

"I started therapy." Why was I telling him this? "I mean. I'm sorry. I started therapy and I realised how fucked up I am. Not only that but I fucked up a tonne of other lives being so fucked up. I'm not even doing this to be vain or whatever, but I ruined your life. I ruined October's life. I ruined the group. I'm so sorry. Charlie, I hope you know that." There were no tears, not even a stinging in my eyes. There were no tears left to cry and this wasn't my situation to be crying over. I'd hurt him, not the other way round. No more victim playing.

"What do you want me to say?" He replied, fingers rubbing at his temples as he lent up against his bed frame. There were dark rings circling his eyes and he was in sweats and a vest. This was not an outfit I'd ever seen Charlie in before, not even on our chill-out days. His room was littered with textbooks and notebooks, scattered across every surface. We were getting closer to finals week, but they were still a couple of weeks away. I'd been trying to study as well, my room not looking too dissimilar to this, but this was Charlie. Books organised in a system, Charlie. Closet organised in a perfect colour system, Charlie. Even when he was studying he was methodological, he'd have books stacked neatly, a schedule of when he'd need to be using each and every book. This was a mess.

"Are you okay?" I asked, observing the rest of his room. His bed was the only tidy thing. It didn't even look like it had been slept in. "I mean, I know twelfth-grade finals start a week earlier, but this looks like an exam meltdown waiting to happen."

"Did you come here to judge me, Logan? Because that's really not helping your case right now. I'm busy, so if you just came to criticise my work environment, then you know where the door is."

"Okay." Deep breath in, deep breath out. I could do this. "The first thing is, which I know I've already said, is that I'm sorry. Christ, you have no idea just how sorry I am. I have caused so much irreparable damage and I don't even know how you can even start to forgive me, but I would really like it if we could try. I'm sorry for how much I hurt you over Isaac and how I ruined the group. I honestly never meant to do that, but I should have known it would come down to this. You can't sleep with someone else's boyfriend and expect it not to come back to bite you. I really fucked up there, didn't I?"

I searched his face for any kind of movement or reaction. But he'd been so still for the whole time I'd been speaking, I should probably have been checking for signs of life. One smile, just a tugging at the corner of his lips was all I needed right now. Some kind of motivation for this ridiculous monologue I was currently giving. I needed something to spur me on in my embarrassment.

"Charlie, you're my best friend. I love you more than anyone else on this planet. I can't even tell you how much your friendship means to me. You've done so much for me." My whole body felt heavy like there were weights strapped to my legs, pulling me down. I wanted to sink into the floor. I wanted to sleep and be done with this conversation. If I could just fix this, fix part of what I'd broken, the weight would be lifted. Even if it were only slightly, it would be a relief.

"I broke up with Beth," he said like it was the simplest thing in the world. An easy, breezy statement. Not that he'd broken up with the girl he'd been with for the whole of his time at Cherrington Academy. I was about to comfort him, about to reach out and support him. I wanted to pull him into a hug and make sure he was okay about all of this. But, the pit of dread in my stomach was holding me back, worry gnawed at my insides as I let myself become overwhelmed with the thoughts of this being about Isaac. Now he knew that Isaac was potentially bisexual, did he think that he had a chance with him? Was he about to start pursuing him? I'd become so checked out of the real world, I had no idea what had been going on with everyone else for the last month or so. I'd lost track of whether he and Isaac had made up, whether the group had reunited or if Isaac and October had managed to sort things out between them.

"Oh wow. I'm sorry Charlie, I had no idea. When did this happen?" I asked. He looked composed. Even his tired eyes didn't make him look upset about this, just exhausted. This was Beth, a girl only he was able to put up with. I couldn't understand how this was such a casual thing for him to be slipping into the conversation.

"Last month. It was time, you know? Things had

fizzled out between us, so I just bit the bullet and broke up with her. It sucked, you know? I just didn't want to keep leading her on when I was no longer in love with her. It wasn't right." He was right. If only we all had the same kind of moral compass as Charlie did. If only I had the balls to be a man like Charlie did, to do the right thing, no matter how hard it would be.

"Can I ask something? This is about to sound really freaking insensitive, but I want to be friends and to do that I think I have to start being honest and real with people. No more lying." It had been something Noah had been drilling into me for the last few weeks. He'd convinced me to go to therapy and to seek help. I'd even been talking to him about it and the crazy thing was that he was actually helping. We were helping each other. I was helping him through his grief and he was helping me through my breakdown. "Are you going to go after Isaac?"

"Wow, Logan, really? That lasted for almost ten seconds. No. No I freaking well am not. We aren't even talking, Lo. I'm not thinking about chasing after him. He's yours. You're very much welcome to him."

"I'm sorry. Fuck, I knew you weren't going to. I just had to be sure."

"You really do love him don't you?"

"More than I want to admit." It was like breathing out. The words were free flowing. It was good to be telling the truth for once, not hiding behind other people, not playing the victim. It was time to be the man that Charlie was, follow in his footsteps, let him be a good example for me. Take charge of the situation, put out the fire, fix this.

"You're an idiot for that. I get it though. I get how lost in all of this you could get, I got lost in it too. I don't blame you anymore, Logan. I wish I never had. I knew his charm, I can see why you fell so hard. I wish it hadn't blown up like this, though." He glanced around me, uneasily, it wasn't easy for him to admit this to me, just as it wasn't easy for me to come here and plead for forgiveness, highlight all the ways I'd screwed up. He shook his head and turned away from me,

"Can we fix this? Charlie, I miss you, like you have no idea. You literally changed my life. I can't repay you for that, but I would love to be your friend. I don't want to leave things like this. I don't want you to graduate and go to university hating me." I hugged my shoulders, curling my chin into my chest. I really didn't want us to part ways like this, I couldn't. He'd been my first friend when I got here, I couldn't let this be the end of our friendship. I knew I'd messed up. I just wanted one chance to fix it. A second chance to put things right between us.

"I want to, Logan. I really do. It'll just take time. I forgive you though, it's been a rough year for all of us really, I wish I'd just been able to see how much everyone was hurting. I should have known from the start that was something going on with Noah, he should have been my priority this year. You should have been too if I'm honest. I knew your back story and how hard it must have been to settle into a new school like this, so far from home. I wish I could have been there for both of you." He gripped me by the shoulders and pulled me into a hug, I gripped at his shirt, fingers clutching into the material. Finally, I allowed the tears to fall freely, this had been all I wanted since I started to lose everything.

"You were there for me, Char. More than anyone else I know, even when you really didn't have to be. You didn't have to come when I was being suspended and I know you sent Noah to look after me as well. Thank you for that." I smiled, for the first time since I'd entered the room, salty tears leaking past the corners of my lips. I was so overwhelmingly grateful for Charlie and what he'd done. If Noah hadn't shown up and shook me out of my spiralling depression I hated to even think about what I'd had done.

"Shields did good for once?" Charlie asked pulling back from the hug, his hands still resting on my shoulders.

"He really did. Who'd have thought I'd have needed Noah Castle to sort me out, turns out he actually has a heart and soul after all." I was grinning through the tears and he was grinning back and then we were both crying and hugging each other once more. This was how it was supposed to be, this was how it was supposed to end after this crazy year. There was no way I was ever going to let him walk out of here and graduate without us sorting out all our differences.

~ Chapter Twenty-Six ~

"Y ou've got to be kidding me." The door was
       slamming in my face before it had even been opened
more than a couple of inches. I really should have
expected this.

"October, please," I pleaded, sticking my foot in the
narrow gap before the heavy wood crushed it. "Fuck, I
swear it never looks like it hurts this much in the movies."

"I can't even believe that you'd have the nerve to
come knocking, Logan, never mind to even think I'd want
to talk to you right now. Go steal somebody else's
boyfriend." The wood was practically splintering into my
leather shoes at this point. Part of me wanted to give up,
to leave this be, let her have time to get over everything
that happened and then come here asking for forgiveness.
But I was riding this high of trying to fix my life and even
if that didn't happen right this moment, I had to get the
ball rolling.

"I just want to talk, October, apologise." I scrubbed
my hands over my face, the pain in my foot blisteringly
sore, I couldn't give up though. I lent my whole-body
weight up against the door and it flew open, October
jumping backwards to avoid being in the path of my
collateral damage yet again.

"Fuck you, Logan. Fuck you. You swooped in here,
this damaged, naive little mouse and we took you in,
made you part of our group, we loved you, Lo. We
thought of you as one of the gang, one of our best

friends. When really behind our backs you were screwing my boyfriend. The man that I've loved for the last two years, the guy who I was planning a future with in my head. Thinking about what would happen when we were both out of here, the life we could have together. You stole that from me, stole my future, my dreams, my life. So forgive me if I no longer want to be part of your life anymore, I'm done." With that said, she pushed me out with all her strength and slammed the door once more. This time I didn't even try to intervene.

"How did you think that was going to go?" Ameliah asked. I mean, I had just been thrown out of Octobers room. Like physically manhandled and thrown to the hallway floor, thrown out of her room. How did she think I thought it went? At least she was offering me a hand. That was something right. I'd take it. She pulled me up off the floor and I brushed down the back of my pants, these were way too expensive for me to be lying on this dirty floor. That definitely wasn't an appropriate thing for me to be thinking right now as the friend I was trying to make up with was blatantly observing me.

"Not at all, but I was on a roll and I thought you know, things come in threes. This was not one of those things."

"It's going to take more than that weak apology to fix things between you two. Although, I think at this point it may be beyond repair."

"What about us?"

"I don't know," she said simply. "I knew, you know? Ever since that huge fucking bruise on his face. I didn't know exactly what was going on then, but I knew you two were more than friends. Part of me wanted to think it was a one-time thing. But, then I'd catch you staring at him, I'd catch him eying you up like he wanted to rip your clothes off. Neither of you were subtle."

"You knew a lot didn't you?" I asked. I'd worked so hard to keep it a secret from her, more so than the others, she had an inquisitive eye, saw more than everyone else.

"You're talking about Charlie, aren't you?" I nodded. "I saw something I wish I hadn't in his second year here. I caught him crying in a secluded corridor when Isaac and Toby first got together and with the longing stares he kept giving him in the early days of Toby and Isaac dating, I pieced it together and I just knew that he harboured feelings for Isaac."

"You never told anybody though? You didn't tell October about your suspicions of me and Isaac either?" That was what truly confused me, she was such a good friend to October, why hadn't she told her?

"I didn't have any proof, no evidence of what was going on. Plus, with Charlie I knew he wasn't actively going after Isaac, so I thought why rock the boat there, you know? October and Isaac were just starting out and Charlie and Beth were happy. It felt silly to ruin that."

"But, you knew about me and Isaac, you saw the hickies, you saw all the looks?"

"That wasn't enough, you'd already told me a fairly believable story about the hickies and the looks weren't enough to prove anything. I honestly thought that if something was going on between you guys it was just, I don't know a fling? I didn't actually realise it was a whole hog deeper than that. Look, Logan, I forgive you, even though I don't really have much to forgive you for, you didn't directly hurt me. Plus, I miss you, we are two peas in a pod when you think about it, things can't just go back to normal, but I'd be willing to try okay?"

I nodded, gratefully, so incredibly thankful that, like Charlie, she was willing to give me a second chance at friendship. "Thank you, Ameliah," I said nodding at her, she wasn't the hugging type.

"How are you though, Lo? I heard about what's been going on. Had a strange text about it from Noah, how that boy got my number I don't even want to know." She was gesturing for me to take a seat in the armchairs in the foyer of the girl's dormitory.

"Better, getting there, went to my first therapy appointment this morning. It was kind of what inspired to me come here if I'm honest after I went to see Charlie. I'm going to be okay though," I said adamantly. "My suspension is over and I'm working through the catch-up work I've missed, just need to try and get ready for finals. Thankfully, Noah is back so we are looking out for each other. Checking in to make sure each other are doing okay."

"I have *so* many questions about all of that. Firstly, Charlie? How did that go?" She asked.

"Good, really good, I think we are going to be okay, Ameliah. I didn't even realise it till I was talking to the therapist this morning just how much Charlie meant to me and how much I desperately needed to fix things with him."

"I'm so glad, Lo. You two are the most perfect best friends, plus if there is anyone who can forgive you it's him, that guys a saint. So, Noah? What the hell is happening there? I heard about his girlfriend, but from what you're saying he sounds like he's some kind of human now?"

"I think Jessie's death and everything that followed has done something to him, like he really cares, Ameliah. I think part of him always has in this messed-up way now I look back at what's gone on between us. But yeah, when I got suspended and Charlie couldn't get through to me he called Noah and since then we've been quite close."

"Wow. Noah Castle has feelings and emotions, that

does shock me."

"Give him a chance, Ameliah, if you saw him now you'd understand he's changed. Don't get me wrong that snark is still there, but it comes from a place of caring."

"I'll take your word for it, Lo. We'll see," she said, smiling slightly. It was good to see her happy for me, it was progress.

"Look, I wanna stay and chat, but I have one more person to go and try and make things right with," I said as I peeled myself out of the armchair.

She just looked at me with knowing eyes and I smiled at her, before I walked away, straight out of Victoria and on the path back to Edwards.

Next up, it was time to go and face him. I hadn't seen him in over a month and if my trembling hands were anything to go by, I'd say I was pretty nervous about seeing him again. It really couldn't go any worse than what had just happened with October.

It was at the point where I was feeling overwhelmed by all the emotions I was holding towards him. I was so angry with him that he hadn't been there for me, that he hadn't tried to make this better for me, hadn't even dropped in to make sure I was still alive.

Red flags popped up everywhere in front of me. I wasn't going to let them stop me though. I didn't ruin a tonne of friendships and a two-year relationship, to not give this a shot. I had to. I owed it to every person that had been hurt in this stupid mess. To Charlie, Callum, October, every single of the group who had been torn apart, because me and Isaac just couldn't keep our hands off each other or our morals in check.

It was bittersweet. Our whole relationship so far had just been this enormous oxymoron. I'd never wanted this. I hadn't asked for the first boy I ever fell in love with to have already been taken by someone else. I knew it was a wave that I shouldn't have even been trying to ride, but here I was again dragging myself back out to sea, even though the waves ahead looked rougher and choppier than they ever had done.

With things starting to sort themselves out with Charlie, the potential of a friendship I may actually want with Noah and Ameliah still wanting to be part of my life. I had to ask myself whether trying to see where things could go with Isaac were worth disturbing the peace I was beginning to build once more.

He looked confused to see me, clearly not sure why I was there, but then he smiled and I realised that he was happy to see me, it wasn't like the reception I'd originally received from Charlie or from October, he wanted to see me. "Hi Isaac," I said softly, smiling wistfully back at him.

"Hey, you," he said, as he reached out for my hands, pulling me close to him, wrapping his arms around my waist. "Long time no see, ay?" He chuckled awkwardly and I felt relief that this wasn't just weird for me.

"Yeah, it's been a while huh? Guess I lost time locking myself in my room," I replied, as light-heartedly as I could about my spiral into severe depression, trying not to think about the fact that he hadn't even come to check on me.

"Yeah, news travels like wildfire here, especially after the Dean suspended you. I thought that was my role here, not yours." He grinned a little and I tried to smile back at him, tried to make this the joke he wanted it to be.

"Tell me about it," I replied simply. "Isaac, I miss you. That's why I'm here if I'm honest. I really just wanted to see you."

"I've missed you too," he whispered into my shoulder and I pulled away from him, could we really just go back to how we were before things were exposed? Did I want that?

"I still have feelings for you, Isaac," I said openly and honestly, that's what had to be the difference here. We had to be open about everything, nothing could stay hidden, trapped behind closed doors, I couldn't put myself back there.

"Me too," he replied, still clutching onto my hands, squeezing them reassuringly.

"We can do this, can't we? We can make it work." There was so much desperation in my voice, it was gross. I may as well have been down on my knees pleading for him to take me back.

"How? How would we make this work? Everyone hates us. If we got together we'd ruin it all once more. Our relationship was born out of damage, do you want to go there again?" He said and I knew it was the truth yet I still wanted it.

I pulled him closer, my hands winding around his neck, our foreheads meeting and I did exactly what I knew would get him back. I crushed his lips with mine, our teeth clattering together angrily, forcing my tongue inside his mouth as they battled together. It was hot and rough and I didn't even care that this wasn't the soft, passionate kiss that I craved when I first got into this relationship. I ignored the nagging feeling inside of me that if this was going to be different it shouldn't have to be like this. I should be getting all those beautiful moments I longed for. But, in that moment I didn't care, I really didn't. I was getting Isaac back and that was all that mattered. I could allow this wave to completely wash over me and knock me off my feet once more, dragging me under. I didn't need to breathe when I was kissing him, the feelings that bubbled inside of me were enough. The warmth inside of me would keep me alive. Isaac would keep me alive.

He pushed me up against the wall, dominating me, just like he always did. Typical alpha male move. His fingers weaved through my curls and damn I'd missed how he would tug at them, it didn't even make me wince anymore when he got too carried away. My hands were trailing down his shirt, throwing open his buttons and tracing over his perfect abs. I didn't even have to think anymore, I knew this path like the back of my hand. I had him all mapped out.

It wasn't what I was expecting to happen, but as I lay with my head on his chest, his arm wrapped around my waist, our chests rising and falling almost in sync. I knew it was what was supposed to happen.

"So, what does this mean?" I asked, disturbing the beautiful silence that had settled around us.

"What do you want it to mean?" That wasn't what I wanted him to say. I wanted him to just straight up say that we were back together and we could take on whatever was about to be thrown at us when we walked out of his bedroom as a couple. His hesitation to do that almost derailed my plans of asking him to be my boyfriend. That wasn't going to happen though. I wanted this to be another thing I accomplished today. I wasn't just going to let him slip away, not after everything I had to go through to try and get him back.

"Well, I'd like us to be a couple. If you wanted that too?" It was like I was pleading with him to take me back. As if I hadn't just gone through hell for this relationship, for his affair, for hurting all our friends and loved ones. I was trying not to let myself look like I was on the verge of desperation to be with him, but if we didn't walk out of this together, what would have all the chaos and disaster been for?

"Okay," he agreed, simply.

It was like a weight slipped off my shoulders, for a second there I thought he was going to reject me. I never wanted to feel that worried again, I couldn't. I was starting the uphill battle against feeling this stressed and anxious. I just hoped that having Isaac at my side now meant that it was a battle I'd be able to fight. It was all the confirmation I needed, confirmation that we could do this, we could get through whatever was about to come next when we stepped out of this room as a couple, we could make it.

~ Chapter Twenty-Seven ~

We'd been having the time of our lives, it was so good to see Noah smiling and happy as we lobbed balls down the polished alley. It was good for him to be getting out, he'd gone home and grieved and I knew every day he was still grieving, but he'd said it himself when he'd come back, Jessie wouldn't want him to just mope around.

Plus, Charlie and Joshua were giving him a chance and I guess in some way giving me a chance as well, to make up for all the damage I'd done, to let me grow from my mistakes. I couldn't say they were happy about the fact that me and Isaac had gotten back together, but I hoped in time they'd accept it and be happy for us. It would just take time.

It had been an amazing night and as we finished the last game my phone began to ring and stupidly I answered it before even looking at the caller ID. It was Isaac and even as he shouted down the phone around the noise of the lanes and the arcade around us I still couldn't hear him.

"Logan?" He shouted and as I moved away from the noise and into the reception area, I could finally hear him as he yelled my name down the phone. "Logan, can you hear me?"

"Hey, sorry, I can hear you now. What's up?" I asked.

"Where are you?" He replied and already the guilt of not inviting him began to gnaw at my stomach. Things still weren't great between him and Charlie and with what

237

I knew I wasn't sure they were going to be for a while, but if he could forgive me, he could forgive Isaac. It would just take more time.

"Uh, I'm at the bowling alley."

"With who?"

Fuck, I hated this, but I couldn't lie to my boyfriend. I wouldn't after all that we'd been through. "I'm with Joshua, Noah and Charlie. Babe, I'm so sorry," I sighed and I heard him sigh too on the other end of the phone. "You know I wish you could be here, but I don't know, Charlie's still so angry with you."

"It's fine." It wasn't, his voice was hoarse as he replied with fake reassurance. "They're your friends, I don't know what I expected, but I don't want you to hide these things from me. You shouldn't have told me you were just studying, Logan. There was no need to lie. Yes, it hurts that you're spending time with the two people I've been best friends with for the whole of High School, plus someone who tormented and blackmailed you for the last six months now seems to be the fourth member of your little group, but I'd have been okay with you spending time with your friends. I just miss you tonight, this history paper just kicked my ass and I thought we could hang out, that's all."

"I'll be back in like an hour, I'll sneak up after curfew and I'll sleep in there okay? I'm so sorry, Isaac." We'd been back together all of a couple weeks and I was already screwing this up. We should have been working harder to push past everything that had happened, to make more time for each other before the year was over and we were no longer just four floors of bedrooms apart.

It didn't stop me from wanting to hang out with the guys though, especially Joshua and Charlie. They'd be leaving too and I knew they would both be off to

University. Joshua had already told me he'd gotten into the University of Toronto with Callum, and it was so good to see him so excited and happy to move on from Cherrington Academy. Gave me a little bit of hope that I too would be excited to move away from the first place I finally felt properly at home, next year.

"Isaac?" I asked into the phone when he didn't reply. "You still there?"

"Sorry, don't worry about it. I'll just start work for my last English paper. See you tomorrow." The call died without another word and I almost started to cry. If we couldn't make this work here, how would we make this work when he was at University with his new friends and I was here for another year with Noah and anyone else I became friends with next year?

I plodded back over to the bowling alley where the guys had been waiting for me to take my last turn.

"You okay?" Noah asked, this look of concern that now seemed to be reserved for me glowing in his emerald eyes.

"Yeah, just Isaac. I didn't tell him I was hanging out with you guys and well he feels left out and I feel bad." I couldn't look at Charlie, this wasn't his fault, he couldn't help how he felt, but I did wish he could just forgive Isaac or at least talk to him.

"You could have invited him, I wouldn't have minded a night at home, I should probably have spent tonight studying anyway." Charlie shrugged and I shook my head at him.

"No, it's not your problem. I just have to find a balance between you guys and him. We created this mess so we should have to deal with it. It'll be fine, I'll make it up to him."

Joshua and Noah gagged behind me and then pounded each other's fists like they'd been bros for years.

It warmed my heart, made me feel so proud of Noah for letting other people in, it was never going to be easy after he lost the one person that had meant the absolute world to him, but he'd done it for me, Charlie and Joshua. Somehow, even after the bad blood it just clicked and they treated him like he'd always been part of the group. I'd never been so grateful.

"I do need to go now though if that's okay? I know we were going to get pizza, but I'm gonna jump the 436 back to school and spend some time with Isaac before curfew." They all nodded around me and we gathered up our stuff. I headed for the bus and they headed to Boston Pizza, it didn't feel great to leave them behind, but I couldn't leave things with Isaac like that.

When I arrived at his room I didn't even knock, I just pushed open the unlocked door and found him hunched over, half asleep at his desk. This was a position I found him in a lot recently during the run-up to the last few weeks of school, it killed me every time. He worked way too hard and nobody even knew. He had the best grades in pretty much every subject and yet all people saw was the boy who hurled condoms from the top floor balcony and snuck out to get drunk every other week. It fucking sucked that this was everyone's opinion of him, but he was so resistant to being anything but the troublemaker or at least being seen to be anything but. He had so much more to give.

I wound my arms around his neck and placed soft kisses to the top of his head. "Time to go to sleep, gorgeous, the books will still be there tomorrow," I sighed into the top of his head, but when he didn't move away from the desk, his hooded eyes still glued to the page like they were going to just jump out at him. "Isaac come on, you're too tired to study, let's sleep now so you

240

can get up early and study before breakfast. Come on this is the last few weeks, the final push, don't work yourself into exhaustion."

I managed to peel the book from the grip of his fingers, but he still stared down at the desk like it was still there. Eventually, I moved to the side of him to get a better look at the sleep-deprived boy, bags the size of shopping bags formed under his dark eyes. "Come on baby, let's go to bed," I said as I pulled his hands away from the desk, he rose to his feet and shuffled into bed, pulling me down with him, but he didn't say a word. Just passed out almost the second his head hit the pillow.

I watched him sleep for hours, just to make sure he got some kind of rest. When I'd stayed up here a few nights ago I'd fallen asleep first and woken up at half three to find him at his desk, biology textbook open, studying for the final that was still two weeks away. At this rate, he was going to pass out before he could sit any of his exams.

I knew it was because he hadn't heard back from McGill or any of the other Universities he'd applied to. Over the last month people had started to get a trickle of replies from their top choices and when Joshua was one of the first to hear back from his first choice Isaac shut down a little, retreated to his room and studied his ass off, even asked if I could make him a study timetable. Which he wasn't sticking to with the ridiculous number of hours he was putting in.

I tried to ask if he'd heard from his Universities sparingly the last couple of weeks because he always got defensive when I asked. Eventually I stopped asking, the topic too sensitive to talk about. He'd tell me when he found out and we'd celebrate no matter where he ended up. That's what I fell asleep thinking about, all the positive thoughts of Isaac getting into University and the crippling amount of studying he'd done being completely worth it.

~ Chapter Twenty-Eight ~

My last final was over. I should have been overjoyed about it, but I wasn't, I was too busy being worried about my boyfriend. That was all I could think about as I left the exam hall for the final time as an eleventh grader.

Last night had been particularly strange. I'd spent the night in his room and after hours of kissing, everything had felt perfect. However, when I finally collapsed next to him in his arms, my head resting on his chest, I'd looked up to see a tear-stricken face as sobs started to rack his body. I'd never seen silent tears quite like it.

I had asked, *what's wrong?* But he'd just shook his head at me and tried to wipe away the tears like I hadn't seen them, but even when I looked away I could still feel his body crying, a wetness to his face as he tried to kiss me once more.

He'd been silent for the rest of the night and at first, I thought he'd fallen asleep, but he hadn't. His eyes were trained to the ceiling like he was waiting for it to fall in on him. I knew that feeling very well from when we were sneaking around behind everyone's back. I'd spent many nights laid in my bed like that, waiting for everything to fall in around me. I'd tried to ask once more if he was okay, but he pulled his arms from around me and rolled on to his side.

When I'd woken up to go to my exam he was already gone, even though he had no classes or exams today. I'd text a couple of times to check-in and received no reply until he messaged to check that my exam had gone okay.

It went fine. Where did you go this morning? Are you okay? -
Logan

No reply. I put it down to him being worried about his own exams. School was almost over and for him, it was almost over forever. I was dreading that next year.

For now, I was free. That's what mattered as I headed back to the dormitory. As I walked into Edwards' all I could feel was relief. It was over. I was done. The academic year was coming to a close. I closed the door behind me, throwing my satchel down on to the floor, flopping onto my bed.

"So, I have two things to talk to you about," Noah said as he shuffled to my bedside on his desk chair.

"Shoot," I replied as I pulled the pillow from my face. This last final had killed me. I always knew that sociology was going to be the death of me. I'd sat in the exam hall, surrounded by everyone, all the desks way too close together. Everyone's nervous ticks catching my eye, from the boy in front of me rocking on his chair, to the girl next to me repeatedly popping the gum in her mouth. I had just about finished the last question when the lead invigilator told me to put our pens down. I was aggravated that I hadn't had the chance to look over my paper, to check that I'd answered all the questions properly and do a quick read-through of everything. Not that it mattered now. This final exam marked the end of my penultimate high school year. I was excited, even if it did signify that the hardest year of my life was about to start soon.

"Do you want the incredible news or the news that is probably going to make you want to hit me?" His mischievous grin was almost haunting of that of the one he'd given me on the day we'd first met. Today, however, there was a softness behind those eyes. We'd grown over the last couple of months and part of me had started to think why hadn't we just been friends all along? Although, now I knew I needed him. He'd kept me grounded in some ways. Hadn't allowed me to drown. His snarky remarks kept me on my feet, sometimes they pushed me to keep going during the day. I hadn't seen that back then.

"Oh god, do I want either of them when you're looking at me like that?" I replied and for some strange reason there were tears pricking the back of my eyes. I felt emotional that this was the end, that we were leaving on good terms and that Noah Castle had incredible news to give me. Before I'd even had the chance to think about what I'd rather hear right now, he was thrusting a stack of papers at me. They were pages and pages of signatures. Names of boys I recognised and tonnes that I didn't. Boys from the choir, boys from classes, boys I'd watched play in lacrosse and soccer matches. Names that meant the most to me. Isaac's, Charlie's, and Joshua's at the top of the page, just below Noah's.

"What is this?" I clutched at the papers, eyes taking in the ridiculous number of signatures. Was this the good or the bad news? I couldn't help but let my mind wander to the fact that this could be a petition to kick me out of residence. Was I going to have to pack up my bags and go back to Calgary? I took a deep breath and slowly released it. That wasn't going to happen.

"Read the forms underneath," he said gesturing to the bottom of the stack of papers where I found an application form, all completely filled in by Noah, just the space for my signature and the date at the bottom of the page.

"Prefect?" I almost wanted to ask if he was kidding me. Had he slept through half of the chaos I'd been a part of, and caused? I didn't even want to know how he'd managed to get all of these other boys on board. Then I remembered that you had to have one hundred signatures. One hundred of the boys in this dormitory wanted me to be their prefect next year? I almost couldn't breathe, there was a tightness in my chest crushing at my heart.

"We would like you to be the Edwards Prefect next year." He was beaming at me. A toothy grin. So un-Noah like.

"We?" He couldn't be serious. "How much did you pay these guys to sign this?" I laughed out, handing the papers back to him. I couldn't be prefect, not in a million years. I was no Charlie at the end of the day. I couldn't be him. I had thought about it, though. At the start of the year, heck even at Christmas I contemplated throwing my name out there. Dropping a few hints in house meetings that I'd love to do the job. Charlie had kind of became someone I looked up to. He was this strong figure within our dormitory and within my life. He was the first person I'd became friends with here and felt like I could be myself around. Part of it had to do with him being a male. He was so different from any man I'd ever met, he played sports, was a debate captain, was an authority figure as a prefect and he was bisexual. Despite all of this, no-one saw it to be an odd combination, he was the most respected and liked boy in the school and I wanted that. I wanted to do everything Charlie did. Put out all those fires, look after all of the boys and be respected. Charlie was my hero and I wanted to be other boys hero, show them that you could be whoever you wanted to be without that constant fear.

"I didn't pay them. We had a house meeting about it last week, whilst you were at your therapy appointment.

Every year to elect house prefect the current prefect puts forward his suggestion and then residents get to put forward theirs. Everyone said you."

"I was Charlie's suggestion?" I was going to cry, the hot tears pooling, before they slid down my cheeks. "Charlie wants me to take over from him next year?" I choked out, the words almost getting lost in the back of my throat.

He was nodding his head, almost too fast for me right now. The dizziness overwhelming me.

"I can't work out if this is the incredible news or the news I'd want to punch you for, because although I could kind of kill you for springing all of this one me without a moment's notice, it's incredible."

"Well, I definitely thought it was going to be the latter kind of news. I prepared a few self-defence moves just in case you attacked me for taking this decision out of your control, I know you're a bit of a control freak," he teased, his words light and mocking, there was no malice in them like there would have been a few months ago.

"Hang on, so what is this incredible news then? What could you have possibly done that would top this?" I asked, I was almost bouncing on the spot where I sat in my bed.

"We are going to be roomies again next year," he said, throwing some jazz hands in at the end of the sentence, his fingers twitching out of sync, we definitely wouldn't be recruiting him for show choir.

"So I won't be getting the prefect room upstairs?" I asked, a tone of sadness in my voice as I lowered my bottom lip. "But that room has the perfect bookshelf for all my books and it has a bigger wardrobe for all my clothes."

"Wow. I thought you'd be happy to have a roommate for another year. I mean especially considering how great

247

I am," he protested, making a turn away from me to head back to his bed.

I grabbed at his arm and stopped him in his tracks before I burst out laughing. "Are you kidding me? Of course, I want us to be roommates again. Let's do it, where do I sign? What room are we moving too?" I said excitedly, as I pulled him into a hug, for once he hardly protested.

"Pull back kid, don't get too excited we are staying put," he said as he wriggled out of the hug. This was probably, definitely, too much affection and emotion for him to cope with from me. He wanted to keep our room though. There was something about this small gesture that caused me to well up once more. The fact that he felt that little bit of sentiment towards our room. "This room deserves a little bit of redemption after the year it's had."

"So the prefect is going to live on the second floor, is that even possible?" From all the stories I'd heard about prefects that had come and gone at this school, not one of them had ever lived outside of the room that Charlie currently resided in.

"Already cleared it with Jules, he's fine with it, I think he thought I was going to be having to convince you to not move up there."

"I mean he's right." I stuck my tongue out at him and he rolled his eyes. "I can always make you have to find another roommate you know, I won't take your cheek now that I'm your prefect," I giggled. Me, a prefect. This was going to be a crazy senior year. Not that it could get much more chaotic than it already had been during my junior year.

"I knew you were going to abuse this power. I've fed your ego way too much during this conversation." We were both crying with laughter and I never wanted this moment to end. I, Logan Shields, was thankful for Noah Castle. That was not something I ever thought I would be thinking at the start of the year.

"So what will happen to the prefect room?" Which student would be lucky enough to live in that huge room? Plus the furniture in there was much more premium than the other rooms. Jules wouldn't be just giving that room away to any old person.

"No clue, Jules said that they'd already found someone to fill it next year. They will be paying through the roof for that room," Noah said as he scooted his way back to his desk. "You know as a Prefect you can stay an extra week after the term ends and come back a week early in August?"

That was something I was looking forward to, that was two weeks less I would have to spend with my parents. "Are you planning at looking at any uni's over the summer?"

My plan was to look at five across the country. None anywhere near home though, I'd already taken the first step by moving here to get away from my folks, there was no way I was going back. I'd start by looking at Brock as it was just next door, then I was thinking Ottawa, Guelph and the University of Toronto. Then just to branch out of Ontario, I'd go take a look at McGill. Absolutely nothing to do with Isaac looking at going there this year.

"I have a couple of plans to look," Noah started. "My brother is trying to convince me to go and look at McGill, but I'm still unsure. I'm thinking of Waterloo, maybe Ottawa. Will look at Brock just to be safe. What are you thinking of majoring in?"

I hadn't even thought of Waterloo. Maybe I should look there too. Being from Calgary I had zero about what Universities were like down here, even with the good amount of research I'd done on them. I just hadn't grown up hearing about them like I had the University of Calgary or Mount Royal.

That was a good question though. I hadn't quite decided on my major yet. Part of me just wanted to say, *fuck it* and throw caution to the wind and do something to do with the theatrical arts, but the other part of me knew I could do that as a hobby. I had this inner voice telling me to do something practical and then join the show choir or musical theatre club at whichever university I went to. If I had to do something practical I'd do something in business management. That way I'd know enough about industry and finance, as well as management to be my own manager when I went into the world of the arts.

"Spit it out, Shields. I thought with all your prepping and planning you would have had this decided years ago." He was right, this was definitely one of those decisions I should have already made by now. There was still time though.

"You're going to laugh, I know it."

"You're going to say some kind of artsy-fartsy program aren't you."

"Actually, I wasn't. I was going to say business management."

"No, you weren't. You, doing business management?" He looked at me like I had just told him I was applying for Hogwarts.

"I have my reasons okay? Plus, I can do all the artsy-fartsy stuff in my spare time, that's what clubs are for," I replied with a roll of my eyes. I knew in my heart that this was the right decision. I'd have a solid, clear path if I didn't end up pursuing theatre or show choir. It was for the best. "I'm going to look at McGill too. Do you- I mean, would you like to maybe road trip up there together? At least then you wouldn't be stuck with your brother as your tour guide." I didn't even know if we were there yet as friends. Would he even want to be stuck in a car with me to drive up there?

"Why not. Then I can see him and get away whenever he begins to do my head in. Good shout, Shields. I knew you were good for something."

I lobbed one of my decorative pillows at his head. *We were there.*

~ Chapter Twenty-Nine ~

Everything with Isaac was so messed up in my head, as I looked back at everything that had happened during my time here, I struggled to see when Isaac had been there for me or when he'd fought for me. It was Charlie who sat in that office and tried to pull me out of the depression I'd spiralled into. It was Noah who Charlie had sent to comfort me, Isaac hadn't even attempted to see me when I'd been absent for so long. He'd come looking for me when he'd missed kissing me whilst I was with Callum, not because he'd missed just being with me. Even when we were on our own on dates, there was somewhat of a rush to get back to the bedroom. Was that all I was to him?

I couldn't be. I remembered the message he'd left on the bottom of the mug. He wanted me to put up with him forever. What did that even mean though? Because as soon as that mug was smashed to smithereens he was nowhere to be seen. He hadn't stuck around or put up with how bad my mental health had got, he hadn't checked in to make sure I was okay when my whole world was falling apart. He couldn't though, things were a mess. That was what I was riding on, that there were a lot of reasons he couldn't do things, not that he didn't want to do these things. I loved him so much and I knew he loved me. I didn't want to think negatively about him. Not towards someone who I loved so much.

I didn't want to be having those thoughts right now. It was supposed to be a day of celebration. We should be popping the champagne and toasting to everything the three senior boys had achieved this year. I could not wait to watch my best friends graduate. It had been a rough and rocky road to get to this point. It was nowhere near perfect, Charlie still couldn't be in the same room with Isaac for too long, but I'd still been trying. Even so, spending time with just Isaac or just Charlie, Joshua and Noah were making things better. I was sure that slowly, but surely, things would get back to some kind of normality, even if they weren't perfect again. I could live with that.

Dean Winters was up on stage, the ceremony was about to start. The class of 2019 was lined up backstage and I was about to watch my boyfriend and my best friends graduate and I was over the moon for them. I was so freaking proud of these guys, of everything they'd been through and accomplished. But first things first, before I could see them graduate, the Dean had to announce the valedictorian for graduating class. As I only had two higher-level classes with these people I had no idea who it was going to be. I asked Joshua about it the other and day and we'd laughed about it being him, but he said although he had a decent GPA, played sports and was a good student it was not going to be him.

"Good morning, friends, family and classmates of the graduating class of 2019." Dean Winters started and everyone clapped, whooping, and hollering erupted from the surrounding proud parents and siblings. "Before the ceremony starts, I have a few words I want to say. This year has been incredible, we took on a record-breaking amount of freshman to the school, we had some incredible wins and successes for all of our sports teams, especially our soccer team that went on to win their league. Not only that, but the debate team made the semi-finals of the national competition. We celebrate academic success for so many students this year and our graduating senior class have the best combined GPA we have ever seen at Cherrington Academy. With that, I could not be prouder to present the valedictorian for the class of 2019, Mr Isaac Miles Wells."

Everything erupted around me, my hands clapping rapidly before I could even think about it. My boyfriend, Isaac, valedictorian. This could not be happening, how was that even possible with his behaviour record, was his GPA even that good? There was no way in hell that Dean Winters would have agreed to this, he'd spent way too much time with Isaac in his office. But there he was, calling Isaac on to the stage, placing the sash over his head.

"You must be really proud of him," he whispered to me and I whipped my head around so fast because that voice definitely shouldn't be talking to me right now. "He did it, valedictorian. He worked so hard for it and never in a million years did he think he'd get it."

Luckily, we were still hidden by the crowd giving Isaac his standing ovation, so the absolute shock on my face was hidden. "Why aren't you backstage and why aren't you in your suit? You can't graduate in those jeans, you look scruffy."

"Well, that's good then because I'm not graduating," Charlie said, his voice calm and his eyes uncaring. What was it with these boys and saying major things like they weren't life-changing problems?

I didn't get a chance to reply and ask him what the hell he was talking about, Isaac's valedictorian speech was starting. He was at the podium with that same telling smirk on his face. I grinned ear to ear, despite the amount of shock that coursed through my body.

"It's an honour to be up here, accepting the title of valedictorian. I was as shocked as all my classmates look right now when I found out I was this year's valedictorian recipient. But, I'm proud of my 4.20 GPA and that I helped in leading our soccer team to win the league this year and to win the provincial championship cup. Not only that, but of the other extracurriculars I've participated in this year." I was beaming up at him, tears brimming in the corners of my eyes and as I turned to look at Charlie I saw the same amount of pride. I was glad that despite their current differences and everything that had happened this year, that he was still proud of Isaac.

"Not many of you know this about me and by not many I mean I've only ever told one of you." His eyes locked with mine from where he was stood on the stage. My eyes glossed over and I silently nodded at him in reply. "But in my spare time, when I'm not causing havoc that is, I write poetry. I write under a pen name and have actually been published in a couple of anthologies."

There were so many gob-smacked and disbelieving faces around me. People looking up at Isaac in wonder. Probably wondering how he had time to write poems when he all but lived in the Dean's office. I felt blessed and grateful that I'd been the person he'd chosen to let in on this secret. The person he's shared one of the more private parts of himself with.

"Now, nobody have a heart attack. I know some of you are already shocked enough that I'm standing up here as valedictorian. But, I've written a piece about my time here at Cherrington that I'd like to share with all of you. I hope it says everything that's been left unsaid by me in this speech."

"I didn't think I'd be here
After all was said and done

255

I had some laughs and played the game
And I got all tangled up.
The new world held such promise
I was blinded by the sun
For a time we had a good thing
But I knew I would screw up.
I hurt the heart I once had loved
To savour the newer I had won.
I didn't think I'd be here
My special talent is in 'mistakes'
And the pranks I played
Seemed harmless
Without twenty/twenty hindsight.
I know I've had my high points
And hurting you was a low,
As I stand here looking out there
I know I have a long way to go.
I didn't think I'd be here
But I'm happy that we made it
I know I'm far from perfect
But I'm ready to try and change that.
There's so much out there beyond us
Beyond what we have been,
Though I know that we're imperfect
I swear that we'll go far.
So take a breath, it's coming
No more time to lay about
There are chains we've forged
To bury now
No more sorry's or goodbyes.
This is the last today
Eternity is in our tomorrow
We've come so far already
And there's still a path to tread

High school is now behind us
Our future, my future, is ahead."

Everyone applauded wildly. My heart swelled with pride as I started to sob. Charlie placed a hand on my shoulder and squeezed it softly, I couldn't have been more thankful in that moment because it was just what I needed from him to collect myself in this crowd. I'd read some of Isaac's material before, seen the poems he'd entered into the competitions, but hearing him say those words, the emotion behind them and how he carried the pace. The words came to life, they weren't just flat on a once blank page.

"He's good," Charlie whispered, hand still on my shoulder. "I don't know why I found it so hard to believe when you told me my best friend was a poet." He almost laughed, almost laughed about a past memory of his once best friend, the guy he loved, the guy I was now dating. Not awkward at all.

It was time. The names were being called out and just like that Joshua and Isaac were no longer students at Cherrington Academy and as they disappeared backstage again, this was my chance to find out what was happening with Charlie. "What happened, Char?" I asked. It was my turn to rub his shoulder in a comforting manner. This couldn't be easy for him, he'd worked so hard.

"I failed all of my senior finals, my GPA plummeted this semester and I didn't have a high enough grade to graduate. Even if I did graduate and just leave school I wouldn't have gotten into University anywhere. Which I didn't by the way, everywhere I applied for rejected me. Turns out not even three years of being prefect can save a failing grade." The hint of bitterness in his voice surprised me, I thought there'd be more. If I were him right now I'd be extremely sour. This wasn't about me though, even though I probably hadn't helped with his failing grade.

257

"So I'm being held back a year, going to stay and do grade 12+. Guess you're stuck with me for another year." He elbowed my ribs lightly, I couldn't laugh about this, if this were me I'd be devastated, but he seemed in good spirits.

"Well, that isn't a bad thing for me. I'm happy to spend another year with you. Hopefully, this one won't be so dramatic." I forced out a laugh, but what I was saying was true. I wanted to fix this friendship. I loved Charlie and previously he'd been my best friend, I severely hoped my current relationship wouldn't get in the way of that during our Senior year. "I want to say thank you, by the way. For nominating me to be Edwards prefect next year. After everything, that means a lot.

There was just a nod for a reply. "Your boyfriends coming," he said as he gestured to what I presumed to be Isaac walking towards me. "I'll see you next year, Lo. Enjoy your summer. Start prepping for being prefect." With that, he walked away and I had everything crossed that this wouldn't be it, that next year would be better for both of us.

I twisted around to see him almost running at me, there was a bubbling in my stomach getting more and more fierce with every step he took and as he got close enough to hear me, it just slipped out. "I love you." And I did. I had for months and months and months. Standing here now, him in his cap and gown, high school diploma in hand, I couldn't hold it back anymore. This was the perfect moment I'd been waiting for. I loved Isaac and it was time.

He went rigidly still. It was almost like he'd just been frozen in time, and as he started to melt the smile dripped off of his face. "I got into McGill, for English. I'm moving there next month to do

258

pre-uni orientation and to get used to living in Quebec. My parents already found me an apartment I can live in until I move into halls in September."

It was almost as if I hadn't actually said anything, as if I'd just stood there silently as I waited for him to walk off the stage to me. "I just said I love you and you tell me that? How long have you known? I'd started to think you hadn't gotten in because I know some universities started contacting students weeks and weeks ago."

"A month. I just wasn't sure when to tell you. When would be the perfect moment to tell you I'm moving hours and hours away to a different province?" *He* was trying to tell *me* about the perfect moment? This was supposed to be ours and whilst I was super happy that he'd gotten into his dream university to do the program he wanted to do, all I wanted right now was for it to be about us. No matter how selfish that was, I'd just said *I love you* for the first time and hadn't heard it back.

"Isaac. Are you even hearing me right now?" We were amongst a crowd of people and I could see some of them starting to stare, mouths wide open at the lover's tiff we were clearly having. "I just said I love you. I'm super happy that you got into McGill, but I'm freaking out that I'm in love with you and you're just staring at me like I'm a mute." Hot angry tears poured down my face like molten lava, my fingernails clenched into my palms. It was happening all over again, the wave of panic was coming, the feeling of complete and utter despair.

"I, uh well, fuck, Logan, I can't." There was no smile, no warmth in his eyes. He didn't reach out to touch me or lean into kiss me. He stood there, motionless, emotionless, and as he stumbled over *I love you too*, I knew that this was it, this was goodbye. And he walked away.

To my Mum, my closest friend and the best person in my life. Without you, I'd be nothing and nowhere. You are the strongest woman I know and my biggest supporter in everything I do and I have no idea how you do both. You always push me to fly, to do everything I dream of even when I don't think I can do it myself and have never doubted that I would shine. Thank you for being the best role model in my life and providing me with the environment to grow into the person I am today. I love you and I hope I continue to always make you proud, one book at a time!

To my family - my Dad, my Brother Drew, Nanny Jean, and Grandma Barbara. I thank you for raising me to be outgoing, talkative, confident, and courageous. I've learnt so much about growth, resilience and being strong from all of you and I hope I continue to take lessons from you all and flourish into someone who makes you proud and optimistic for the future.

To Linda and Kathryn for being the most wonderful God Mothers to me and Drew and for being the best kind of extended family - the ones you choose in life.

To my best friend Ona, we met in the final six weeks of my exchange year in Canada and I knew from the second we first spoke we were going to be forever friends. Not even 4,000 miles stops us talking every single day and being in each other's lives. I am beyond grateful for your friendship, for your endless support, for cheering me on from every side-line and for ALWAYS being there through every part of my life good or bad. I love you and you'll forever hold a piece of my heart no matter where we are in the world.

To Bryn, Matt and Kecha, they say the people make the place and without you guys and Ona in it, St-Catharine's would not have become my second home. You're my Canadian Brother and Sisters, you drive me up the wall and keep me sane and were the best kind of family I could have asked for when I moved to Canada and knew no-one. We are the most mis fitted group of friends, but we complement each other perfectly and I hope I did a good job of creating a friendship group in this book that reflects our crazy gang. I love you guys and I'm so glad every once in a while I get to come home to y'all.

To Ella, Liv and Paige. Ella, you got me through four wild years at University, we had some of the best days and nights together and have supported each other through some of the worst. To Liv, who made going to work bearable and turned out to be one of the best people in and outside of the office. To Paige whom without fourth year of University wouldn't have been the same. The three of you helped me grow during my time at University, kept me mostly on the right track and pushed me to be the best version of myself.

To Brock University and St Catharine's, the birthplace of this book and the home of my characters and their home Cherrington Academy. I'm always going to be indebted to Brock University as it gave me four wonderful friends that I will treasure till my last breath and the idea for a boarding school full of hope, love, and friendship. St Catharine's provided with me the most beautiful town for the setting of my ideas and allowed me to encompass all my favourite places to eat and visit in my first ever book!

To SRL Publishing who took a chance on a new writer and her book baby and helped her showcase it to the world. I can never say thank you enough for giving Logan, Isaac, and the rest of the gang at Cherrington Academy a place on the shelf to shine.

To my wonderful Beta Readers: Catriona, Kate, Diane, Charley, Leanne, Abigail, Anthony, Alicja, Megan, Mary Kate, and Jessa. Also, to Tasha Mapes who lent me her wonderful poetic skills and wrote the graduation poem.

And finally, to the Writing Community of Twitter. From Ecrivains to Royal Chaos, to my NaNoWriMo stars to my Contemporary YA ladies! To the thousands of other writers that I've connected with since joining the community in December 2018. The support I've received from all you amazing writers is both incredible and overwhelming and I'm so thankful for every single one of you who identify as a part of the Twitter Writing Community. You are all inspiring and motivating and have pushed me to keep writing even when times were tough. You are all the brightest lights in the constellation of future authors!

ABOUT THE AUTHOR

Rebecca Caffery is a BA Politics graduate and enthusiast, who can always be found curled up reading somewhere when she isn't working on a new novel idea. She grew up in Birmingham, UK, where she's been writing since the age of fourteen. It wasn't, however, until she moved to Canada for a year that she found her voice and passion for writing again and was inspired to write Cherrington Academy.

Outside of the writing and reading world she is a Netflix addict and loves to watch anything with a heart wrenching romance plot, just like the books she writes. Cherrington Academy is her first book.

Where else to find her?

Twitter - @BeckaWrites

Book Blog – www.BeckaWritesAndReads.co.uk

9 781916 337343